MW00329687

FROM THE YONDER

A Collection of Horror from Around the World

Volume II

War Monkey Publications, LLC
Orem, Utah

©2021 War Monkey Publications, LLC

First Print, 2021

Cover by Fabio Krieger
www.selfpubbookcovers.com/BravoCovers

ISBN **978-1-954043-04-6** (Paperback Cover)
ISBN **978-1-954043-05-3** (ePub)

www.warmonkeypublications.com

AUTHOR COPYRIGHTS

TABLE OF CONTENTS

A NOTE FROM THE EDITOR

2020 has been an interesting year to be sure. A world-wide pandemic and civil & social unrest. Work on the anthology has been delayed several times, by COVID-19 and by services and care being unavailable due to priority given to treatment of the pandemic.

But, finally, we are approaching conclusion of the work. And in the end, the anthology has only been delayed by a month.

It has been wonderful working with all the authors. We had so many great submissions, it would have been fabulous to have included more stories. Yet, in the end, our judges decided on a great selection.

I consider it a privilege to have read and helped in the editing of the contents of this book. And I look forward to future projects.

I hope that you, the reader, get as much of a thrill reading this volume.

Sincerely,

Joshua P. Sorensen

AUTHOR BIOS

ANDREW M. BOWEN- Andrew M. Bowen has published about 125 poems and is seeking to publish two novels. He is also an actor and an insurance agent.

JASON BROWN- Jason Brown is a poet and playwright from Donegal, Ireland. Much of his poetry and short fiction is available on Cosmofunnel.com. His work has been published in The Brooklyn Review and The Literary Hatchet.

J. PERRY CARR- J. Perry Carr is a medical communications SVP by day, budding sci-fi/horror/mystery writer at night, which sounds like the beginnings of a superhero's bio. But alas, her only superpower is remembering random facts (like the human body contains trillions of microorganisms that outnumber our own cells by 10 to 1!). She has a PhD in molecular neurobiology from Yale University. She's a Minnesota native living in North Texas. Her short story "Blue Serpent" won honorable mention in the 2020 L. Ron Hubbard Writers of the Future contest. She is currently working on a sci-fi trilogy.

L.F. FALCONER- L.F. Falconer is a lifelong resident of northern Nevada where she enjoys exploring the back roads, ghost towns, and the lonely places. An Indie author of dark fiction, she is a member of High Sierra Writers and has published seven novels and one collection of short stories. Her work has appeared in *Weirdbook Magazine* and *Shallow Waters Flash Fiction Anthology, Volume 4.* Discover more at www.lffalconer.com

LINDA KAY HARDIE- Recently Linda Kay Hardie has had stories published in A MURDER OF CROWS (Darkhouse Books, 2019) and STRANGE STORIES VOL. 1 (Forty-Two Books, 2019). Linda is the author of the picture book LOUIE LARKEY AND THE BAD DREAM PATROL (Moon Mountain Pub., 2001). Other credits include an essay in the book CAT WOMEN: FEMALE WRITERS ON THEIR FELINE FRIENDS and pieces in national magazines CAT FANCY and CHILE PEPPER. She is a professional member of SCBWI and of International Cat Writers Association, and holds a Master's Degree in English (Creative Writing). Her writing has won awards from the Cat Writers Association, the Association for California School Administrators, the California Association of Community Colleges, and more. She won her first writing trophy in fifth grade, with first place for an essay on fire safety.

Linda Kay Hardie has been featured on the Food

Network about the National Chicken Cooking Contest, for which she was the Nevada winner in 2001. She is also the Spam Cooking Champion for Nevada (yes, the tasty treat canned mystery meat). Linda been a disk jockey and newspaper reporter. A lifelong book lover, she is now an adjunct professor teaching English composition and core humanities to unwilling students in Reno, Nevada, where she lives with Abyssinian cats.

SARAH JANE HUNTINGTON- Sarah Jane loves horror and traditional Japanese folklore. She likes to bring tales of Yokai into our modern era.
She has two cats and one rescue dog. She works in a secure unit as a nurse and currently has a collection of horror stories out called Paint it Black.
Sarah spends all her time, reading, writing, and walking.

MAGGIE IRIBARNE- Maggie Iribarne is a lifelong writer, happiest with a blank journal and a new pen in hand. She loves her husband, son, and working as a writing tutor at Le Moyne College. She practices her craft on the third-floor attic of her home in Syracuse, New York.
Her website, www.maggienerziribarne.com, is evolving, but accessible.

SHASHI KADAPA- Based in Pune, India, Shashi Kadapa is the managing editor of ActiveMuse, a journal of literature. He is the 2021 International Fellow of the International Human Rights Foundation, NY. Thrice nominated thrice for Pushcart Prize, he is a two-time award winner of the IHRAF, NY short story competition. Writing across various genres, his works have appeared or forthcoming in anthologies of Casagrande Press, Anthroposphere (Oxford Climate Review), Alien Dimensions #11, Agorist Writers, Escaped Ink, War Monkey, Carpathia Publishing, Sirens Call Publications, Samie Sands, Mitzi Szerto, and others. Please follow these links to review his works:

http://www.activemuse.org/Shashi/Shashi_Pubs.html

JESS LINDSAY- Jess has been practicing her writing since she was thirteen. Her husband introduced her to the horror genre when they started dating, and Halloween is her favorite holiday. She is a third-generation author and book-wyrm and loves making new friends.

DEAN MACALLISTER- Dean MacAllister lives in Melbourne, Australia. He is a seasoned world traveller, scuba diver and avid lover of writing and reading fiction. He has previously published stories in multiple anthologies, zines and competitions worldwide, including EWR, AWR, WWC, Untitled, Jitter Press,

Creepy Cabin, Haunted MTL, is a regular in Weirdbook and his first novel 'The Misadventures of a Reluctant Traveller' is now available on Amazon. For more of his works make sure you check out http://www.deanmacallister.com

PAUL MCCABE- Paul McCabe is a writer living in Northern Ireland. Having completed a postgraduate degree specializing on the work of H.P. Lovecraft, August Derleth and Robert Bloch, he now teaches English in Belfast. His stories have appeared in Belfast's 2015 Papergirl Exhibition, Grotesque Magazine, and Econoclash Review. Others are due to be published in AEL Press' 'Omens' Anthology and Trigger Warning's 'Hallucinations' Anthology. When he's not working on his latest novel, he loves long walks on the beach and fishing for Deep Ones off the coast of Donegal.

KEVIN PATRICK MCCANN- Kevin Patrick McCann has published eight collections of poems for adults, one for children (Diary of a Shapeshifter, Beul Aithris), a book of ghost stories (It's Gone Dark, The Otherside Books), Teach Yourself Self-Publishing (Hodder) co-written with the playwright Tom Green and Ov (Beul Aithris Publications) a fantasy novel for children.

He now publishes under the name of Kevin Patrick McCann to avoid further confusion between himself and other Kevin McCann's currently roaming cyberspace.

LESLEY MORRISON- Lesley Morrison lives and works in New York City, dreaming of an eventual escape to somewhere with palm trees. She writes speculative fiction and has a tendency to be a bit obsessive about certain authors, series, shows or games. Her short stories have appeared in Canadian magazines TransVersions and On Spec, and in The New School's DIAL Magazine in NYC.

CHRISTOPHER R. MUSCATO- Christopher R. Muscato is a writer and adjunct professor living in the mountains of Colorado. He was the 2017 writer-in-residence for the High Plains Library District and has published numerous short stories in print and online journals and anthologies. His first alebrije was a bobblehead armadillo, given to him by his grandmother.

STEVE ODEN- Steve Oden is a retired newspaper and magazine executive who began writing speculative fiction because a lifelong love of SF, fantasy, horror and related genres. His work has appeared in several anthologies, including Black Veins, Scary Snippets (family and holiday editions) and The Devil You Know, in addition to print and online magazines such as Constellary Tales, Harbinger Press and Tales from the Canyons of the Damned. New stories will be published by Wicked Taxidermy Press and Black Hare Press in 2021. He writes from Wartrace, Tennessee.

SERGIO PALUMBO- Sergio is an Italian public servant who graduated from Law School working in the public real estate branch, who published a Fantasy RolePlaying illustrated Manual, WarBlades, of more than 700 pages. Some of his short-stories have been published on American Aphelion Webzine, WeirdYear, Quantum Muse, Antipodean SF, Schlock!Webzine, SQ Mag, etc.,and in print inside 70 American Horror, Sci-Fi, Fantasy, and Steampunk Anthologies, 50 British Horror/Sci-Fi Anthologies, 2 Canadian Urban Fantasy/Horror Anthologies and 4 Australian Sci-Fi Anthologies by various publishers, and 30 more to follow in 2021/2022. He was also a co-Editor, together with Mrs. Michele DUTCHER, of the Steampunk Anthology "Steam-powered Dream Engines", published by Rogue Planet Press, an Imprint of British Horrified Press, of the Fantasy/Sci-Fi Anthology "Fantastical Savannahs and Jungles" and also of the Horror/Sci-Fi Anthology "Xenobiology – Stranger Creatures", by the same Publisher.

He is also a scale modeler who likes to build mostly Science Fiction and Real Space models.

The internet site of his Scale Model Club "La Centuria": www.lacenturia.it

DEREK PATERSON- Derek Paterson lives in Scotland, a land of mountains, forests, glens, and rain. He's been writing Sci-Fi and Fantasy since original Trek inspired his first fanfic stories, thankfully lost in the mists of time. He's had a few short stories published and is currently working on a veritable plethora of novels, which he hopes to finish before the sun goes nova. The idea for "The Search" came from Scottish mythological creature legends.

GARY POWER- Gary Power is UK author of over 25 weird, disturbing and occasionally wonderful short stories that have been published in anthologies such as When Graveyards Yawn (Crowswing Books), 'The Black Book of Horror' (Mortbury Press), The Horror zine (as featured author of the month) and The Year's Best Body Horror 2017 (Gehenna and Hinnom publishing).
Most recently, his darkly fantastic novella, Art of Anatomy, has been published by Mannison Press, LLC.
He has been a member of the British Fantasy Society since 2006 and is also a proud member of Allen Ashley's Clockhouse London Writers group.

You can check out freebies, a rogue's gallery and more at garygpower.com or on Amazon as an Amazon author. You can also find him being interviewed on the YouTube channel, Tim Mendees 'After Hours'.

NIDHEESH SAMANT- Nidheesh Samant is a marketing professional from India. He obsesses over soup and enjoys crafting dark tales. You can find him blogging at https://thedarknetizen.wordpress.com/

AUSTIN SHIREY- Austin Shirey has been telling stories ever since he first read THE HOBBIT as a kid. If he's not writing, he's probably reading or enjoying time with his wife, their daughters, and their cats in Northern Virginia. His fiction has appeared in Orca: A Lterary Journal, All Worlds Wayfarer Literary Magazine, Stonecoast Review, Blind Corner Literary Magazine, and is forthcoming in anthologies from Black Hare Press and Eerie River Publishing. You can find him and his work online at www.austinshirey.com

KEN TEUTSCH- Ken Teutsch is a writer, performer, and filmmaker whose stories have appeared in such diverse publications as Mystery Weekly, Andromeda Spaceways Magazine, Cowboy Jamboree, and Halfway Down the Stairs, as well as in the anthologies *Shadow People, Old Weird South, First*

Came Fear, and Strangely Funny. Ken also composes songs and performs in the guise of the perennially "emerging" (any time now) country music star, Rudy Terwilliger. His novella, *S-10 to Valhalla,* is coming soon from Shotgun Honey Books.

MARK TULIN- Mark Tulin's books include Magical Yogis, Awkward Grace, The Asthmatic Kid and Other Stories, Junkyard Souls. He is a Pushcart nominee, and his work appears in *Amethyst Review, Strands Publishers, Fiction on the Web, Necro Magazine, Ariel Chart, Dreams in Fiction, The Opiate, Terror House Magazine, Raven Cage Zine, The Writing Disorder, Disquiet Arts, Active Muse,* and Trembling with Fear. A poetry publisher compared his writing to the artist, Edward Hopper, on how he grasps unusual aspects of people and their lives. Mark is a retired psychotherapist who lives in Ventura, California with his wife. Follow him at www.crowonthewire.com,

DJ TYRER- DJ Tyrer is the person behind *Atlantean Publishing*, was placed second in the 2019 'Dead of Winter' horror story competition, and has been widely published in anthologies and magazines around the world, such as *Winter's Grasp* (Fantasia Divinity), *Tales of the Black Arts* (Hazardous Press), *Pagan* (Zimbell House), *Misunderstood* (Wolfsinger), *Sorecery & Sanctity: A Homage to Arthur Machen* (Hieroglyphics Press), and issues of *Fantasia Divinity,*

Kzine, Broadswords and Blasters, and *BFS Horizons.* And in addition, has a novella available in paperback and on Kindle, *The Yellow House* (Dunhams Manor). DJ Tyrer's website is at https://djtyrer.blogspot.co.uk/

BERNARDO VILLELA- Bernardo Villela has published a novella *The Isle of Helyr,* and three short story collections, *The Bloodmaster Trilogy* and *Teenage Death Songs, Vols. 1 & 2;* and has short fiction included in stories in *Coffin Bell Journal*, *The Dark Corner Zine, Constraint 280* and forthcoming in *Rivet* and *42 Stories Anthology.* You can read more about these works and various other pursuits at www.miller-villela.com.

JAMIE ZACCARIA- Jamie Zaccaria is a wildlife biologist by trade and writer by pleasure. She currently works for a wildlife conservation organization and writes fiction in her spare time. She is also a part-time Staff Writer for The Rational Online. For a complete portfolio, please visit www.jamiezaccaria.com.

THE WHISPERING WOOD

by Gary Power

"North of the village of Bagshot in Surrey is a sprawling forest, and deep within that forest is a dark and secret place. The trees there grow in mysterious ways: branches reach out like mutant limbs, bark peels from wood as skin might be flayed from flesh and tangled roots rise from a mattress of thorny bracken like flailing tendrils wrenching themselves from the sodden earth.

East of the forest is a rise of land known as Chapel Hill, and on that hill there are gallows that have stood for three centuries. From that place a path leads into the heart of the forest where there can be found a tavern. "Ye Hangman's Rest" has been there for as long as the gallows have stood. The ancient oak beams and creaking floorboards have been warped by time, and some say by malevolence. The air within is musty and has about it the odour of iniquitous history. Because of a constant and unholy chill, a fire is always burning in the hearth.

It is said that George III had occasion to drink there; history tells that soon afterwards his behaviour became irrational; his madness thereafter is well documented. Algernon Blackwood, writer of dark and fantastic things was fascinated by the ghostly wilderness of the forest, and it is speculated that much of his inspiration came from that irreverent place.

Occasionally there are those who happen upon that heathen Inn and cross its unholy threshold; may God protect their souls.

Excerpt from "The Legend of the Whispering Wood" circa 1910

Dragging his fingers through his unkempt mop of raven hair, Luke cast a cynical gaze and handed back the dog-eared paperback.

"Yeah, very interesting, mate. But I still say it's a load of old folklore tosh."

Ben shook his head and crossed his brawny arms across a black T-shirt emblazoned with a white sabbatic goat's head.

"I know what you, Emily and Ivy think, Luke, but this guy in the pub last Sunday was so genned up; we understood each other."

Luke snorted at that.

"So, you're saying you conversed with a similarly troubled soul in the Woodcutter about the five of us meeting in a dodgy car park on the edge of Swinley forest and searching for a place that's a cross between Silent Hill and Mordor?"

"Yeah...why not? He knows stuff and I don't want to pass up this opportunity. He could be helpful and - and you wouldn't understand because you don't want to."

"Ben, you're a man of mystery; it's like you've appeared out of some kind of witness protection set up, and we're okay with that. We've had a blast these last few months, and you look after the girls like a doting parent. But this thing with the Whispering Wood has become an obsession; you need to let it go. So, let's make a deal. Just today, we'll play along. We'll go into Swinley forest and look for this place. But if nothing comes of it, we draw a line under the whole thing. No more Whispering Wood. Deal?"

Ben studied Luke's face and his stern grin gave way to a gracious smile.

"Deal." he replied.

"Anyway Ben, you shouldn't go talking to strange men." remarked Emily, a tall, ashen-faced young woman, "But then again, I guess he was talking to you, and you're strange."

Ivy tossed back her tousled mane of auburn hair and shrieked excitedly when she caught sight of a tall figure strolling along the London road in their direction.

"There, over there. I bet that's him."

"Swampy's arrived," scoffed Luke. "and by the look of him, medieval tunics are back in fashion."

"Looks fit." observed Emily, reluctantly shifting attention away from her mobile and preening her pixie cut hair. "Strange and fit is… not so bad."

Shading the scorching midday sun from his eyes, Luke squinted so that he could see the approaching man better.

"Hmm, I'm thinking Rasputin meets Charles Manson. Has he got a name mate?"

"Terran." muttered Ben awkwardly.

Luke roared at that.

"Terran? Where does that come from? Terran from some weird fucking inbred, serial killing family? I reckon he saw you coming, pal. Better mind out it's not you on the menu tonight."

"Look, he's a regular guy with Pagan beliefs. And just to enlighten you, his name means "of the earth.", and he's proud of that, so maybe a few more manners and a little less taking the piss, eh?"

Luke held up his hands. "Dude, don't be so touchy. I'm only joking – sort of. And while I'm at it, what's with those grey hairs sprouting on your bonce, mate. Something on your mind you want to tell us about?"

Terran, a lean, long haired man with a swarthy complexion and soulful eyes, greeted Ben with a warm handshake and briefly cast a wary gaze over the others, paying particularly attention to Ivy. Leading them from the car park into the outer fringes of the woods he turned, pulled a long blade machete from his canvas shoulder bag and holding it aloft told them:

"So, guys, get ready for an adventure; we're going off-piste."

*****

Having followed the Windle Brook river as far as Rapley Lake the group turned west and followed a tortuous path, their progress becoming increasingly hindered by savage patches of thorny bracken through which seeped a creeping mist. Terran strode confidently ahead thrashing a path through the dense undergrowth. Beneath the forest canopy the air had become oppressively humid and quite stifling.

"Can't remember stormy weather being forecast." declared Luke as the rumble of distant thunder filtered through the forest.

"… and this mist is spooky." said Emily, dragging her hand through the haze, watching it cling to her skin like an amoebic limb drawn to the warmth of her flesh. "I thought we were in Swinley forest for God's sake, not the bloody Amazon jungle; I swear these barbed creepers are moving, it's like the woods are alive. If my legs get scratched, I'll -"

Ben span around, glaring daggers at her.

"Will you stop whinging, woman." he bawled, "Keep quiet and know your place!"

It hadn't gone unnoticed that Ben had become grouchy just lately, but this sudden explosive outburst shocked them all and left Emily close to tears.

"Whoaa, chill a little, mate." said Luke, stepping between them and turning to face Ben, "We've been walking for ages and it's not exactly the Sunday jaunt we were expecting. And what's this "*know your place*" crap?"

Ben glowered back; his fury barely contained.

Further conflict was averted when an obviously flustered man appeared from out of the forest and confronted the group. Terran raised a cautionary hand and with machete raised, approached the stranger. After brief but intense conversation the man continued on his way making a comment to Ivy as he pushed by. It was a remark that seemed to disconcert her.

"What did the nutter say, Ivy?" asked Luke, "Want me to have a word?"

Ivy shook her head dismissively but flattered by his concern replied, "Thanks, Luke."

As they ventured on, the enveloping mist thickened reducing their vision to just a few feet. Eventually, passing through the stifling fug, the group found themselves on a gravelled path that led up to a dilapidated traveller's inn. A weathered sign, that depicted a corpse swinging from a gibbet, creaked as it swung on rusty hinges.

"Well, that was all a bit weird." remarked Luke.

"Ye Olde Hangman's Rest," interrupted Terran before anyone else had chance to pass comment. "Once frequented by footpads and highwaymen on their way to London. Gentlemen would be relieved of their wealth and ladies of their virtue by those philandering lawbreakers. Their spoils would often be sold in inns like this."

Turning to Ben he told him, "This is as far as I go, friend. You'll get all the help you need inside." and then, with a cursory glance at the others, headed back into the forest.

With Terran barely out of earshot, Luke called after him, "Don't be a stranger, mate. Give my regards to Bubba." And then gleefully rubbing his hands together declared, "Now this is what I call a result. First round's on you, Ben me old mucker. Reckon you need a drink too; I swear your hair's turning greyer by the minute."

Ben and Luke entered first with Ivy and Emily following close behind, chattering and giggling as they sat themselves at a table next to a huge inglenook fireplace. Emily fell silent as her eyes grew accustomed to the murkiness within. Ivy, similarly unsettled by the gloomy atmosphere, whispered to the others, "I don't like it in here."

A burly man wearing a distressed, leather long-coat and carrying four pewter tankards invited himself over to their table. Unshaven and unkempt, it was apparent that he was a man who cared little for appearances. His teeth were decayed and his breath, even from a distance, had about it the reek of stale meat.

He grinned lewdly at Ivy with her loose blouse and generous tease of flesh, his gaze lingering long enough to make her feel uncomfortable. Luke laughed at his audacity and the old man chuckled with him.

"Don't reckon you're dressed right for the weather that's headin' this way, lass - nor for the chill in here."

With a ribald chuckle and gesturing at the drinks he told them, "Warm spiced cider, a little token from me so you'll stay awhile and keep this ol' man happy. We don't get visitors that often, 'specially young'uns."

With drinks graciously accepted, the man drew up a chair close to the fire. Gently placing a small sack on the floor from which protruded a beech sapling he proudly announced, "There's goin' t'be a new tree in the forest."

"Whoopee," quipped Emily while checking her fingernails. Her blatant display of disinterest didn't go unnoticed. The man glared angrily at her and then remarked to the others, "It's my guess you people are lookin' for the Whisperin' Wood?"

With the cider going straight to her head, Ivy told him: "A weird guy in the woods told me we shouldn't look for it - that it'll find us first and then we'll be sorry."

With a nod and a chuckle, he replied, "Aye, there's lots o'things said about the woods, an' like this place, it ain't easy t'find. Tell me, did he have a strange way about him?"

"Well, he stared like he knew me, and he called me Lily, then he went off like he'd seen a ghost."

The old man laughed again, not just at her juvenile exuberance but because he too had seen the similarity.

"That'll be Eugene," drawled a gaunt man propped slovenly against the bar, "Mad as a hatter, he is. Haven't seen him in a while." and then he too laughed, but his mirth was deep and resonant, like the throaty growl of a beast.

Ivy grabbed Emily's hand beneath the table and gripped hard.

"So, I guess you want to know a little more about the place your lookin' for?" asked the old man.

"We've heard the folklore stories and I have this book, but we'd certainly be interested to hear what you have to say." enthused Ben.

"Yeah, fascinated." added Luke lethargically.

Emily started prodding the screen of her mobile phone, much to the old man's disdain. Rapping his cane on the table he told her, "We don't like those things in here girl!"

Glowering back, she replied, "I'm texting my folks; I said I'd let them know where I was."

The man scowled and spat into the fire. His phlegm hissed and sent up a cloud of fetid steam.

Clenching the crook of his walking stick with both hands he hunched forwards and stared into her eyes. With shadows dancing like demons on the wall behind, and brooding thunder accompanying his words, he told her,

"Won't work in here anyway. None o'those gadget things ever do. You got somethin' to say 'round these parts then you say it t'their face."

"This phone's state of the art; it works anywhere." she replied arrogantly. But her smug expression faltered when the display faded and died. "No way." she groaned, "No fucking way."

Luke leaned over and whispered something about "using jungle drums" to her and they both laughed. With surprising agility, the old man grabbed Luke's wrist. His grip was tight, and his grubby fingernails dug into his skin. "If you got somethin' to say son, you say it so's we can all hear. Now tell me your name so that we can be acquainted better."

Wrenching his arm free Luke replied, "Beckham, mate. David to you, though. And him over there, his name's Rooney Toon.Wayne Rooney Toon."

For a few seconds there followed an uneasy silence, but youthful wit was no match for the menace behind the old man's intimidating stare.

Conceding defeat, he mumbled back grudgingly, "I'm Luke and he's Ben."

The old man seemed intrigued by that.

"Benjamin." he mused. And then, as if he'd had a moment of epiphany, straightened his back and smiled broadly.

"Well, young people, you're almost there, and with my help you'll find what you're lookin' for. But I'll tell you this as a warning. Y'should show folks more respect; y'never know when y'might need their help."

With a smug grin, the old timer slouched back into the shadows. "You're a cocky young man, Luke, and handsome too, but I was better lookin' when I was your age. Y'would've had a fight on y'hands for these two women of yours. And believe me, if we'd come to blows, I'd have given you a thrashin'."

Turning his attention to Emily, he told her. "Y'got witches' eyes, girl, an' skin that looks like it ain't never seen the sun."

That seemed to please her. "There were people who used to live here who'd o' given anything for a complexion like yours. Tell us y'name girl."

"Emily." she said reluctantly, but she didn't look at him. Staring into his soulless eyes was like looking into a bad place.

"An' you?" he said to Ivy.

Feeling distinctly woozy from the cider, Ivy giggled and mumbled her name.

The old man nodded and lowered his gaze from her face, his eyes drawn to her voluptuous figure. "You're a comely young woman, Ivy. Back in the early days o' this place you would o' made a fine servin' wench. What with that fiery hair, y'might 'ave made a few bob on the side as well."

Her blossoming flush deepened and that amused him. "We speak how we see 'round here, lass, so don't be offended. That's just our way of bein' friendly." he told her, and then turning his attention to the others continued, "I got a grand tale to tell you 'bout how the Whisperin' Wood got its name."

Striking his walking stick twice on the floor the man signalled for more cider to be brought to the table. With firelight flickering across his face and flames dancing in his eyes, he began:

"Two and a half centuries ago most these parts were owned by a country squire by the name of Eleazer Fox, 'Lazar' to those who knew him well. He made the Devil's business his own an' he pleasured himself with liquor an' women. If you girls had been around then, he'd o' had his way with y'both. He took women when he wanted because that was his way, and there wasn't no-one to say whether he could or couldn't. Things was different then y'see."

"Hashtag Me Too." remarked Emily, and for that earned another livid glare.

"Obsessed with livin' forever he was." he continued, and then studying Ben's T-shirt remarked, "Would've sold his soul t'the devil he would."

He stared at Ben a little longer, this time narrowing his vision to a thoughtful squint. "Lazar, had a home not far from here. A manor house as grand and stately as ever you might see. Just a ruin now it is; forest has taken it for its own."

A sudden gust of wind, like the screaming howl of a banshee, forced its way through the rattling window frames. For one unearthly moment, the din became a woeful chorus of suffering that swirled about the heads of the four young people. Just as the discordant clamour reached a deafening crescendo the old man struck his empty tankard against the wooden table and in that instance the wailing ceased.

"Virgins!" he exclaimed as he cast an incriminating glare at the two girls sat opposite.

"Unlikely." said Luke, and then with a nod towards Emily added,"'specially that one."

The old man chuckled and continued,

"Lazar had a preference for virgins, particularly redheads."

Ivy shuffled uncomfortably in her seat.

"It was in the Summer of 1768 that Lazar held a party for the forest folk. The squire spent most of his adult life studying the black arts and developed an

·

obsession for the occult, 'specially where it related to immortality. Got it from a book that he could perform a ritual and live forever, so that's exactly what he did."

"Grimorium Verum?" suggested Ben. "The book I mean."

Catching his eye and with a smug grin, the old man nodded. "Aye, the Grimorium Verum."

Stoking the fire and stirring up a cloud of sparks, he continued.

"The woods were alive with music an' laughter that night. There was gypsies playin' music and actin' the fool, and a hog on a spit roast, and a bonfire big as a house. Lazar liked the Romani folk; they did his bidding without question and he gave them land to live on. They knew better than to ask questions; curse them forever if they crossed him, he would, and their kinfolk too.

In the early hours o' the morning he took ten o' the young'uns deep into the forest; much like y'selves they were. Lazar got 'em drunk on tainted liquor. Those young people danced under the moonlight like things possessed. By three in the morning, they was scant of clothes and leapin' around like the devil had got hold o'their souls.

"Took 'em to a clearing in the woods, he did. Then he stood 'em in a big circle. They did what he said willingly. It was like their minds was in another place."

A chilling silence ensued, broken only by the crisp crackling of the fire. The old man, seeing he had their attention, let the moment ride, and then when the time was right, he leaned forwards and told them,

"Slit their throats he did, like they was pigs in the slaughterhouse, and not one o'them tried to escape. Some was even laughin' as they bled t'death."

The old man chuckled at that and poked the fire with his stick sending up another burst of sparks. "Got his men to bury them right where they stood. By morning there were ten beech saplings freshly planted in those graves, an' that, friends, is the part o' the forest that's become known as the Whisperin' Wood. Harken to the trees and they might speak to you, it's said. Legend tells they lure people in an' feed on their flesh, so you've been properly warned. Lazar left soon after that. Went off to travel the world and study demonology, he did, an' that was the last time he was seen."

Hawking up another ball of phlegm, he spat into the flames and continued.

"Just one more thing y'need to know before you go. Nearly thirty years ago, there was a great storm in these parts. Most o'the trees in the Whisperin' Wood survived, but one was felled. A young man happened on it the next day while he was out with his girl. The roots was wrenched from the earth and the soil sodden with storm water. Sometime later they found the man wanderin' in a daze an' talking gibberish. '*Her eyes is in the mud*' is all he kept sayin', '*Her pretty eyes is in the mud.*' They found his girl cradled high in the branches of one o' the trees, her clothes all tattered and hangin' from her, and her face contorted with such terror that it was like she'd seen the devil himself. Two bloody holes was all that was all that was left where her eyes had been. Course there were those that said her man did it, but no mortal could ever have put her up in that tree. That man's name was Eugene, and he was never right from that day onwards." Looking at Ivy he added, "It was him you met in the forest. His girl's name was Lily, an' I have to say you got more than a passing likeness to her."

When a splintering crack of thunder shook the walls of the Inn, the old man anxiously pulled the sapling closer and warned them, "You young people better get a move on 'fore the weather breaks. When you leave here, you'll see a narrow path straight before you. That leads to Chapel Hill. At the top you'll find gallows that was put there as a warnin' to highwaymen.

From Chapel Hill you'll see a great Oak risin' above the forest. You can't miss it."

With a heavy sigh he told them,

"Keep heading towards that tree and you'll pass straight through the Whisperin' wood."

*****

Inebriated and curiously euphoric from the cider, the four of them made easy work of climbing Chapel Hill. But with dark clouds gathering and the air becoming uncomfortably oppressive, it was clear that a storm was about to break - and Chapel Hill was the most vulnerable place to be.

As soon as Luke caught sight of the gallows cast bleakly against the leaden sky he was off as though the devil was snapping at his heals. When the others caught up they found him swinging by an arm from the gibbet with his tongue poking from his mouth and his eyes crossed.

Ivy shot him an amused look of disgust.

"We should get away from this place. The weather's getting worse." warned Ben.

Emily, oblivious to the impending storm, was wandering aimlessly, standing on tiptoe and holding her mobile phone high in vain attempt to get a signal.

"Is this place off the fucking map or what!" she cursed.

Amused by her mounting frustration, Luke dropped from the gallows.

"You heard what the old geezer said, Em." and then he growled, "*We don't like those things 'round here. Modern magic they are. Harken to the trees, I tell ya, harken to the trees.*"

"Bollocks." she snapped.

When the storm finally struck, it did so with ferocious intensity. Lightning flashed followed a split-second later by a blistering crack of thunder. Howling wind and thrashing rain swept across Chapel Hill like a marauding beast scattering the group in all directions.

Emily shrieked when a squally gust sent her tumbling onto the muddy earth. Cursing, she clambered to her feet and took flight for the shelter of the trees. The others, now resigned to getting a soaking, watched her desperate retreat and laughed amongst themselves, until they heard her cry out and saw her lashing out at the forest edge as though trying to fend off an unseen assailant.

'Emily, get your arse back here.' Luke called after her, but it soon became obvious she was struggling to escape from something.

She screamed out desperately as branches reached out like skeletal limbs and dragged her deeper into the forest.

Panicked by her predicament, Luke and Ivy ran to the rescue, but how the unrelenting wind wailed, as though in mockery, when they reached the spot where she had last been seen.

Ben, having reached the forest edge, stood defiantly against the elements and beckoned Luke and Ivy closer, raising his voice to make himself heard above the sound of the storm rushing through the trees. Entry to the forest was made all the more difficult by a vicious barrier of nettle and thorn bushes.

Pointing towards a patch of flattened bracken, and with stinging rain driving into his face, he bellowed, "She must have gone that way."

"She didn't go anywhere," called Ivy, tugging a scrap of blood-stained material from a gorse bush, "...she was dragged through."

With brute force being the only option, Ben trampled a section of the barbed thicket into the ground until it was flat enough for them to climb over.

"I took a bearing from the top of the hill. The Oak tree the old man told us about is straight ahead. It looks like she's headed for the Whispering Wood."

Pointing to his legs, Ivy mouthed, "You're bleeding."

Thin blood mixed with rain was streaming from several gashes in his muscled calves, but Ben just waved his hand dismissively and shook his head.

Having forced his way through, he beckoned for Luke and Ivy to follow closely. With little option they did as he said, moving further into the forest where the air eventually became still and the sound of the storm muted.

Ivy shrieked when she came across Emily's possessions strewn across the forest floor and spotted her backpack hanging high in the branches of a tree. More disconcertingly, she saw in the barbed thicket what looked like shreds of skin and flesh.

With mounting concern Luke and Ivy continued the search; but Ben, distracted by a nearby clearing, wandered off.

"Hey mate, we're looking for Emily. *We* being the three of us." protested Luke. "We'll continue your little adventure once we've found her."

Ben was neither concerned nor interested, acting as if they weren't even there.

"Look how healthy the forest is here," he said, "...so lush and green. And the trees - nine of them *proud and strong and one fallen*". The circle is fragile; I can feel it."

With a haughty grin he pointed to a shallow pit where a storm-felled tree had been. "That's where Eugene and Lily were. The trees must have taken her as a sacrifice, but her flesh was sullied; and for that she paid the price."

Luke couldn't believe what he was hearing.

"You've lost the plot mate; we're looking for Emily and you're more interested in a hole in the fucking ground and a plot straight out of a crappy old Netflix movie."

Ignoring him, Ben continued,

"Abe's got the sapling that'll make the circle of trees strong again."

Luke looked puzzled.

"Who's Abe?"

"The old man back at the inn...Abraham."

"Not with you, mate. He didn't tell us his name."

23

Ben glared back at him.

"His name's Abraham. He told us clear enough. You weren't listening."

"That cider's sent you doolally, Ben, and right now I'm not finding you very funny."

Ivy, trembling and on the verge of tears, stepped between them.

"Both of you, stop. We've got to find Emily. That's all that matters."

She fumbled for her phone and stabbed awkwardly at the keys. "Maybe her mobile's working."

Ben continued to pace around, occasionally crouching down and holding his head as though in pain, not reacting at all when a trill jingle broke the pensive silence.

"That's it." cried Ivy excitedly, "That's Em's phone."

With a look of relief on her face, Ivy called out, "Say something Emily… anything."

A brisk breeze penetrated the forest canopy, filtering through the higher branches and rustling the leaves. At first the noise was that of gentle whooshing, but as the wind picked up so another sound resonated throughout the forest.

A sound that took on phonetic form and filled the air with whispering voices.

"*…with us…with us… she'll soon be with us…*" they said.

Luke looked to the trees.

"What the hell's that?"

"*She's here… she's with us now… come to join us…*"

The words whooshed about them, clear as day. Sometimes distant and at other times as though just inches away.

Luke shook his head.

"Someone's playing games with us. Has this got something to do with you, Ben? You and your weird fucking forest friend playing mind games?"

As the sibilant chorus reached a crescendo an object the size of a large marble struck Luke's foot. Almost immediately the ground came to life and several squirming roots emerged from beneath the sodden earth, darting towards the fallen object.

Luke was quicker and snatched it up.

The ball was warm and slimy in his clenched fist. Unfurling his fingers, he found in his grasp the gristly remains of a human eye. Denied of their quarry, more flaying roots erupted from the earth and constricted tightly about Luke's wrists and ankles. Restrained and unable to fight back one of the barbed tendrils coiled tightly about the glistening orb and with a sickening "pop" claimed it for the hungry earth.

Ben, far from concerned or fazed by the bizarre turn of events, looked up towards the trees, his attention drawn to a certain spot by the whispering voices. Ivy, now on the brink of hysteria, followed his line of vision towards the forest canopy. And she cried out in horror.

Emily's body was there, cradled high in the branches. Her clothes in tatters and her body covered in cuts and bruises. Barely alive and groaning in pain she turned her head as though to look down. But hers was a world of darkness for gnarled branches, like old man's fingers, had burrowed deep into her eyeless sockets.

Roused by Ivy's hysterical cries, Emily began to move. Branches creaked and groaned as she tried to free herself, unaware that she was cradled so high above the ground.

"Ivy, it…hurts so…bad." she called, her voice weak and barely audible, "I can't see. Why can't I see?"

"Don't move!" screamed Ivy. "We'll get you down. Just keep still."

But hearing her best friend's voice only made Emily more agitated; thrashing about she struggled free of the tree's hold, her fall broken as she crashed through several branches onto the forest floor.

Luke and Ivy, restrained by a fresh attack of writhing roots, were forced to watch as a dense tangle of glistening bracken smothered Emily's body. Emily screamed in agony as acrid sap burned through clothes, skin, flesh and bone. There was to be no escape as the forest fed voraciously upon her until all that remained was a bloody pool that drained slowly into the earth leaving no trace.

Ben laughed, his mirth becoming more vulgar as he watched Luke and Ivy struggling to break free.

"You'll only make things worse if you try to escape." he told them, "… vicious bastards, they are."

Catching sight of a figure emerging from the forest, Ben beckoned him over like an old friend.

"So y'found the Whisperin' wood." remarked the old man from the inn, amused by Ivy and Luke's predicament

Through her tears, Ivy begged Ben to free them and then venting her anger at the old timer she screamed, "What happened to Emily?"

"That friend of yours got what was coming to her," he snapped.

Unaffected by Emily's merciless demise, Ben paced thoughtfully around the circle of trees.

"You've done well while I've been away, Abraham." he said. "But you can leave us now. I have work to do."

The old man avoided eye contact. His manner was servile and his demeanour humble. "Thank you, Mr Fox. I done my best to look after the place just like you asked. It's been a long time, but I'm still here thanks to you. Strong as ever, too."

Luke couldn't believe what he was hearing.

"Ben?" he said, "What's going on?"

But Ben's appearance had changed. There was a maturity about his face and a dark look in his eyes. His brow was heavy and his jaw stronger. His hair was longer and streaked grey and black.

"There is no Ben, Luke. I am Eleazer Fox. You saw what I wanted you to see. You all did. I played with your minds; a little trick I learned on my travels." Looking at Ivy he declared, "Now I have my prize, I no longer have any use of you."

Ivy screamed when a monstrous root erupted from the earth, coiled itself around Luke's waist and dragged him to the ground. Constricting slowly as he struggled frantically to free himself, the arboreal serpent crushed his ribs with terrifying ease.

All Ivy could do was cry Luke's name as Ben strolled over to Luke and stood over him.

"You didn't have a clue, did you?" he scoffed, "Ivy worshipped you. You were my biggest threat if you'd only known it. But she was mine from the beginning; there was to be no other outcome."

Unable to breath and struggling to speak Luke looked at Ivy and through a flood of tears tried to smile. With blood foaming from his mouth and his eyes red from haemorrhage it was clear that death was imminent; and yet still he clung to life.

Ben chuckled, wallowing in his pain and suffering.

"Oh, Luke, you are so heroic, and I respect you for that. But time, as they say, waits for no man…apart for me, of course."

An assault of wildly flaying roots tore Luke apart with the ferocity of a pack of wolves and then, just as they had done with Emily, smaller ones attacked like squirming worms; smothering, consuming and finally dragging the human detritus deep into the earth.

Ivy had become insentient, her mind and body paralyzed by the profound shock of what she had just witnessed. For a while there prevailed a stillness and silence in the forest that was quite unnatural and then Eleazer raised his hands commanding the leaves to turn, shutting out daylight and changing day to dusk.

Poised like a predatory beast he stood before Ivy, a spade in one hand and the seedling in the other.

"And as the sign that ye are truly free ye shall be naked in your rites." he growled.

And throughout the woods came a chorus of hushed rejoicing.

His gaze lingered as the roots delicately removed her clothes and jewellery.

The unworldly light gave her flesh a soft, velvet sheen. It pleased Eleazer to see her so unfettered and vulnerable. "I protected you as a father would his own child and I chose well." he said as he caressed her skin with the rough callus of his fingertips, and then passing her a flax vestment to wear added, "So many years I've waited for such a fine specimen and so many times I have been disappointed. Because of you Ivy, the circle will become strong again; I will be strong again and able to continue my work here. I have such magnificent plans."

Ivy was peaceful now. No longer angry or terrified she stood motionless as the sacrificial gown was slipped over her head.

Staring vacantly into his eyes she told him, "I give my life willingly, and my love unconditionally."

Gone was her juvenile exuberance. Now she was relaxed and softly spoken.

Lazar's gaze reached within and took hold of her. Looking to where the tenth tree had fallen, he nodded towards the shallow pit that was there, indicating for her to go and take her place.

As a light mist drifted in from the forest so the circle of trees became obscured from view. After a while the haze thinned and Eleazer, to his immense pleasure, saw standing in a circle nine youthful forest folk, each bearing a livid wound where their throats had been crudely slashed. Their faces were pale and bloodless like lifeless mannequins and their black, soulless, eyes stared vacantly into space. Ivy stood amongst them making the circle ten.

Eleazer took his place behind Ivy and then, unsheathing a serrated hunting knife from a pouch, pulled gently on her hair so raising her chin. An impassioned sigh slipped from between her lips as she felt the cold, steel blade press into her throat.

Tiny beads of blood burst onto her skin like a string of scarlet pearls. Lazar tightened his grip and prepared to make the final sacrificial cut, but with a gargled grunt and a sudden tremor of his hand he faltered. It was as though he was unable to carry out the heinous act; wracked perhaps with guilt at carrying out such a cruel and coldblooded sacrifice.

Ivy blinked and drew a deep breath, the sudden shock of pain rousing her from her spellbound state. At the same time Eleazer Fox, with a look of stark terror in his eyes, spit a fine mist of blood into the air and collapsed to the ground next to her.

A dagger had been thrust to the hilt into the back of his neck.

The bloodied blade having severed his spinal cord jutted several inches from the front of his throat. Dazed but slowly emerging from her entranced state, Ivy turned and saw Eugene, the man who had spoken to her in the forest. He was smiling in a way that suggested insanity and at the same time adoring affection.

Wrapping his jacket about her shoulders, he told her, "Don't you worry no more, Lily". And then holding up Abraham's sapling and giving Eleazer's lifeless body a hefty kick so that it rolled into the shallow grave, told her, "There's goin' to be a new tree in the forest."

THE SISTERS PURIFOY

by Steve Oden

Three old women rode the jouncing buckboard's bench seat. One held the team's reins. Another snapped a flexible buggy whip at horseflies trying to alight on the withers of the mules. The third sat between her sisters, cursing loudly whenever a wagon wheel thumped in a deep hole or trundled over large rocks.

"Christ on the cross, it's me piles!" she wailed after landing hard against the bare wooden seat.

"Shad-up, sister. I weary of your moans an' groans. That boo-hooing ain't gettin' sympathy from me," complained the crone with the whip. A horsefly the size of a hummingbird exploded bloodily in midair above the righthand mule's flank when she flicked the bone-tipped whip.

"Hate these damned blood-suckers," the wagon driver croaked, flapping her gingham bonnet at the flies and gnats swarming around her sweaty, wrinkled face.

The middle sister cried, "Ooh, it's all me poor bony bum can take. Stop this damned torture wagon, let me off!"

Time to rest the mules and make camp, the other sisters agreed with a wink and nod. The eldest, Poteet Purifoy, sawed the reins and guided the mules off the trail into a clearing under ancient oak trees.

The youngest, Pearl Purifoy, stowed her whip and nimbly jumped to the dusty ground. She began to unload bedrolls and cooking gear from the buckboard's coffin-shaped storage box.

The middle sister stood with hands on skinny hips and squalled. This was Scold Purifoy, who was never happy or content.

"Stick a plug in your goozle, sister. Nobody wants to hear how bad that scrawny old bench duster hurts. I offered use of me parlor cushion when we started out. Oh, no! You said it weren't fluffy enough," huffed Poteet, whose pendulous breasts had made dark half-moon sweat circles on the fabric of her high-waisted dress.

Pearl lifted a bucket of axle grease – thick, black, and smelly – and laughed. "Bend over that rotten log, sister. I will say a little charm and slather this stuff on your backside. Ought to make you good as new by morning."

Scold uttered an oath damning all buckboards, mules and rutty Appalachia mountain trails.

"I tell ye, a woman is born to pain! The cramps of moon cycles. Birthin' young'uns. Dryin' up of teats and womb. Raw hands from scaldin' water and the damned washboard. Dry itchy skin, flat feet, flaky scalp, rheumatiz, toothache, hot flashes an' piles—not to mention old men," she said.

Her sisters chuckled, wondering if she would pitch in to help make camp or was working up another excuse for not helping. No one would call Scold a lazy woman, but her domineering ways could produce the same result.

First, she had to criticize the camp site and instruct her sisters on how to build the fire (not like they hadn't done it hundreds of times). Scold complained about the distance to the nearest creek for water. She had to check the branches overhead for hornet nests and investigate the ground for stinging nettles or biting bugs. Finally, she reminded the other sisters to brush and feed the haltered mules.

Then, after not lifting a finger, she demanded to know what was for supper.

"We is havin' a fine fatty roast seared in the Dutch oven and cooked in its own gravy, m'dear," said Poteet, chief cook and bottle washer during their annual journeys. "With cathead biscuits an' what, Pearl?"

Pearl, the forager, sang a chant about "fresh boiled cattail roots, gizzard from a full-grown coot, mushrooms grow'd on rotted logs an' watercress picked in April fog…"

Scold sniffed. "Well, I get to season the meat. It ain't spiced right 'lessen I use my secret herbs and old salt box."

Gatherer, Cooker, and Seasoner. These were the individual duties of each of the three Purifoy sisters on their treks. It had been this way for years and likely would not change while they still lived.

*****

Soon, flames crackled in a speedily dug pit. Fragrant hickory wood sent tendrils of smoke into the evening sky. A cast-iron stew pot was on the boil, dangling by a hook from a tripod. Poteet had filled a blackened tin coffee pot with grounds and creek water to bubble in the embers.

Pearl added chopped roots and watercress to the pot, throwing in dried morel mushrooms collected deep in the woodlands and ramsons picked along the shady lanes they traveled.

Scold hauled out the chopping block made from a wedge of swamp cypress, further waterproofed by regular applications of wild goose fat. Poteet revealed the roast from its wrapping of flour-sack towels and layers of peppery moss to keep it cool and fresh.

The sisters gathered around the joint of meat, clasped hands and bowed grey heads. In a ritual observed by their family for generations, they honored the creature that had provided the sustenance and thanked the Wilde Magick that never failed to provide.

Scold eagerly brought forth her salt box, an ancient wooden grinder that crushed rock-sized chunks hacked from natural licks frequented by deer and other wild animals. She also arranged her prized containers of wild herbs and spices, mixing what she wanted for seasoning the roast.

"Many have grumped about Sister Scold, but they never tasted her camp roast," declared Pearl, stirring the stew pot's contents. Poteet shaped the dough, preparing the biscuits to be baked in a covered tin dish in the coals on top of the Dutch oven.

Ramps and previously boiled young poke plant leaves went into the cooking vessel with the roast. Scold poured the secret spices into her palm, said a prayer and dusted it over the meat. Using a hickory cudgel, she positioned the oven in the heart of the fire and covered it with embers.

"When Scorpius rises, the meat will be done and we will feast," she said.

The other sisters clapped and waited a respectful time before passing around a jug of east Tennessee corn whiskey.

"Ahhh," Poteet sighed, smacking her lips.

"Medicine for what ails ye," agreed Scold, rubbing tenderly between her buttocks.

"Wash those filthy hands before ye carve the meat," warned Pearl, enjoying the liquor's warmth in the center of her thin chest.

The aroma of sizzling fat and herbs soon pervaded the clearing, was picked up by the evening breeze and pushed up the trail.

*****

"Times like these put me in the mood for a wee tune," Pearl said. She always let the spirits go to her head. Possessed of a fine voice, she insisted they sing the old songs of humor and heartache.

Poteet dragged her squeeze box from the wagon. It was a tiny contraption of bellows, reeds and buttons from which she teased rollicky music that her sisters loved. For all their lives, they had made up songs and ditties. For no one but themselves.

"Do the one about Preacher John and the accursed outhouse!" Scold wheedled. She was partial to musical renditions of favorite legends from the hills and hollows. The coarser and more raucous, the better.

Sister Pearl objected, "Oh, 'tis not a fitting song for gentle ladies of our upbringing."

She lifted a knowing eyebrow at Poteet. Not only did Scold love songs with scatological and sexual references, she possessed a loud and grating voice variously described as a cross between a mountain wildcat in heat and a wild hog being castrated. This was being generous, too.

Poteet's squeeze box wheezed and whistled as she tuned, also spitting on the wooden hinges to loosen them. "How 'bout *Curdy Brown's Candlestick?*" Before anyone could reply, she whirled across the campsite, trilling out a snappy melody and singing.

41

Ol' Curdy Brown, he went to town, for to buy a candle.
Curdy left at break of day to blunder through the
brambles.
He took ne'er dram nor crust o' bread to sup on in his
rambles.
Ol' Curdy wasted plumb away afore he bought that
candle!

The sisters' voices—even Scold's harsh croaks—came together in a melody that pleased them, if not the nocturnal creatures around the camp. Her finger's flickering across the keyboard, Poteet led them in a merry dance around the campfire. Three shadows capered after them. They skipped and bowed, holding their dress hems above hobnail boots.

For a while, it seemed they were little girls again, happy with a simple tune and nonsense words. The magic of youth was long past, never to return, but worth remembering for three old women whose wagon trundled between mountain communities where they sold their wares and special services.

The squeeze box wheezed to a stop. The three sisters collapsed where they stood, laughing and breathless. Even Scold. She cast another log on the fire and lifted the oven lid to check her roast.

"That 'un was a right good song, Sister Poteet," Scold said, a compliment rare from someone who found fault faster that flies found syrup. "Thankee for the tune. Nuthin' better before a feast!"

The sisters clapped their agreement and passed around the jug.

*****

"Hello, the camp!" came a shout, followed by the clomp of iron-shod hooves.

Into the pool of firelight limped a gangly man, leading a tired roan mare. The sisters' mules smelled the interloper and bared blunt yellow teeth. Poteet shushed them, picked up the hickory cudgel and stood ready to use it.

Pearl's whip was in her hand. Scold made a warding sign with her long fingers and addressed the stranger.

"By what right do ye advance on our camp, sirrah? We three sisters be wayfarers on journey to Gideon, where kinfolk await. The trail is terrible hard on oldsters, and the route be dangerous. But we know how to defend."

She let him see the long-bladed butcher knife in her right hand.

"I claim the right of traveler's hospitality, ma'am. Help on the road for anyone in need. It is an ancient tradition, old as these mountains. I had hoped that three stately ladies of seasoned age would remember when guests once found welcome in lonely places."

Scold sneered, "Ye have smooth talk and somewhat of the old ways. But who else is out there in the dark, waiting for us to let down our guard?"

"Only me, an accident victim." He turned his side toward the fire, where a dark smear on his dirty linen shirt was visible. It dripped blood. "Horse threw me. Landed on a sharp granite rock that pierced my hide. Needs sewing up and a tonic."

The sisters, who'd been ready to mob the stranger and strike him down, visibly relaxed.

"Aye, ye seem to be in a sorry way," called out Poteet.

The sisters' eyes met and a silent decision was made.

They devoutly believed in the Old Way. The rules had to be observed and for good reason.

Life on the trail, in what was mostly wilderness in this part of Appalachia, could be hard and dangerous. Beasts and evil spirits, robbers and bad men, damned souls cursed to wander the earth, monsters not of this world; all such threats lurked just outside the firelight.

Powder and ball blasted from old musket barrels could not guarantee safety. Traveling together and following the Old Way helped. People aided others, especially on the trail. The Purifoy sisters were known far and wide for the Wild Magick they wielded to aid the young and innocent, feeble and helpless.

"Enter the circle of fire and welcome, stranger."

*****

Two of the sisters bustled around the man. Pearl cleaned the wound, which was more a bloody bruise than puncture. She applied a plaster of plantain leaves and mud, dried ironweed petals, jewel weed pulp and snuff. She wrapped strips cut from a burlap sack around his rib cage and helped him get his shirt on.

In a tin cup, Poteet mixed a tonic of whiskey and creek water, seasoned with sassafras powder and elm bark. The stranger drank it down and smacked his lips. Held the cup out for a refill.

Scold was naturally suspicious. It was her nature. She stood off and peered at the interloper.

He had not offered his name, and the right of hospitality demanded the sharing of identity and explanation of your business on the trail. Many a traveler offering aid had been waylaid when they failed to probe their guests for information. Scold believed in the Old Way but liked to keep a sharp knife handy.

He was an unimpressive specimen, she thought. Too skinny through the shoulders, knobs of his spine protruding down his back, no hips to speak of, and a long face and jutting underjaw. He was a tobacco-chewer, too.

Scold detested a lazy man who'd spit in the fire where food was cooking just to hear the sizzle. The rivulets of brown juice leaking out the sides of his thin-lipped mouth disgusted her. But despite her personal feelings and growing unease, she was bound to help a fellow traveler.

His horse stood outside the firelight, still saddled like he expected the sisters to take care of his animal and tack. Scold found this not only impolite but an indicator of flawed character. Then, there was the scuffed and scarred leather rider's satchel slung over his shoulder. It bulged with contents. When Poteet had tried to take it in order to remove the bloody shirt, he shrugged her off.

"Sirrah, we are ready to enjoy an evening's repast of roast meat, biscuits and wild vegetables. What we have, we will gladly share. Just sit and let us fix a plate," said Pearl, assuming a coquettish pose.

Leave it to Pearl to still have the juice to summon up a pert but wrinkled smile and wink, observed Scold.

They piled high a battered tin plate, opened a jar of homemade plum jelly for the biscuits and poured the stranger coffee.

He ate like a hog, using fingers instead of the fork. Holding out the empty plate, he grunted for more. The coffee, he hardly touched, greedily eyeing the whiskey jug instead. The sisters declined to offer him more of the spirits.

With the last biscuit – he had downed six of the fluffy things – he sopped the gravy clean and tossed the empty plate toward Scold. No thanks, just the metallic sound of tin hitting a rock.

The stranger stretched out his long legs and belched loudly, reared up on his side and broke wind toward the coffee pot. He fed a plug of tobacco into his mouth while staring across the fire at Scold.

"Was the roast joint tasty, sirrah? I seasoned it me-self," she said.

He chewed, and new tobacco dribbles ran. He wiped with a dirty hand and gestured to the empty Dutch oven. "Not the best I ever had, but tender and juicy, all the same. The gravy and biscuits really set that pork off, I'll confess. Your seasoning was tasty. What did you use?"

His lips smiled around the disgusting lump in his mouth, but his eyes did not.

"Oh, this an' that, ye know. Herbs and spices of the forest, things that grow in the shadows of mountains, along the trails, rivers and creeks."

She pronounced the word "herbs" as "yarbs," in the Old Way of speaking. Her fingers twiddled in the cooling air, tracing a pattern that could have been a blessing or curse. It was clearly a symbolic counterpoint to the reality of what the stranger had slipped out of his leather sack and held in a steady hand.

The revolver's black eye looked straightly at Scold's forehead.

*****

"I heard about you three, an' learned a lot about the herb ladies who ride the trails this time of year. You're sellin' homemade concoctions. Tonics, potions an' such. The Injuns call you medicine women. Pregnant gals seek out certain cures from you that preachers would damn them for, as much as for their sin of making the two-backed beast without being married."

The gun wobbled slightly as he laughed. It was a curdled sound, as if the meanness in him wanted to be expelled but was too rooted. The sisters instinctively closed ranks, but the pistol continued to point at Scold.

"Y'all are right famous from here to Kentucky, and even up West Virginia way. I hear tell, you got a thrivin' business. Lotta folks want your remedies. They even say you might be witch women."

Poteet eased toward her cudgel, but the stranger shook his head in warning.

"I also heard that you travel with a lot of silver, gold, an' scrip. This is what I want. All you got. Don't hold back nothin'. Maybe I'll let you live!"

He spit a stream of stinking saliva in the fire and drew lips back from crooked, stained teeth. The sisters realized they'd invited a feral thing into their camp. Perhaps still human, but someone tainted by the Devil. They huddled closer together but showed no fear.

"We gave you hospitality. You were hurt and we aided. Our meat and bread, you ate and was nourished." Scold's words, carefully intoned, sounded much like Bible scripture.

The stranger's face reflected cruelty bubbling from a dark soul. "Don't give a shit about hospitality or none of them old commandments! My rule is to take what I want. Sometimes, it's easy. Other times, it ain't."

"Your wound?" Pearl asked.

"Like I said, sometimes there's bloody work to be done." He touched the injury. "This here happened when a ridge-runner kid hit me with a really long shot from his pappy's squirrel-huntin' rifle. Light powder charge, and the distance too far. Miracle he hit me. Hurt like hell, but the damage could a been worse."

Cocking his head, he laughed at the black velvet sky. "I ran the squirt down and bashed his brains out, just like I did his pa and ma. Lucky for you, I let her live a while and had my pleasure. Otherwise, it might've been one of you old hags!" he said.

"You drag out that treasure right now," he hissed.

The gun's barrel continued to point at Scold's head, but it wobbled. It was difficult to hold a heavy gun steady with one hand.

"Nuthin' but a thief and murderer, you be," said Pearl, shaking her head sadly. She picked up the wagon whip.

The stranger tried to point the revolver at her, but the weapon now trembled, pointing up and then down like he could no longer control where it aimed. He lurched to his feet and nearly fell in the fire.

Body parts would not obey commands from his brain. The gun dropped from nerveless fingers. There was buzzing in his ears, and he began to choke on the cud of tobacco.

He heard scurrying and whispers, felt his arms and ankles tied. He tried to speak but couldn't, something stuffed in his mouth. What was happening? How was this possible? So many times, he had lulled his victims and taken their treasure and lives.

Three wrinkled old women bent over him, smiling. Their eyes shined like fiery stars. Then blackness came.

*****

He awoke when the buckboard hit a washed-out ditch on the lonely trail to Gideon. Hog-tied, naked, and gagged, he rode in the coffin storage box. He rested atop mildewed blankets and bundles of old clothes.

Pinpoints of sunlight that shafted through nail holes and imperfect carpentry joints provided some brightness inside the box. Dust motes danced before his eyes. He moaned and thrashed, surprised at the intense pain from his back, hips and trussed legs.

His arms were securely bound. He wanted so badly to stretch and work out the pain and stiffness.

He heard the buckboard's creaking, felt the hard bounce as steel-rimmed, wooden wheels trundled over rocks and ditches. He did not know the time nor the day. Then, he remembered the three sisters.

Rather than despair, hope rekindled in his brain. He was ever the smooth talker, could wheedle, lie, and convince women, even ancient crones, that black was white and up was down. He was a rogue, after all. Dangerous even without a pistol. He'd charm them into complacency and turn the tables.

The wagon stopped. A voice cursed all mules, rocky trails, and the world in general. The other

Purifoy sisters laughed. Another long summer day was ending; shadows along the trail lengthened.

"Listen!" Poteet said, hushing her sisters. They heard a barred owl's "hoo-hoo-hoo," an invitation for darkness to fall. Soon it would be time for the owl to hunt, to satisfy the imperative of nature for survival.

"Time to make camp!" Poteet hollered, and her voice echoed between steep hillsides. The sisters went about their duties, including Scold whose job was to roundly criticize her sisters at their tasks.

The stranger heard the jests and laughter of old women comfortable with themselves and their lifestyle. He smelled hickory smoke as the campfire blazed. Heard cast-iron skillets and lids clanking, the racket of tin plates and cups.

He prepared himself. They'd soon be in his thrall. He had a magic of his own, especially when it came to womenfolk. All that happened back at the camp had been a misunderstanding, a fanciful tale he'd concocted for their entertainment. It was the corn liquor talking. Plus, they drugged him. He wasn't in his right mind.

He would fault the sisters for their suspicion, lay the blame off on them. He was a brave man and companion. Good to have on the trail to provide protection.

The hinges of the storage box squealed as the top opened.

"Our guest is awake!" Poteet looked down at him and smiled, jowls wobbling.

"How's our fellow traveler doing?" Pearl tittered, assuming her coquettish pose.

Scold hauled herself on the buckboard with a groan and peeked in the box. This was the woman whom the stranger most feared. The one he'd held at gunpoint until the potion had taken effect. He should have known the three old bitches would be distrustful and feed him something to dull his wits and render him helpless. Probably put it the moonshine.

"You seem nice and fresh, sirrah, for all the miles you've rode in the box. Now, 'tis time to prepare our evening meal. Stranger, you relished our camp hospitality last time and are invited to join us again."

He'd heard much about these three old women from gossip, stories, and local lore. Thought he knew enough to make them easy victims. But now came the realization that he'd never really known who they were or why they traveled the backroads and lonely trails. His newfound confidence began to dwindle.

When Scold started to strop the butcher knife, he knew what hospitality really meant to the Purifoy sisters. In the twilight, he could see the mutilation when he stared down at his body. Where the pain throbbed, the stump of his right thigh had been sewn and tied carefully to staunch the bleeding. Nothing remained below.

Awareness dawned. The old ladies had fresh meat in the pot when he walked into their camp. From where? Three elderly women couldn't feed themselves off the land. He should have known.

He had been to supper again yesterday, while still unconscious. This realization caused him to beg when the sisters took hold of him. The stranger screamed himself to oblivion when Scold expertly removed the next choice roast.

THE HERO

by Ken Teutsch

Let me tell you something. If you do something good in this world, don't expect no credit for it. What I done was a brave deed, and all I got for it is whatchacallit.

Vilified. Yeah. Vilified.

Here's what happened. First off: She started it.

Hey, look: I never liked the old woman. Sure, I'll admit that. I always knowed there was something off about her. More than just being foreign, I mean. (Though I didn't know just how off she was.) Even so, I never done her any real dirt. I might make a joke here and there or something. Just messing around. And that's how it started, see? She couldn't take a God damn joke.

It was at the little store at the crossroads where everything costs more than in town, but sometimes you don't want to drive all the way to town, so you suck it up and pay it. I walked in the store as she was coming out. Little scrawny thing, come up to about my armpit. Long grey hair. Most women her age (whatever that was...she looked about two hundred) wear it up or cut

57

it short, but she wore hers pulled back over her shoulders and down her back.

"Mizz Fontananny," I said, and I stepped aside to let her by.

"Fonta*nini*!" she kind of snapped back, her little black eyes shining at me, and she hustled on past. Like it's my fault she has a funny name! So, I called after her, "Sorry, my eye-talian is a little rusty. *Beenie weenie! Ats-a spicy meat-a-ball!*"

She stopped there next to her old truck and she turned around and looked at me. I give her a smile, you know. Like I said. Kidding around. But she come out with a string of eye-talian words, kind of halfway spitting them at me, then turned around and got in her truck and left.

I may not speak eye-talian, but I know when I been cussed at.

"What's her God damn problem?" I asked Lowell. Lowell runs the store. He just kind of looked at me.

"You really asking?" he said. Lowell doesn't like me because I pay for my gas with money at the cash register. He'd be happier if everybody paid with plastic out at the pump and he didn't have to do nothing but sit on his ass.

He kind of shrugged at me. "For one thing," he said, "You call her 'eye-talian'."

"That's what she is, ain't she?"

"Yeah, sure." he said. "What bothers her is the way you say it."

"Say what? Eye-talian?"

"Yeah. '*Eye*-talian' instead of 'Italian.' Sounds disrespectful. Like you're making fun of her."

I threwed up my hands. "Eye-talian! E-talian! What's the difference? And anyway, who's a damn dago to tell me how to talk English?"

"I don't know," he said, and he kind of sighed and rolled his eyes and started looking over my shoulder like I should maybe move on and make room for the next customer, only there wasn't no next customer.

"Anyway," I said, "you mark my words: There's something squirrely about that old woman."

"Uh huh," he said. He picked up a little notebook and started flipping through it like it was real important and pressing stuff, which I doubted severely.

"You just mark my words," I told him again.

"I'm markin' 'em," he said, and he picked up a pencil and started poking at the notebook. "See? Markin' 'em."

Smartass.

And that's what got that witch on my whatchacallit. Radar.

Of course, I didn't know right then that she was a witch. But she was. A real one, God damn it, and not just name-calling. She may have had some foreign word for it, but a witch is a witch in my book (which is the Good Book, which has some things to say about witches). Believe me or don't; I don't give a shit. I know what I know.

*****

This eye-talian woman in question (who was a witch, whatever she called herself) lived way back on a dirt road in a house that used to belong to a fellow named Moses Brooks. Moses was already a geezer when I was just a kid, and I'm getting up there myself now. Moses had two boys and one of them got killed invading Africa. (Lot of people forget we invaded Africa in World War II before anywhere else.) The other boy, Jefferson, lived through invading Africa and went ahead and invaded Italy. And when he come home, he brought this girl home with him that he had married over there.

Or maybe they didn't even marry. She called herself Fontananny after all, not Brooks.

They didn't move in with Moses and Mrs. Moses back then. They lived off somewhere. But then Mr. and Mrs. Moses finally both died, and Jefferson died, too. So here come this eye-talian woman to claim Moses's place, and there she's been, all alone way back there in the woods, for years now.

And she was a witch, damn it! Thinking back, I should have known it even before I knew it.

For one thing, ain't nobody as old as she had to be got any business being as spry as she was. She drove that ancient damn pickup truck that she kept running somehow, had to sit on a pillow to see over the dashboard, and she would come to town maybe once a month to buy stuff, two carts full sometimes, which she would load in the truck by herself, a little scrawny woman in a black dress hefting them bags into the truck bed, shooing off the bag boy at Harp's with never mind, never mind, *is good, is good.* Still not talking English right, and her living over here since Truman was president.

She had a big garden out there that she took care of all by herself, hoeing and digging one thing or another damn near all day damn near every day, working like ought to wear out a woman half as old as she had to be. Everybody who ever went out that way went on about that woman's garden and how beautiful it was, and she give away all kinds of vegetables to her neighbors. She had nearly an acre of all kinds of stuff, including weird eye-talian stuff. Herbs and shit.

Fennel. She grew a big patch of fennel.

What the hell is fennel?

And she didn't go to church like everybody else. Now you might think, "Well, she's eye-talian, so she'd go to a Catholic church." Well, Faye Fields at the bank is one of them and goes to the nearest one, down across the Louisiana line in Preston, and she said she'd never seen the old woman down there. Said maybe she goes to a different mass (I guess they have a dozen or so a week or some damn thing). Yeah, maybe. But I doubt it.

After I left the store that day I started thinking. Who the hell did that smartass Lowell think he was? And who the hell did that eye-talian witch think *she* was? (Though I didn't know yet that she was a *sure enough* witch.) And I started getting more and more pissed off.

Let me tell you something about myself: I'm a Christian. I go to church, when I go, at the Right Apostolic Freewill Tabernacle. A tabernacle is like a church, only more so, and us Right Apostolic Freewill Christians are Christians, only more so. Because the other denominations call themselves Christian, but they have got it all wrong. And ain't no denomination got it all wronger than the Catholics do, which was what this eye-talian woman was, if she was anything at all. Which she wasn't. Witch.

So, like I say: I'm a Christian. But now let me tell you something else: I don't take no shit off nobody.

That same night, after I went in Lowell's store and he smarted off to me, somebody busted the lock on the gas reservoir and poured about ten pounds of sand into his gasoline. I could say more, but I won't.

And the next day, I drove out Hornbill Road to old Moses Brooks' place. Or rather past the place. Just to take a look, you know.

There wasn't that much to see. The house was back a bit from the road, and the great big garden was all around it, greened up and thriving like the damn

Amazon or something. Corn was all tasseled out, even early as it was. There was a barn out back with some goats wandering around it, and what I guessed was a chicken house. I didn't see the old woman, but she could have been in the garden and you couldn't have seen her over the tomato plants. I sort of slowed down a bit and then kept going. On a road like that, people notice when a car goes by.

Driving on, I give it some thought. Thought about that snotty little eye-talian woman and her goddamn garden. Be a shame if anything happened to that garden.

*****

That night about dark I went across the county line down to The Rack, which is a pool hall and tavern that I go to from time to time. I had a few beers and shot a little eight-ball. Then I flipped Leonard Davis for whiskey shots and won four in a row before he accused me of cheating and wanted to switch to using his own quarter. I told him to kiss my ass, took my gimmicked quarter and left.

From there I went to the drive-thru liquor store and bought a pint of Kentucky Tavern.

From there I drove back to my house and got the gas can I keep out in the shed with the lawn mower. It was about three quarters full. From there, I drove out Hornbill Road.

It was along about eleven o'clock by now. past bedtime, I figured, for eye-talian fossil women. The moon was nearly full, and it was just getting up to where it peeped over the trees on the east side of the road. I pulled off the road a ways down from her house, got my gas can and started walking. I sang really quiet under my breath: *There's gonna be a hot time in the old town tonight!* That's the only line in the song I could remember, so I just sang it over and over.

Then there it was. The award-winning (or would be if they give awards for that) garden. The house was all dark just like I figured it would be. I moved through the road ditch without falling down (a little surprising) and crept into the rows between the corn stalks. More cover there, and I figured the tall corn would make the highest flames. All this stuff was green, but three gallons of gasoline can cancel out a lot of chlorophyll. I took the cap off the gas can and was getting ready to pour, when I heard something moving in among the stalks.

I got my flashlight out of my pocket. I hadn't needed it on the road, but it was dark in among the corn. Something rustled a little ways off. Then it rustled a little closer. Then the stalks shifted and wiggled just a few feet away down the row. And then I seen the goat.

Listen now. This is when shit starts to get weird.

I didn't really see the goat at first. I just seen the eyes, which kind of freaked me out because you know, goat eyes. You ever seen goat eyes? They're weird colors, and the black part goes sideways. The eyes were glowing at me from about ten feet away in the shadows between the corn stalks. But man, I just thought I was freaking out, because about the time my brain told me "stop freaking out, it's just goat eyes," another pair of eyes all of a sudden opened up right over the goat eyes! And these was cat eyes. I know you've seen cat eyes. They're weird, too.

Then the four-eyed goat cat stepped out from the corn stalks into the row, and I got the flashlight turned on it.

Well, it was a goat with a cat on it. I mean a cat riding on the back of a goat. Black goat, black cat. Big fucking goat and big fucking cat. And they was both looking at me with them glowing eyes. Goat eyes, cat eyes. Both of them, goat and cat, just looking at me.

"The fuck?" I said, and I took a step back and dropped the gas can. It give a liquid-sounding *bong* and just set there. And me and the goat and the cat all just looked at one another. Then the cat stood up on the goat's back and give a sort of growl. Then it jumped.

O.K. I know what you're gonna say about this next part. I'd been drinking, right? But let me tell you something: I took my first drink when I was eleven years old and I started drinking more or less regular when I was sixteen. I drink often and I drink a lot. Usually, a lot more than I had been drinking that night. And never do I ever see anything that ain't there. Now I'll admit that I sometimes don't see things that are there, like porch steps or police cars, but never once did I ever see snakes or pink elephants or any of that crap and I sure as shit never seen anything like what I seen when that cat jumped off the goat's back.

Because when it landed, it wasn't a cat no more. It was that eye-talian woman.

She was standing there big as life, or little as life, her grey hair all loose and down around her face and over her shoulders. She was wearing a black nightgown kind of deal and was barefooted. The flashlight beam was shaking, because I was shaking, but the light still hit her. I could see her sharp little yellow teeth in a grimace, and her eyes was still glowing. And the black parts still went up and down like a cat's eyes! She hissed at me like a cat, too.

I didn't do nothing because I couldn't move. I wanted to run; I won't lie. I wanted very much to turn and haul ass, but I simply could not move. Pretty much everything on me shut down when that cat jumped up a cat and come down an old eye-talian woman. So I just stood there. Then the woman all of a sudden snapped an arm up, and I felt a sharp sting across the side of my face and there was dust in my eyes and a sudden whiff of something peppery. She had smacked me with something, and now I seen that she held in one hand stalks of some kind of plant. She had smacked me with that, and it hurt like hell.

She cocked her head and looked at me, then at the gas can, and she snapped out an eye-talian word. Then she looked up at me again and yapped another eye-talian word: *"Bastardo!"* That one I could understand. She kind of crouched down a little, and I braced myself for something really, really bad to happen.

Something happened, but it didn't happen to me. Right then there come a noise through the air like a yell from off in the distance, and the old woman and the goat both jerked and turned away from me. They both of them looked up in the sky. So, I looked up in the sky, too, but I didn't see nothing but the moon. When I looked back down, the corn stalks were still moving, and the goat and the old woman were gone.

So, I began to be gone, too. Gone just as far and as fast as I could possibly make myself gone.

I tore through the corn in the direction of the road, arms up to keep the leaves from slicing my face. I busted out into the open and directly into the road ditch. This time I did fall and slammed into the far side of the ditch so hard I thought I'd busted something. But I dragged myself up and began to climb out onto the road, busted rib or not. Then I heard screeching, stopped, and turned around, in spite of myself.

All right. Here's what I seen. No shit now. Here's what I seen.

I seen something up in the air over the old woman's garden. There was people up there. Yeah, you heard me. People up in the air. Three of them, silhouetted against the moonlight and trailing sort of streamers behind them that might have been strips of their clothes or might have been hair. They were holding big, leafy stalks of some kind and were waving them around over their heads, and as I looked, they swooped down over the garden. And then up from the garden came another shape, blacker than the others. It was that eye-talian woman, and she was riding on the back of that fucking goat.

And what happened then was...I guess you might call it a witch's dogfight.

They circled and swirled around one another, and the air was filled with noise like from a flock of mad screech owls. The three flying people would each dive down at the ground, and that woman and her goat would swoop down to meet them. They'd swing those stalks and flail at each other like crazy. The old woman was swinging that handful of brush she smacked me with, and every time she landed a thwack on one of them flying people, he-she-it would wail like a banshee and go spinning off. One zoomed by right over my head and crashed into the trees on the other side of the road.

It was like them flying people were trying to get at the old woman's garden, and she was knocking shit out of them with them weeds of hers before they could get there. It was the damnedest fight I ever seen, and I couldn't stop looking. But before too long them three whatever the hell they was seemed to give up. They screeched louder than ever, and then shot straight up into the sky like they wasn't going to stop until they got to the moon. Things got kind of quiet then, and I lost sight of the old woman and the goat.

Enough standing around. I started running.

I was panting like a dog and my side was hurting like a son of a bitch when I got to the truck. I come up on the passenger side and stopped to catch my breath. However drunk I might have been before, I was stone cold sober now. I just wanted to get the hell away and never come near that woman, her house, or her goat ever again. So, I near about pissed myself when I heard her right behind me.

She was standing there in the middle of the road. Just her. The goat wasn't around. Her hair was all wild and windblown now, and the handful of whatever kind of plant she was holding was shredded and busted in her hand. She was walking toward me slow and looking at me with her head kind of tipped forward. The moonlight was behind her, so I couldn't see if her eyes was still cat eyes or people eyes again.

"Why?" she said. "Why you want to burn-a me?" And somehow all I could think was, *Still with that God damn Chico Marx accent?*

"Ma'am," I said, holding out my hands, "I wasn't gonna… I was just…. Listen, it's just a big misunderstanding!"

She laughed at that and muttered something in eye-talian. She started walking toward me a little faster, and I about freaked. I started hollering. "Stay away from me, God dammit! Stay away, you witch!"

She stopped and cocked her head like she done in the cornfield. "Witch-a?" she said, kind of quizzical-like. After a second she all of a sudden looked up at the sky and held her arms out. I ducked and looked up, too, thinking them whatever-the-hell might be coming back, but from her voice I could tell she was just being exasperated. She kind of cried out to heaven. "*Quante volte devo ascoltare questo?*" Then all of a sudden, she hopped right up to me—quick-stepped, like a jumping spider—and I give out a little shriek and would have climbed backward up onto the truck hood if I could.

"I am not a witch!" she said, and for that long at least, that accent was gone. She pointed up into the air toward her place. "They! They are *malandanti! They* are witch!" She poked me with a boney finger. "*Idiota*! I am *benandanta*. I fight-a the *stregone*! I fight-a the witch! Since forever we fight-a the witch! Since before there is a Pope, we fight-a the witch!" She backed off then and looked at me. I couldn't see her face very well in the shadows, but I could feel the whatchacallit. Contempt. I could feel the contempt and hear it in her voice. "Always the people like you come. Always. Come...and *burn*! But what will you do when we are-a no more? Hah? Who then will-a burn? Hah? *Culo!*" She snapped her fingers at me and tossed her head, then turned away, swishing her skirt. She dropped the ragged plant she had been holding, made a sort of "up yours" gesture without looking back, and started walking back down the road. That's when I remembered.

I remembered the pistol I keep in the glove box of my truck. I reached in through the window, pulled it out, and I put three right in the middle of that witch's back.

*****

They got me a couple of days later. I forgot about the gas can, and they found my fingerprints all over it. They had them on file from two or three other troubles I got into. And some of the people who were at The Rack come forward and said I did some talking while I was playing pool about teaching that old eye-talian bitch a lesson. (I don't remember that, but I guess I probably did.) And also, they found the gun and matched it up. I guess I should have got rid of it, but my Daddy give it to me.

I told them I shot the old woman because she was a witch, and the Sheriff just said, "Nice try, you piece of shit." I guess he thought I was going for an insanity plea or something, but I was just telling them like it was. He said everybody the old woman ever gave a tomato to was volunteering to push the plunger on my injection.

Smartass.

So here I am. And ain't nobody come to see me in here except my lawyer, who also don't like me, and Leonard Davis. Leonard said they were going to put the old woman's place up for auction, and he drove by there to take a look at it.

"Brown," he said. "Whole place is just as brown as Arizona. Kind of a shame, when it used to be so pretty." Said it wasn't just her place, though. Everything was browning out, it seems. It was starting to look like the year's whole cotton and soybean crops would be a loss if it didn't rain soon. Hadn't rained at all since, well, since I shot the old lady, come to think of it. I told him to forgive me if I wasn't particularly interested in his fucking weather report.

Then he asked me: "How come you to want to shoot her, anyway?"

"'Cause she was a *God damned witch*."

They ought to give me a medal is what they ought to do, the bastards.

End

UNMASKED

by Austin Shirey

It's a little after one in the morning when the luchador stumbles into Cantina del Brujas. The bottles of cheap whiskey he's drained alone in his apartment earlier that evening have left Marco Alvarez more than a little unsteady.

The cantina is grimy; dimly lit by yellowed lights and a stylized, slow-dying, red neon sign of a calaca skull just above the bar. There are only four patrons at this hour, tucked away in booths nursing their demons—five, actually: a woman Marco hadn't noticed just a moment ago is sitting at the bar a few stools down from him. She's dressed in a faded black suit and matching wide-brimmed hat. Her dark hair is held in a ponytail by a red ribbon as garish as a slit wrist. She's very pale, and uneasiness flutters in his stomach as she looks at him.

"Jack, neat," Marco says to the bartender as he climbs up a stool and slaps his last thousand pesos onto the scoured and pock-marked bar. "As many as that will get me."

The bartender is old, her face lined and cratered by age. She's reading a romance novel, one of those with the bodice-ripping artwork on the front cover. She sighs, palms Marco's money and puts the book down on the counter near the cash register. She pours his drink, slides it to him across the bar and returns to her paperback.

Marco downs the whole glass, slides it back to the bartender for a refill. She ignores him, focused on her book. Marco *tinks* the glass loudly with a dirty fingernail.

The bartender huffs, tosses the book back onto the counter, and refills his whiskey. She's about to turn back when Marco says, "Must be getting to the good part, huh?"

The bartender's back goes straight as a board. She moves after a silent moment of collection, grabs three more glasses and fills them. She turns and lines the glasses up in front of Marco, grabs her book and retreats to the other end of the bar, fleeing his orbit.

Fine with him. He downs another glass.

"Rough day?"

The voice is a jolt of electricity up his spine, a nail scratching across concrete.

Marco turns as he grabs his next whiskey. The woman in black is looking at him, lips curled in an inviting smile.

"Not good," Marco says. He downs his drink.

Next in line.

"Wouldn't be here if it wasn't." The woman gestures at their poorly lit, poorly maintained surroundings.

Marco laughs. "This is true."

The woman pats the barstool next to hers. Marco notices the black nails on her pale fingers are chipping. There's something about her that excites him, then he remembers he's out of money and downs another drink. Can't afford such pleasures, not after today. Not for a while.

"Thanks, but no," he says, sliding his empty glass across the bar. He reaches for his next drink, comes back with an empty one. He frowns.

"I bought a bottle," the woman says, and Marco notices she's holding an unopened bottle of Don Julio. She motions to two empty glasses on the bar in front of her. "Won't be able to finish it all myself, and you look like you need it more than I do."

Marco hesitates. Something about this woman, the way she smiles, is too inviting. It feels...*off*. Then again, she's offering free drink. Expensive drink. He's got a good buzz going, drunk by most standards, but he's nowhere near the oblivion he thirsts for.

"Can't say no to that," Marco says with a quick smile, dismounting his stool and moving next to her.

The woman smiles, opens the bottle of Don Julio and pours them both a glass. Marco watches, almost mesmerized by the strange way her skin seems to shimmer up close, like he can see through it to the skull beneath. Who is this woman who looks so much like a painting of Santa Muerta?

"To stories," the woman says, handing him a glass.

"To drinking," Marco says, and they *clink* their glasses together and drink.

The Don Julio is smooth and warm and flavorful, like liquid silver running down his throat; like consuming a pleasant summer breeze.

"Just how bad was your day, Marco?"

Somewhere in his head, Marco recoils. He's sure he hasn't introduced himself. But everything's so hazy.

"Bad," he says, finishing his drink and eagerly accepting her generous refill. "Lost a big match."

"Match?"

"Wrestling."

"Ah, I thought you looked like a fighter." She winks at him. "What promotion do you wrestle for?"

"None. It's street wrestling."

"Oh, I see."

"Street's a good way to make quick money. If you're really good, you can maybe make a name for yourself, if you build a following."

"Maybe catch the attention of a big promotion?"

"Maybe." Marco takes a drink. The world takes on a dreamlike quality, almost as if he's looking through an empty bottle smudged with fingerprints. "But not likely."

"Then why do it?"

"Just something I'm good at. And it helps pay the bills."

"So you had a bad match," the woman says, dismissing the idea with a languid wave of her hand. "Surely that's not the end of the world."

Marco grunts. "You'd think."

"Giving up so easy?"

"Don't have a choice."

"Of course, you have a choice."

"Not when you lose your mask in a lucha de apuesta." He punctuates this by downing the rest of his drink. He motions for another refill.

The woman pours him another.

"I've seen that happen in the arena matches on TV," she says. "But those luchadores still have a career afterwards."

Marco nods. "Those are the guys in the promotions. Me…"

"You're just a street fighter."

"Right. And losing your mask in a betting match on the street means you're through. The mystery, the shine, it's all gone. No-one cares who's under the mask. It's the mask that counts. It's the mask the fans follow. Once that's gone, you're out for good. No one will pay to watch you anymore."

The woman pouts her bluish lips, and Marco feels an overwhelming urge to kiss them. He drinks more instead.

"Rough day," she finally agrees.

"Yeah."

"What will you do?"

Marco shrugs. "Bounce for a few more places, probably. That's what I did when I wasn't wrestling. The worst thing is that the prize money would have kept me afloat for a good, long while. Could've let me focus on wrestling."

"Prize money?"

"Yeah, from the match. Winner keeps his mask and gets twenty-three-thousand pesos."

"So, this guy that beat you—"

"Guerrero Grande."

The woman gives him a look. "Really?"

Marco shrugs. "Luis. His name is Luis Rivera."

"So, Luis got your mask and your money?"

Marco drowns the harsh truth in his tequila. "Yeah."

The woman empties her glass and sets it on the bar. She eyes Marco for a moment, her sharp, gray eyes burning through him.

"Marco," she says slowly, softly, focusing on the bottle in her hand as she refills both their glasses.

"Yeah?"

"What would you say if I could get you that money back?"

Marco laughs. "I'd say you're full of it."

"I'm not." She faces him again, eyes hard and unflinching.

Marco wants to look away, to wither under the heat of her gaze, but he forces himself not to.

"How?" he asks. Almost a whisper.

The woman drinks deep. "Tell me, do you like this Luis Rivera?"

"No. Not at all. He's a real pendejo."

The woman smiles. "Good."

Marco feels like a swarm of cockroaches is skittering down his spine. "*What?*"

"Well, I assume your dislike of Luis means you won't mind anything unpleasant befalling him."

Marco feels suddenly unmoored from reality, drowning in possibilities. "I, uh, I don't know."

"Sure, you do. You need that money. But you also need Luis gone in a way that doesn't point back to you. Which is where I come in."

The weight of Marco's world seems to collapse upon his shoulders: the rent due next week; the overwhelming reality that he's lost his most reliable means of income, and will probably be evicted; this strange, unsettling woman offering him a way out of the hole he now found himself in—the very hole he'd walked into this bar hoping to fill with alcohol—and the harsh truth that her offer was actually tempting.

He takes a drink, his first *small* sip of the night. "How?"

"Have you ever heard the tale of El Silbón?" the woman asks.

Marco shakes his head.

"It's said it originated in Venezuela, but who can know such things? It's one of my favorites. Would you like to hear it?"

Marco shrugs, continues drinking.

"Well, there once was a very poor family. A father, a mother, their young son, the grandfather and the grandfather's hound. They didn't have a lot, but every year for the boy's birthday the father always went hunting for deer. It was the only real gift they could give the boy. So the boy's birthday comes around, and just as he does every year, the father leaves early in the morning with his bow and arrows to go hunting. Only this time, he takes the boy with him, figuring he's old enough for his first hunt. The boy is jubilant; but after hours and hours of tracking and waiting, they come up empty handed. And now the sun is setting, and it's time they return home. But the boy, he flies into a rage and beats his father to death in the woods with a rock. Then he takes his father's hunting knife and guts him and takes his father's heart and liver back to his home. The boy gives the heart and liver to the mother to cook for his birthday dinner and tells her and his grandfather that his father will come along after he has finished dressing the rest of the deer.

"As the three of them begin to eat, the mother remarks about how tough the meat is and how it's so unlike the father to take so long. The grandfather agrees and decides to go into the woods to search for the father. But just as the grandfather is leaving, he notices the boy is wearing the father's hunting knife, the very knife the grandfather himself had given him.

"It is then that the grandfather realizes what the boy has done and what they have been eating. The grandfather begins to beat the boy, and, eventually, the boy confesses everything to him and the mother. The mother begs the grandfather to punish the boy further. So, the grandfather ties the boy to a tree and whips him mercilessly, until the flesh of his back is raw and seeping. The grandfather then calls for the mother to bring him hot peppers, which he crushes and rubs into

the boy's wounds. Once he is done, the grandfather
and the mother force the boy to lead them to the
father's body. They make him place the father's bones
in a sack which the boy must sling over his wounded
back. Then the grandfather whistles three notes, and
sics his hound on the boy. As the boy runs through the
forest, the hound on his heels, his back burning under
the weight of the bag of his father's bones, the mother
casts a powerful curse on him. So, now, El Silbón
wanders the night, whistling. If you hear him, it means
he's coming for you. When he catches you, he will
break you open, consume your organs and take your
bones, placing them in the bloody bag he carries over
his shoulder, the bag that continues to grow heavier
and heavier, doubling him over as he wanders the
darkness."

Marco feels hollowed out, his buzz gone. He
feels stone-cold sober.

"That's one of mine," the woman says.

"One of yours, what?"

"My stories."

"*Your* stories?"

"Yes. I conjure them."

Marco gulps down the rest of his tequila and sits clutching the empty glass.

"I could send El Silbón for Luis, if you'd like."

"I see." Marco slowly places his glass on the bar, never taking his eyes off the woman. "And what's in it for you?"

"Nothing, really. Just another story to tell."

"Okay," Marco says. He glances up at the clock over the cantina's back door. It's three A.M. But how is that even possible? "I, uh, better get home before I black out in a gutter. Thanks for the drinks."

"And Luis?" the woman asks. "Shall I send him a story tonight?"

Marco stands. "Uh, sure, whatever."

The woman smiles. "Very good. You can get your money in a day's time."

She blows Marco a kiss.

"Whatever you say," Marco says over his shoulder as he pushes through the door of Cantina del Brujas, determined to get as far away from the strange woman as fast as possible.

When he glances back to make sure she's not following him, the woman in black is already gone.

*****

A cockroach scuttles across the back of Marco's hand and rouses him from his sleep. He's on his kitchen floor, still wearing his clothes from the night before. He grunts, flicking the roach across the room where it lands on its back just under the fridge, then rights itself and disappears.

Marco envies the pest as he slowly gets to his feet, envies their seeming invincibility: he'd heard somewhere they'd have no problem withstanding a nuclear holocaust. They'd prevail—*thrive*, even—as the world burned to ashes around them.

Sunlight streams in between the broken blinds over the window above the sink and lasers Marco in the eyes. The light cracks through his skull like a glowing bullet, his hangover rumbling anew in his head like a roach with a jackhammer crawled in through his ear while he was sleeping. He puts an arm out to steady himself against the fridge.

Images of the dimly lit Cantina del Brujas, a pale woman in a black suit and hat at the bar coalesce in the fog of his memory and then, just as quickly, dissipate. He can't remember much of their conversation—just bits and pieces, really—but he can recall just how unsettled he'd felt sitting next to the woman.

That feeling creeps back into his stomach now.

He wonders if she's still at the cantina, if she'd be there if he visited this afternoon.

Marco tells himself she couldn't be there, that she's just in his head, a figment of his imagination. A bad dream.

Besides, he doesn't have time to go to the cantina today. He needs to find another job. Maybe run security for one of the back-alley drug and gambling dens that sprout like weeds in this neighborhood; maybe bounce for a couple more cantinas, on top of the ones he was already bouncing for. Whatever it is, he knows he'll need several more jobs just to make up what he's lost now that wrestling's not an option.

And rent's due at the end of next week.

And his landlord has a zero-tolerance policy.

If he can't pay, he'll be evicted, and he'll be back on the street, homeless and hungry. Marco promised himself a long time ago that he'd never end up back on the street. He intends to keep that promise; kill for it if he has to.

Marco's stomach clenches and the woman in black's ice-cold stare comes back to him. A gaping hole seems to dilate inside of him, a sinkhole in his soul. He knows there's no way he'll be able to get enough money in time to pay his rent. Maybe if he had two weeks instead of one, it might be possible, just barely. But one week? No way. And in Mexico City? No way in hell. He was just one in a sea of innumerable people trying to make ends meet, to stay afloat, to survive. On any given day there were uncountable Marco Alvarezes he'd have to compete with for the lowliest of jobs. Wrestling had been the only thing that set him apart; the only thing that had given him a leg up. It wasn't something everyone could do, let alone do it well. Marco could.

But it's gone now. All gone.

And Luis Rivera took it from him.

Marco vomits in the sink.

He wipes his sleeve across his mouth, splashes water in his face.

Luis.

That pendejo.

Luis is probably still riding high on his victory, rolling in his twenty-three-thousand pesos without a care in the world, drinking, drugging, and whoring. Living la vida grande while Marco's left with nothing, not even the mask he'd sewn himself all those years ago, and days away from being evicted.

Something inside Marco clenches again, wringing him like a wet rag.

He's never going back on the streets.

Never.

*****

Luis lives in an apartment complex very much like Marco's, in a barrio about twenty minutes away. The moon has just come up as Marco makes for the stairwell. The snub-nosed revolver he's tucked in the back of his jeans is rubbing his skin raw.

He takes the three flights of stairs at a brisk pace, past crumbling hallways covered in graffiti. Someone is cooking something that smells incredible: the smell of cumin, chili peppers, and lime makes Marco's stomach grumble. His pantry and fridge are bare, but he hopes to remedy that, here and now.

The building pulses with noise: large families together in small quarters; whores loudly plying their trade; children laughing and screaming; someone playing a guitar and singing off-key.

Marco stops at Luis's door, hesitates. He steels himself, goes numb, and retreats to that place inside that kept him alive during the worst days and nights of his life. He is a passenger in his own body, safe and sound. Untouchable. He reaches back under his jacket and shirt, reassures himself the revolver is still there, still with him.

He lets out a heavy breath, pulls his shoulders back, straightens his spine, and pounds the door.

No answer.

Marco keeps himself tucked deep, focuses only on the fact that he must survive.

He pounds the door again.

Nothing.

Although...

With the noise emanating from the apartments around him, he can't be sure. He thinks he heard something. Maybe whistling?

Marco leans forward, placing his right ear flush against the door.

Silence.

He grunts. Okay, so maybe no-one is home. This could still work to his advantage—especially if Luis left some of his winnings behind. And what are the chances someone here would even notice the sound of a door being bust in?

Marco looks around, leans over the railing of the stairwell, checks the stairs down to the first floor.

No-one.

Nothing but noise.

Home free.

Marco pulls out the revolver just in case, then kicks in the door. The wood around the lock splinters under the force of his boot. A second latch on the inside catches and keeps the door from fully opening. He tears the latch off the frame with another kick and lets himself in.

*****

Blood, everywhere. The bodies of Luis' entourage broken apart in the kitchen and living room, bones pulled free of flesh in antlered architectures. Chewed organs slopped on the floor.

Down the hallway, past the kitchen, Luis is suspended between two bedrooms, his skin cut loose from his body and stretched taut from wall to wall. His body trembles, his musculature glistening red and wet, his ribs cracked and pried open. His face is still intact. Blood pours from his mouth, from the stump that used to be his tongue. His throat has been carefully mutilated, leaving him alive, but unable to so much as whimper.

But it isn't the blood that terrifies Marco; it isn't even the sight of Luis flayed alive and tacked to the wall by jagged shards of his own ribs like a human butterfly. No, it's the look in Luis's eyes that terrifies Marco to the point that he pisses himself.

He has only seen that look one other time in his life, back before he was a luchador or even a bouncer, back when the only job he could find one summer was working at a slaughterhouse.

Something whistles a triad of discordant notes behind Marco and he spins reflexively. The thing is massive, hunchbacked, dressed in a black deeper and darker than the void between stars. Blood and viscera glisten on its clothing.

Oblivion burns at the edges of Marco's vision like black smoke. The thing brings down a bone and caves in Marco's skull.

He's alive just long enough to feel his flesh pulled open and his spine ripped from his body.

MERMAID NOODLE CASSEROLE: REVENGE OF THE WATER BABIES[1]

by Linda Kay Hardie

"I don't believe it for a second," George said. "Someone would definitely notice a mermaid in Pyramid Lake. And a bunch of scaly little babies with gills living in the lake, eating people."

Katherine sighed. "Good grief, George. It's a fable, a myth. A foundation story. It explains why the Paiute had such bad luck with the white man coming to massacre them and take their land. You take things too literally."

"And why don't the babies grow up?"

Katherine sighed again. "Just drive, George."

They were driving back to Reno from Pyramid Lake on a spring evening after a day on the reservation. George had been out on the lake fishing, and Katherine found an old woman working on a basket along the shore. They got to talking, and the woman told her the story.

---

[1] This story is a follow-on to "Beware the Water Babies of Pyramid Lake", published in From the Yonder: Volume 1.

*****

"Back when the cui-ui were plentiful," the woman said, "there was a man of the Numu, the People who Ate Cui-ui, the ancient fish of Pyramid Lake. He fell in love with a mermaid-serpent in Pyramid Lake. He took her back to his village so they could be married, but the Numu were horrified and chased the couple back to the lake. The mermaid cursed the people and the lake and disappeared from their lives. The Numu lived in fear for a season, but their luck didn't go bad and life went back to normal."

The old woman stopped speaking, and Katherine pressed her for more.

"But something must have happened."

"Yes," the woman said. "One day a young mother was feeding her baby on the shore of the lake. She set the child down and turned away for a moment, and that's when a serpent slithered out of the lake and swallowed the child. Just as the mother began to turn back, the serpent assumed the form of the baby. The mother picked up the child and started to put it to her breast, but she saw the changes. Gills, scales, claws, and sharp teeth. She dropped the baby. The serpent-baby said it would spare her if she left it alone. She fled to the village screaming, and the serpent, now a water baby, crawled back into the lake."

"Are the water babies still around?" Katherine asked.

"It is said that if man or beast hears the water babies, he will be cursed with bad luck. If he sees the water babies, he will die," the old woman said.

"Does the mermaid still exist?"

The old woman shrugged. "The lake is large and deep. Babies need a mother."

"Is that all the bad luck there was, just the one baby being eaten?"

"No. The worst luck started in the white man's year of 1844. First one man with his guide, then hordes of white men. They cut down the piñon trees, from which the Numu harvested sweet nuts, and their large beasts, the cattle, destroyed the grazing lands with their hooves and teeth. They killed the People and told horrific stories about us. They said that the water babies sought revenge on us because the Numu drowned disabled babies in the lake to keep our race pure." The woman stopped and looked Katherine in the eye. "The Paiutes are not the ones with racial purity issues documented in their history."

*****

Katherine recounted this story to George as they drove back to Reno from the reservation. But then she told him how the Paiute myth was used to explain the disappearances of modern-day fishermen, who vanish in freak accidents every year. The mundane explanation for these is weather that can change from mild to menacing within minutes, the water gets deep fast close to the shore, where it drops from wading depth to 350 feet deep, and (of course) alcohol consumed by fishermen that leads to accidents.

She'd learned this part of the myth from a waitress. She'd gone into the lodge after the old woman left, and since it was quiet, she ordered a cup of coffee and talked with the waitress, Shirley. She asked about the old woman, if she was a regular around there, but Shirley wasn't familiar with her. Shirley was the one who had the everyday explanations for the water deaths.

*****

Tonight, George had talked Katherine into cooking his trout from this trip. Lahontan cutthroat trout are good eating, even if your girlfriend doesn't like fish. George felt that if Katherine didn't like fish, she could just lump it. "Like it or lump it," his father used to say. George wasn't sure exactly what that meant, but it was nothing good anyway.

George had gotten Katherine to be a decent fish cook. She was an okay cook otherwise, and he made her figure out how to cook fish right. He let her make one of her fancy vegetarian casseroles for dinner on nights that he had fish. Her casseroles weren't bad as a side dish to his trout, but it wasn't right to not eat meat of some sort for dinner.

Ironically, the only kind of fish Katherine liked was canned tuna. Something to do with what she was brought up on, George guessed. He did like her tuna noodle casserole, if she served it with a hearty salad, something with lots of chunks of blue cheese and tomatoes and other vegetables besides just plain lettuce.

Tonight, to go with the trout, she made what she called stir-fried corn and peppers. It was too early for fresh corn, but she used frozen corn with the jalapenos and red bell peppers and garlic and stuff, and it was pretty good overall. She made herself sauteed chicken livers, something that he'd tried hard to stamp out of her, but she dug her heels in. Fuck the liver, he thought; she should just suck it up and eat the fish.

*****

George drove to Pyramid Lake by himself Friday afternoon, because Katherine had laundry to do this weekend. Even though they didn't live together, he'd gotten her used to doing his laundry, too, so it was a good deal. He checked into the lodge and put his suitcase in the cabin. Then he rented a boat and went out on the lake to fish.

The weather was nice, a typical Washoe County spring day. Cloudless blue sky, temperature warm enough to be comfortable. Of course, any minute it could cloud up, winds could bluster, and a storm could blow in. George cracked a beer, the best part of fishing.

Three beers later, there was a tug on his line, and he reeled in a cutthroat. It was 19 inches long, so it was a keeper. He picked up a chunk of wood he kept in the boat and smacked the fish's head. That felt so good, he hit it again. Whoops! Fish brains all over the boat.

Two beers later, he'd caught his limit, pulling in another Lahontan cutthroat also 19 inches. He'd hoped for larger, but there was tomorrow morning. He always had better luck in the predawn hour. George put the fish on ice and took the boat back to the dock. Time for dinner in the lodge.

As he ate his steak, he overheard the waitress telling a couple at the next table about the killer water babies. She told them earnestly that a fisherman had disappeared on the lake just last weekend. He snorted. Probably some guy trying to disappear to avoid paying alimony or something. Good for him.

In his cabin, he set his phone's alarm to 4:30 so he could be on the lake by 5, an hour before sunrise. Best fishing time.

*****

George sat up in bed. He heard children laughing. Just as he reached for his phone to see what time it was, the alarm beeped. What were brats doing outside at this ungodly hour? He didn't see anyone as he walked to his boat on the dock.

When he was out on the lake, he heard laughter again. It must be some kind of bird, he thought. He knew there were lots of birds on the lake, but that's all he knew about birds.

He got a bite. He started reeling in the line. Boy, this was a big one. The record Lahontan cutthroat trout from Pyramid was 41 pounds, and George was hopeful he was going to break that record.

Wow. It must be huge, because it was fucking heavy. He kept reeling, and suddenly a hand grabbed

103

the side of the boat. A head appeared, and he saw the end of the line going to its mouth. Another hand appeared. He dropped his pole, and the mermaid pulled herself into the boat, the hook in her mouth, blood seeping down her chin.

She opened her mouth to reveal sharp teeth. George grabbed his block of wood and whacked her hard between the eyes. Down she went.

The mermaid looked like a 10-year-old girl, except with gills and razor claws. Oh, and a fish tail. The fish half looked like a 35- or 40-pound Lahontan cutthroat trout, about three feet long. Too bad George couldn't claim the whole fish – mermaid, whatever – which must be about 75 pounds. But he'd killed the thing, and since it looked semi-human, he didn't think that would be a good thing for people to find out.

George heard murmuring. He looked around. Had someone witnessed his murder of the mermaid? He didn't see anyone. The murmuring turned to grumbling. He couldn't make out any words, but it sounded angry. He still didn't see anyone. Must be birds again.

He was going to dump the whole mermaid overboard, but that fish tail just looked too good. What if he cut the girl-part off and took the tail home? How would he get this past the ranger? George noticed that the fins on the mermaid tail were slightly different than the fins on the trout, so he decided that he could claim the fish's head was deformed and ugly, and that he cut it off and threw it back without thinking.

He began sawing at the waist of the fish-girl. Blood gushed everywhere, and guts spewed onto the bottom of the boat. It was far messier than he anticipated. He tipped the girl part overboard and turned to the mess. Fortunately, he had a can that he was able to use to bail out the viscera, the entrails, the offal... Different words for guts splashed through his brain, and he had to swallow hard to keep from vomiting all over the gore.

Once he got it cleaner – he didn't think he would ever get all the fish guts and blood out of the boat or off his hands – he pounded down two beers. That steadied his shaking hands. He'd had enough of fishing for now, and it wasn't even dawn yet.

*****

Back home with his two Lahontan cutthroats and his one mermaid tail, George realized that the mermaid had a vastly different skeleton than the trout. He couldn't let Katherine fillet this one. She'd know something was very wrong right away. He filleted the trout, wrapped them up, and stuck them in the bottom of the refrigerator before tackling the mermaid. He would have called it a messy business if it weren't for the gorefest in the boat. This was a piece of cake in comparison. He swallowed hard at the thought of cake at this moment.

Over at Katherine's apartment with the mermaid fillets, George had an idea.

"Honey, why don't you make your tuna noodle casserole out of cooked, flaked trout?" he said. "That really sounds good to me. What do you think?"

She wrinkled her forehead. "Well, okay. I can give it a try," she said.

"Tell you what. I'll grill the fish so you don't have to do all the work."

Katherine smiled. "Okay."

She ran to the store for the sour cream, which she didn't usually keep on hand, as well as a variety of vegetables and crumbled blue cheese for a nice salad. She also picked up a bottle of a decent fume blanc wine to go with dinner. George was pleased.

Katherine threw together the casserole, which was a simple one, and put it in the oven. She tossed the salad and opened the wine. They drank wine and watched *Jeopardy* on TV while the casserole cooked.

She brought the casserole to the table with oven mitts and set it on a trivet next to the salad. She gave George a decent-sized serving and herself a small amount. She laughed.

"Just in case," she said.

But when she took a bite, she smiled. "It's good!"

George stopped shoveling casserole into his mouth to smile, too.

"How was the fishing trip? Good, I assume," Katherine said, eating more of the casserole.

George's stomach lurched. Could he tell her? He had to tell someone.

"It was weird," he said. "Remember that legend you told me, of the mermaid and the water babies? I think I heard water babies laughing, and then I caught a mermaid."

Katherine dropped her fork. "You're kidding."

"I wish I were. Somehow, I hooked a real mermaid and pulled it in. It looked like a 10-year-old girl, except for the fish tail."

George looked down at his plate.

"That's what we're eating," he said.

"No?!"

"Yes!"

She leaped up and ran to the kitchen sink, where she vomited up mermaid casserole, salad, and wine. She kept puking until she'd emptied her stomach, then she had the dry heaves until she was exhausted.

Katherine wiped her mouth with a paper towel and turned back to George.

"Get out," she said.

"What?"

"You heard me. Get out of here. We're through. I can't believe you made me eat–" And she turned back to the sink to heave again.

George could tell she was serious when she pulled a big knife out of the knife block and waved it at him. He fled.

*****

George wasn't able to sleep that night. He woke up early Sunday morning feeling queasy. He also felt restless, as though he were forgetting something, some obligation. Was he supposed to do something today? There was nothing on his phone, not even for

Monday. He finally decided to go fishing again. That's what he needed, an afternoon on the lake with a six-pack of beer.

At the lake, he took a boat out again, and relaxed with his pole and his cooler of beer. Yes. This was what he needed.

After his third beer, he heard chuckling. The laughter of children. The wind picked up, and clouds appeared out of nowhere to cover the sun. George thought he'd better get back to shore before the wind got too gusty.

Just then, a tiny razor-clawed hand grabbed the side of the boat. A second hand appeared. A small head with sharp teeth poked up over the edge. The water baby levered itself into the boat. Another one followed. And more. The boat filled up with vicious water babies, showing their teeth. Four, five, six – George wasn't sure how many there were. Lots.

He grabbed for his block of wood, but a water baby reached it first and tossed it overboard.

"I didn't mean it. It was an accident," he said.

The water babies swarmed over him, knocking him down. They began chewing on him with their pointed teeth. He screamed. Water babies chewed through his belly and gnawed on his internal organs.

George's screams turned to gurgles as water babies started biting his throat and his face.

George stopped squirming, and the water babies stopped their assault. They leaned over the side of the boat and chuckled at the water. Blood dripped off their faces and splashed into the lake. An adult mermaid appeared and chuckled back at them. They held a conversation in the chuckle-language, then the mermaid disappeared. Moments later, she reappeared with a large serpent.

The water babies gaily leaped out of the boat into the lake, and the serpent used its head to rock the boat until it tipped over, dumping what was left of George into the cold depths of the lake. The water babies and the mermaid laughed, then disappeared into the depths.

NAGLOPER

by DJ Tyrer

The figure moved with long loping strides reminiscent of a hyena skulking through the night shadows, unseen by the men paid to watch for it.

An owl screeched, breaking the silence that that had fallen upon the night as the figure passed by.

One of the two men standing at the entrance to the burial kraal looked up, his wide and fearful eyes glinting with the light of the fragment of moon peeking out from behind the dark smear of clouds.

The man gripped his knobkerrie more tightly.

"Did you hear that? An owl."

His colleague turned his head. "The night is alive with evil."

His tone said he cared little as long as it remained afar.

The figure moved in a wide arc about the thorny kraal fence, swinging around to its rear. Something jangled softly at its neck: a necklace strung with small bones.

With the lithe movements of a baboon, it crept over to the fence and took hold of the branches, pulling itself over it, flowing over the thorny barricade like a shadow.

Piles of large rocks pressed down heavily upon the graves of the dead, preventing dark spirits from raising them from the dust and scavenging beasts from feasting upon their decaying flesh.

The figure reached out with taloned hands and pushed aside the rocks from one grave with the ease of a man shoving an empty basket out of his way.

"Did you hear something?" one of the guards asked, a tremor in his voice as he glanced over his shoulder.

"No?" It was a hopeful question. No man wished to meet one of the dreaded nightwalkers.

"Should we…" The guard looked at the deep shadows of the graveyard. "Should we go investigate?"

"No." This time the word was a statement. "It was likely nothing. Or, maybe, a leopard nosing about. Nothing we need concern ourselves with."

His companion chose not to disagree.

The nightwalker completed its task of shifting the stones aside to reveal a patch of recently disturbed earth.

Long fingers set to work, scraping the dirt away to reveal the decayed flesh of a leg.

Smiling a fanged smile to itself as its fingers sought the foot, the toes, the nightwalker broke one away, peeled back skin and flesh to extract a bone that it added to the necklace it wore.

The nightwalker had what it had come for.

Turning its gaze to the kraal entrance, it considered the two men on guard duty. Tempting. Hunger gnawed within its stomach. The nightwalker could smell the blood that ran through their veins. Tantalising.

But no. They stank of fear, fouling the taste.

It wanted sweet blood.

Let them discover the open grave, let fear chill their blood, let them learn no precautions could stand against those who walked the night.

Over the thorny fence it flowed, once more. Into the night of the veldt, it disappeared. Swift and unseen Just another of the predators that moved across the landscape.

The nightwalker's destination was another kraal, this one a home to the living.

Like the burial kraal, men stood guard at its entrance, eyes watching for nocturnal threats.

The nightwalker knew their names: By day, whilst the tarry worm of its dark nature buried itself in the putrid detritus of a cave floor, it sent out a portion of itself in human form to move amongst the people who dwelt in the region, learning all it could about them, their strengths and weaknesses, their virtues and their vices.

No matter how keen their sight or hearing, the guards held no concern for the nightwalker as it approached the kraal. A taloned finger rose to tap the freshly stolen toe bone, drawn from the corpse of the village headman. Through it, the singular essence of the place and that of the predator were drawn together in a vile union. No guard would see it, unless it chose to show itself, and no magical ward would bar its way. The kraal was its domain, now.

Once again, it moved over the thorny barricade that enclosed the kraal with the effortless grace of a shadow.

It paused and sniffed, revelling at the sweet scent of the blood of those who lay dreaming. It could sense every person within the fence, sense their blood flowing, sense the faint kiss of dream. It knew the name of every one.

Long limbs reached out across the kraal, clutching the entranceway of a hut, before pulling itself toward it, an elongated and barely human shadow.

The nightwalker paused at the threshold of the hut.

It could barely see the ward marked in the dirt of the floor, but knew it was there, nonetheless. The magic flared to life before the shadow. Powerful, yet impotent.

With a throaty chuckle, it stepped over the ward, untouched.

It knew all those who lay within the hut, what they yearned for, what aroused them.

It made a choice.

"Darling. Darling, wake up." The voice was soft, yet clear, a summons for a soul hidden in the depths of a slumbering mind. "Draw back to me."

A woman shifted and moaned, softly, as the nightwalker entered the room, suddenly handsome and straight-limbed.

Outside, the owl screeched a mocking laugh.

The handsome man moved quietly towards the sleeping woman, a cruel smile upon his lips, tongue moistening them in anticipation.

"Darling. Darling, wake up."

A long and perfect finger caressed the toe bone that hung from his necklace.

"Darling. Darling, wake up."

The woman shifted again, stretched, almost awake.

Beside her, a well-muscled man also moved, hand twitching towards half-healed wounds upon his chest, fingers scratching at ragged flesh.

The nightwalker became immediately still and hissed.

The man shifted, again, scratched once more, eyes flickering open, blearily.

The nightwalker stared at the wounds on the man's chest, the pretence of form gone from it.

They knew! They knew!

It had thought itself unsuspected, heard no rumours as it walked amongst them by day, had met no sangoma witch with the power to create such muti, but here it was before it: The only way to detect a nightwalker. A medicine that it could not defeat.

Awakened by the warning itch of the muti rubbed into his wounded flesh, the man sat up with a start and stared at the nightwalker with a mixture of anger and fear.

The nightwalker screeched and slashed with a taloned hand, marking the man's cheek with jagged tears.

The man cried out with pain, but a short-shafted assegai was in his hand and he slashed and stabbed at the hideous being looming over him with the broad head of the weapon.

The nightwalker leapt back, stung as much by the man's force of will as the keenness of the spear.

It hissed, then turned and fled from the hut, the assegai sailing after it, striking its leg, but it ignored the wound and bounded towards the encircling fence.

Behind it, the kraal burst into a riot of life as men grabbed whatever weapons lay close to hand or lit torches.

But it was over the thorny fence and off into the night before they could catch it. None of the men could follow it through the darkness it commanded.

Wounded and abashed, the nightwalker fled back to its cave, where it would bury its evil nature, before sending forth its shell of human-seeming to learn the location of its enemy, the sangoma that had suspected its presence and prepared for it.

The nightwalker hissed in anger as it vomited up its tarry core. They would know it was stalking them, now, not just the graves of their dead. More guards would be posted, guards whose flesh would be lacerated and rubbed with muti to detect it. More men would undergo the rite, becoming a threat instead of victims.

Hunger gnawed at its belly.

The predator was thwarted this night. But, as always, the predator would return and there would always be prey weak or foolish enough for it to take.

Let them do what they would.

It chuckled to itself in the echoing darkness of its cave.

Yes, let them do what they would: It would feast soon enough.

It always did.

Ends

PHILOXENIA AND THE VRYKOLAKAS

by Maraki Piedras

"I think we've finally lost it!"

Panting, Adelphina crash-landed on a battered old couch, which someone had conveniently thrown out, leaving it just outside their house in a sort of back alley. "Ksen? Comrade X?"

Ksenija, her best friend and partner-in-crime, limped over, holding a torn sports sandal. Though normally much more athletic than Phina, now she did not so much drop as *melt* down next to her, stretching out her poor blistered feet.

"I sure hope so," she grumbled, "'cause I don't know about you, but I'm *beat*."

Wordlessly, Phina helped her remove her backpack, but instead of reaching for the source of their current troubles, 'safely' wrapped in an old striped tee-shirt, she merely rummaged around the front pocket for a bandage, or the closest thing that they had.

Ksenija rolled her shoulders with a tired crunch. They were running out of water, and this being a small Greek island, it wouldn't have anything so nice as a drinking fountain or even a hose you could leech off—oh no, it would have to wait until morning, when the neighbourhood shop deigned to open and sell them some overpriced *neraki* and maybe some food.

If there *was* a morning for the pair of them.

Sighing inwardly, Phina went for the small bottle of "emergency" *ouzo*, and grimaced at the anise-y aftertaste, sickly sweet; but the high alcohol content did soothe the chill that was gnawing at her bones from the inside.

The night was low on moonlight, yet star-strewn. She hadn't *ever* seen this many bunched together, grape-like, in real life, only on Instagram.

"Should we just bury it?" Ksenija whispered, taking the tiny bottle from her. "Or, like, throw it into a well and forget it ever existed?"

"Are you freaking serious—after everything we've been through?" Adelphina shuddered to remember Athens and the mad dash to catch the last ferry off the mainland. "Look, *Kyrios Striggos* has a really fucking long memory, okay? He's got to be a witch or a warlock, or I don't know what! So the least we can do is get something out of it, yeah?"

Her friend let out an unhappy huff that turned into a yawn. "Wake me up when he starts stabbing our voodoo dolls with pointy things, K?" She proceeded to curl in on herself, folding her tall body with cat-like neatness. A portable model, that was her Ksen, and as Adelphina adjusted Ksen's jacket to cover more exposed skin, she regretted ever having hatched her Grand Theft Tablet scheme.

It had begun innocently enough, with a seasonal job of picking olives for an intense, semi-creepy character with an enormous garden plot. The pay had more than covered the creepiness. Mind you, most Greeks would rather ask some relative to do it for free, but Kyrios Striggos was not that kind of Greek. There were stories around the 'hood about ghosts and strange noises and lights, especially after midnight; but who could blame a girl without any stable sources of income?

So she had rolled her sleeves, went at the olives, chased off the white peacocks, fed the three sleek black dobermans without losing any limbs in the process—and then the curse tablet came into the story, banished to a brick shed, where he normally kept the empty bottles and other what-nots.

In an hour or so, wind rose to slapping gusts, jerking Phina back to her ouzo. Her phone battery had died hours ago, but she had stuck the cheap pink earphones into her ears anyway, just to feel like she wasn't about to die a horrible death without a word to her Grandma.

Ksen was muttering in her sleep, shivering miserably under the thin, inadequate cover.

But that was the least of their problems right now: the dogs had started barking again, which meant that the *thing* had caught up with them. Phina's throat closed, her stomach lurching nauseously. Last time, it had killed the lights on the whole *street* and made their tram pull to an emergency stop, without anybody understanding why.

A noise like a baby crying was the last straw—it was high time to shake Ksen awake and leg it.

"Wait," Ksen whispered, "it's only a cat—look, it's stuck up a tree!" She gestured at a spiky-leaved palm, clearly decorative.

"And?" Phina snapped. "It's after us—don't you dare—"

Her words fell on deaf ears as the mewling grew in volume. Cursing, she followed her friend to the foot of the tree only to watch her jump up like a pro basketball player and catch the tom cat mid-fall.

God, she really was amazing.

Black with a white chest and a regal mark on his forehead in the same colour, and faintly demonic yellow-green eyes, the dude in distress had no collar. He didn't need it, though: he all but flowed out of Ksenija's arms and strutted off without so much as a thank-you.

For the lack of a better plan, they followed him to a small, isolated cottage that broke away from the typical rows of houses.

"I think we can stay here," Ksen whispered, fingering her evil-eye talisman (lifted off a street vendor at one of the central metro stations, for all the good that it had done her).

"Are you kidding me?" Phina grumbled. "Now we're following a magic cat you've rescued?"

"All cats are magic; didn't your Grandpa tell you?"

Hell, Phina was ready to crawl into the motorboat parked at the back and sleep there, so long as no formless monsters got her.

Instead, they stumbled upon a surprisingly nice lean-to, drowning in wild grapevine and bougainvillea, as well as dusty pillows and blankets. Phina picked very late, sugar-sweet figs and allowed herself a moment's bliss.

"*Zhivem!*" she exclaimed, high-fiving Ksen. "This is the life!"

The cat climbed onto Ksen's lap and headbutted her palm, as if to say: *Haven't I done a splendid job of looking after you two losers?*

Phina strained her ears, wondering if the sudden sense of safety *was* anything to be trusted. She kissed her baptismal cross, praying to her dead grandfather or whomever was listening to hide them from the *thing*.

The morning dawned bright and early. The sound of a garden hose resolved itself into a small, wizened old man wearing a canny expression on his face, like you would expect from a fisherman who was about to sell you yesterday's octopus that he hadn't cooked himself. Phina couldn't quite make out his features, but that was just her myopia and lack of glasses.

"Look what the cat dragged in!" he said to himself, likely not suspecting them of speaking his ancient and noble language.

"Good morning, *kyrie*," Adelphina greeted, in a slow, measured Greek. "We are *so* very sorry, sir, but we got lost on our way to the hotel—"

"And brought a *δαίμων* ghost to my doorstep, eh?" He was still holding the hose, as though he were about to turn it on them. "Where are you from?"

The question was paramount to any true Hellene. Your origins said *everything* that he might want to know about you at this stage of the acquaintance/barging-in and dictated the terms of your conversation from that point onwards.

"Odessos," she answered reluctantly, well aware that it would immediately push her to the rock bottom of the food chain, well below, say, Australia or America. Ksen seemed to be holding her breath. Their paperwork situation was such that they were obliged to lie about it, or face the consequences that would not be pleasant. "Please, grandfather, we're no trouble at all!"

"Your cat likes us!" Ksenija blurted out. "He invited us here, after we got him off that tree." She waved towards it.

He narrowed his eyes. "You did? I *keep* telling him to quit that nonsense." To the cat, "you're not a kitten anymore, are you, Vasileos Pavlaki?"

The cat ignored him with all the dignity of a proper monarch (Pause of Greece being the father of its last king).

"Come closer," the old man commanded. "Let me look at the two of you. And bring whatever you took from the δαίμων ghost."

Warily, they disentangled themselves from the blanket nest and inched forward. Towering over him, Ksen unwrapped the simple, locally manufactured computer tablet with multiple scratch marks on the lead-coloured case and spiderweb cracks on the screen. It had taken them several tries to even boot it up the first time around, but they didn't dare to try it not.

"There's only one app," Phina explained, being the designated tech guru. "When you start it, it asks you the name and date of birth—not yours, the person you want to curse—and gives you a choice of a few standard formulas, in Ancient Greek, so I couldn't decipher it all. And then you get chased by a weird shadow, like from *Spirited Away*!"

"*A pa pa!*" The old man was shaking his head. "In my day, we just made them from lead…"

"Your day? Adelphina asked. "Hold long ago was that, in the dark ages?"

He tried to count on his fingers, but quickly gave up. "*Ela, paidia,* I'll put the coffee on."

His kitchen was a rather spartan affair, conjoined with the dining and living rooms—just large enough for a rusty sink, a leaking refrigerator, a rickety small table, a tiny off-white wall cabinet for plates, with peeling paint, and a two-burner stove run off a gas bottle. The floor, though, was a pretty polished cement mosaic, ranging from black to Hellenic teal, and the cracks in the walls were covered with ornate plates and evil-eye talismans from all over the Mediterranean, from Morocco to Istanbul.

"I used to travel a lot," their owner declared with an unmistakable touch of pride. "But then I came back home, and that's that."

"Do you live alone?" Phina asked, casting about for an obvious woman's touch.

"Ah, Katerina *mou.*" His tone turned wistfully amused, pointing to an old, framed photo on the wall. "Fainted dead away when I showed up to my own funeral. Cookie?" He opened a bakery paper bag of mixed cinnamon and pistachio ones.

An awkward silence blanketed the house.

"Ookay," Ksen dragged out, holding on her chair's back instead of sitting down.

"Your funeral?" Adelphina prompted, in faint hopes of an innocent explanation.

"Oh, haven't I mentioned?" He leaned against the kitchen counter to roll up a brown-coloured cigarette. "I'm a vrykolakas, one of the several that live here in Agia Marina. That's why your ghost couldn't get any closer. We undead are very territorial creatures, aren't we, Pavlaki?"

But he seemed so absolutely normal, like someone who could sell you catch, a melon, or a live chicken out of the back of his old truck. Hell, he probably did grow fruit and raise chickens.

The cat settled on Phina's lap now, shameless in his demands for attention.

"*Ela*, Pavlaki! Don't encourage him, or he'll eat you out of the house!" He seemed to love the pistachio flavour the best, eating right out of Adelphina's suddenly slack hand.

"Hang on," she said, with a creeping feeling climbing up her spine, "Is your *cat* a regular animal, at least?"

"Hm?" The old man blew out a puff of smoke—a messy, imperfect ringlet. "I don't really know, *paidi mou*. He was just at my doorstep one day and refused to leave until I fed him."

"If you're a *vrykolakas*," Ksen cut in, "are you planning to drink our blood?"

He burst out laughing. "*Oh, koukla mou!* You read too many American stories! I don't drink blood—I eat livers. Human, preferably, but chicken will do. Fresh, on a good day, but that's a matter of luck."

Adelphina jerked to her feet. "Well, are you after ours?"

"I'd love to," he replied without a trace of malice, "but I wouldn't want your δαίμων to haunt me instead and scare away my potential food sources, now would I? The coffee, *malaka*! Forget my own head!" He rushed to rescue it.

He had very few books in his house, but in matters of folk wisdom, he was as good as any from a library. He explained, "In the olden days, the magician would not always know whose spirit he was binding to his evil task, so he would use the general 'δαίμων', or 'ghost', which could be either male or female. And if he wasn't sure that the ghost could do the job alone, he would also call on the gods of the dead, like Hermes Katochos. But particularly, he would seek maidens and young men whose lives had ended violently and/or prematurely. Their unfulfilled potential was the key to their power, making them easier to rouse to anger."

"Like us," Ksen whispered, and not without a point.

These δαίμονες supposedly couldn't enter Hades and had no place to rest in the afterlife. But that wasn't to say that they enjoyed being put to work by some black magic practitioner. Quite often, they could only be induced to do it in exchange for a promise never to call them up again to serve the living.

"Great," Phina said, "some freaking *Jumanji* this turned out to be! But why's it after us? We haven't made it do anything, yet!"

"Maybe the tablet's defective," Ksen muttered. "I mean, have you seen those cracks? I'm not sure our buyer would've been too happy about them."

"We've got to make it leave us alone," Phina said firmly. "Bind it better somehow. Or at least ask why it's been after us from the day we touched it, exactly. Can you help us with that, grandfather?"

"I might," he said, lighting another cigarette from the gas burner. "But what do I get in return, if not your livers?"

Money, they had none. And while they convened in the corner, closer to the door, with Pavlaki looping figure eights between their ankles, the Vrykolakas added, "Or you could just write a name in. Any name will do, but it has to be a real one, or it'll come back."

"Wouldn't that get us in trouble?" Phina asked, skeptical.

He cackled. "Only with the gods of the netherworld! But you'll not be meeting them at all if you wait much longer, eh?"

"*Odyssey!*" Phina slapped her own forehead. "Remember, he gave the shades milk, honey, wine… and water, too, I think?

Ksen frowned. "Yeah, but I'm not doing any animal sacrifices, Phi!"

"Comrade X." Phina stood up on her tiptoes to put her hands on her friend's shoulders like they did on the telly. "If you don't buck up, we're both finished—you realize that, don't you?"

"What about your buyer from America? What if there's nothing for it, but destroy the freaky gadget?"

"Then we destroy it." The words had cost Phina more than she was ever going to admit. "But only as the last resort—and only if we're sure it won't keep attacking us anyway!"

Ksen let out another one of her little huffs. "*You* do it. And don't make me watch!"

"If it comes to that, I will do it." She turned to the expectant-looking Vrykolakas. "And you, grandfather, can have the chicken liver. Or better yet, just let Ksen do her famous chicken pâté. I guarantee you it's so delicious you wouldn't want to eat anything else, ever."

"Bold words," he said, considering the offer. "Wonder if ghosts like pâté?"

The preparations were messy, but only because Phina cut herself twice while chopping the carrots for the signature dish. The rest of the offerings, the Vrykolakas had on hand, and some of the wine, they drank on the spot, while he told them a little more about his travels.

The ritual was carried out at night, on the nearest crossroads, and the cat, Pavlaki, had to be physically restrained from sniffing at everything and trying the milk.

Soon, it appeared. After the first sip of milk, the indistinct shape gained more form. Honey and wine added colour, outlining a young woman, like Phina and Ksenija, starkly against the dusty light brown road. She looked more tired than angry.

"Who are you?" Phina asked, planting the final morsel in front of it. "What's your name? And what do you want with us?"

The young woman frowned at the plate and pointed at her throat, shaking her head. "All the more for me," the Vrykolakas commented happily, snatching it up and retreating to his usual nighttime smoking place on the porch.

"Can you write?" Ksenija chimed in, holding up the tablet. "Maybe here?"

"Nastya," appeared in the input field. "Warn you. Killed snooping."

Phina and Ksenija exchanged looks, not quite buying such innocent motives. Ksen gestured at her to continue.

"And if we were to write in a name," Phina said speculatively, mentally waving goodbye to her wonderful bargain, "say, Kyrios Striggos, could you take him on?"

Nastya considered it, then erased the previous text. "Ask help. Other ghosts."

"Well, then," Phina went on brightly, "which cemetery is it going to be?"

THE WORLD'S CRAZIEST RIDE

by Maggie Nerz Iribarne

The rain poured down. A pisser, as Jackie would have said, when they were teens. *Jackie.* Cheryl pushed the memory of her sister from her mind. Jackie remained stuck (She called it imprisoned) at Franklin House. Apparently, as long as she "resisted stabilization," living independently stayed off the table. Sometimes they called it early-onset dementia. *But come on, at age forty? Whatever.*

Yes, the rain pissed heavily, yet Cheryl drove Sam to Sylvan Beach anyway. He loved it there, they'd been coming since he was a baby, and even more since Reggie died. Cheryl found it comforting, too. Her family owned a small house at Sylvan in the eighties. Cheryl and Jackie swam in the lake, got ice cream cones, and rode the wooden roller coaster, all summer, every summer. To Cheryl, Sylvan Beach shimmered and exuded something special, something lost in time. She felt at home there, and she thought Sam did, too

The rain. Back to the rain. Sam held her hand as they bought an ice cream and split it under the protective eaves of the stand. Their inadequate clothes dripped with water, even though they had been there for just a few minutes. After discarding their paper cups and plastic spoons, they walked the deserted beach of Lake Oneida. Empty boats bobbed in the water, moored to their slips. Cheryl and Sam envied the houses right on the beach, with their doused tiki torches and signs pointing to Margaritaville. They noticed the usually packed Sunset Grill's patio, slick with rainwater, its Irish and Italian and American flags hung soaked and limp from their poles.

"Daddy loved it here, too," she reminded her son.

"Tell me more," Sam said. At eight years old, memories of his father existed only through his mother's stories. Reggie died of cancer when Sam was just two.

"Well, we met here. We went on our first dates here. Daddy and I ate dinner at the Sunset, and we sat on the beach and we swam and we rode a bunch of rides."

"Tell me about the roller coaster."

"See? It's right there. It's really old-wooden-very unique. Daddy and I rode it even though we're both scared of roller coasters. We were both pretending to be cool."

Sam laughed. "You are *not* cool."

"Daddy was. Right?"

"I think so. What about your sunglasses?"

"Oh, right. I lost them that night. They flew right off, never to be seen again! Bwahahaha!" Cheryl turned toward Sam and turned her mouth into a freakish expression. He faked terror and ran away, up the beach.

They finished walking by the water and continued around through the amusement rides. Everything was shut. They passed the Rock-o-plane, the Galaxi Coaster (the wooden one), the Tilt-a-whirl, the Tip-top, and Crazy Dazy. They ended up at Cheryl's most favorite, most avoided ride, Laffland.

"Tell me about Laffland," Sam asked as they stood outside its closed doors, the ticket booth inaccessible through a barred gate. Cheryl looked at her wet, wide-eyed son.

"Oh. You know all about it," she said.

"I know, but I like to hear it all again."

"Ok," Cheryl sighed, affected boredom. This was precisely where she wanted to be, exactly what she wanted to talk about.

"Well, it's a dark ride. Which means that all the lights are out, it's as dark as can be. Your eyes can't see anything and you're not even sure how big the room is or where you're going. You ride a little wagon, and it twists and turns through a tunnel and there are loud noises and devils and witches and other scary things popping out. But the best part is…is…something else." Cheryl gazed at her son, water running down her cheeks. Her eyes mirrored Sam's stare. She never told him this part before.

"What, Mom?" he asked.

"The best part is the thoughts you have, or that I had, have, when I ride Laffland."

"Like what? Tell me."

"When I was about your age, I finally convinced Grandma to let me ride it. When I got on, first it just felt just like anything else, no big deal, but then, I started to feel different."

"Like how?" Sam focused on his mother, oblivious to his sopping hair and clothes.

"Warm. I felt warm. I could remember being held as a baby by Grandma. It's a strange thing because I didn't even know I had those memories. And when Daddy and I rode it I felt the same way again. Warm. And with Jackie, I was laughing, laughing so hard with such, such, joy, but I am not even sure what I was laughing about. But..."

"But then Daddy got sick," Sam said, his tone confused, uneasy.

"And Aunt Jackie, too," Cheryl said.

"Well, it's closed anyway." Sam said. *Always so sensible.*

"That's right, honey. It's getting late, let's go to Canal View for supper," Cheryl said.

"Not the Crazy Clam," Sam smiled. One of their private jokes.

"No, too crazy."

They walked away, turned their backs on the entrance to Laffland, the clowns hovered over the letters spelling out the ride's name, smiled down on them, watched them as they moved on.

*****

Cheryl and Jackie approached Laffland, when they were 26 and 25, wondering as they walked through the park, why Jackienever rode it before.

"How could you go to Sylvan Beach, live here every summer, *with me*, without going to Laffland?" Cheryl said. Jackie didn't respond. It seemed many people Cheryl asked hadn't ridden Laffland, some

didn't even know about it. In contrast, Cheryl longed
for, obsessed about the ride. Laffland scared and
attracted Cheryl, lured her, lingered in the back of her
mind, always.

"Come on! Let's do this!" Cheryl grabbed
Jackie's hand and pulled her up to the counter. They
handed over their two raffle-type tickets to a young
boy working at the stand, an innocent looking high
school student chewing gum, and jumped in the small
cart with the Pretzel Amusement Ride Company logo
on the side, their slender thighs touching as they fit
perfectly together. Before they knew it, the cart
swayed and pitched into the darkness, squeaking down
the old tracks into the inky space ahead.

*Was it right away? When did it begin again?
The warmth. The exhilaration.* Cheryl couldn't
remember, but as the car pulled deeper in the darkness
and her eyes surveyed the 1952-era witches and devils
and old timey visual tricks her insides glowed. An
almost sexual feeling shivered up her body. She felt
cocooned, secure, perfectly warm, but not, not ever
hot. Cheryl experienced her mother's chest rising and
falling. *Was she inside her? Was she lying on her
chest?* Her father hovered above, holding and kissing
her over and over. She was a baby. It was magnificent.
Dreamy hugs and kisses smothered her and she began

to laugh. Her face glistened with tears as they pulled into the light. Overcome with a rush of self-consciousness, Cheryl blinked, aware of young ride operator's critical gaze. She turned to Jackie, also startled by the light, but frozen in a different look. She appeared unhappy, confused, even alarmed. A mask of fear enshrouded Jackie's expression. The sisters looked at each other in silence for a moment and then cracked up laughing.

"Jeez. I'm sweating like a pig. I need a drink," Jackie said, snapping out of it, and they headed off to the Sunset for a beer.

*****

"Reggie, have you ever had a perfect moment of faith?" Half asleep, Reggie exhaled,

"What?" he said, slightly annoyed.

"I mean it. Like have you ever had a moment where everything made sense?"

Reggie rolled from his side to his back, took her hand, "Wasn't that the other night?"

Cheryl shifted to her side, faced his profile,

"Ha ha, no, I'm serious," she said.

"Well, I guess when we found out about the baby."

"You guess?" Cheryl said, miffed at her husband but also at herself. She never compared the feeling at Laffland with the feeling about the baby. A darkness crept into her brain. *The feeling at Laffland was better than the baby.*

"So, when did *you* have this perfect feeling?"

"Of course, when we took the pregnancy test," Cheryl said, ashamed, rubbing her belly.

Laffland. She wanted to get there, before the baby. Something was urging, surging inside her. She would suggest it to Reggie. After all, they had a history there. Reggie held Cheryl in his arms in the lake while she felt light as a feather. She vividly recalled the electricity between them that first time their bodies touched. Cold beers and burgers out on the porch of the Sunset. Reggie sang softly to her as her eyes drooped on the 45-minute drive home. That night existed in her life story as the one date that "sealed the deal." They intentionally did not ride Laffland that day. Cheryl did not want anything to overpower that moment with Reggie.

"Wouldn't it be fun to go back to Sylvan Beach?" Cheryl asked the next morning over coffee.

"Um…you cannot ride a roller coaster," Reggie said.

"No. No way. Or drink beer. I just think it would be nice before I get too huge. Go for a swim?" she winked at him and he smiled.

"How 'bout Saturday?" Reggie said, always easily convinced.

They retraced their steps from that first time. The beach. The water. Getting showered and changed in the public bath houses. Feeling sunned and tanned and clean and refreshed. It *was* a good idea, a nice treat before the baby. They veered from tradition and went to the Crazy Clam (Seltzer for Cheryl), enjoyed watching other people get drunk and loud. Afterwards, avoiding the roller coaster, they went to Carello's Carousel (Cheryl thought it was bad luck for the baby to consult Zoltar the gypsy for a fortune) and the Playland and Fascination arcades and to the Bonanza shooting gallery. Cheryl kept quiet about Laffland, but led her husband toward it, hoping it would become his suggestion.

Finally, they stood in front of its peeling, clowned structure. *Laffland. The World's Craziest Ride*. Cheryl's breath became uneven, stuck between what felt like extreme excitement and a minor panic attack.

"This is a weird old place, huh? For little kids I guess," Reggie said.

"No. It's supposed to be like a scary ride where things pop out but it's so old. It's not scary. Jackie and I went on it once." She resisted the urge to give more information, reveal the extent of her knowledge, her over-interest. Reggie looked at his wife, worried the mention of her sister would be sad.

"Really? Do you want to ride it, honey?"

"Yeah, I think I do. Why not?"

Reggie passed the ticket to the kid before they forced themselves into the little wagon, barely fitting this time. Cheryl's hand slid down to feel the pretzel side of the cart. Her breath smoothed in a sigh of relief as she squeezed her husband's hand and they jerked and lurched forward. The baby inside Cheryl moved slightly. She positioned her hands over her belly, forming a kind of arc of love, or protection.

*****

Cheryl tried to go see her sister about once a month. This was a struggle, and if she was honest with herself, Cheryl dreaded it. Each visit began with Jackie's constant rehashing of the same anxiety-producing topics. She repeated her litany of complaints: She wished she could have a drink, she

wanted to see Sam, she grieved for Reggie, Cheryl did
not visit enough, she was so lonely. She inevitably
started to cry, wail, sob, finally talking about fire. *Fire,
Cher, Fire. All I can see when I close my eyes. Fire.* At
this, Cheryl immediately rushed into the hall to find a
nurse and then kept going, out the door, to the car.
After each visit with Jackie at Franklin House, Cheryl
cried all the way home and felt depressed the rest of
the day.

Everyone was gone, everyone except Sam.
Cheryl grieved the loss of her sister and husband. She
wished she could talk to Jackie about Reggie and to
Reggie about Jackie. She wanted to reminisce about
Mom and Dad. Cheryl ached with gratitude for her
son, although she felt sorry for him, having to grow up
without a father, grandparents, and aunt. She knew she
was inadequate, spaced out, not enough for this little
boy who lost so much.

When did Jackie start falling apart? Cheryl
surmised it was in their thirties, after Mom and Dad,
before Reggie. Jackie liked her drinks, that was for
sure. She started with that "Wine all the time" business
a lot of women get into. It's all jokey-jokey until it's
not, Cheryl knew. Then, she and her husband broke up,
she was calling him late at night, chasing him around.
Cheryl told her, the night Jackie crashed the car, that

she was turning into a big cliché. Jackie got so angry and started throwing things. Cheryl figured it was the booze, nothing else. Jackie so often repeated, "I'm just so hot all the time, Cher. I am not comfortable in my skin. I am boiling, Suffocating."

Things just got worse from there. Next, Jackie got into the opioids. She was caught stealing from a workmate. Then, after Reggie got sick, she called Cheryl at all hours, picking fights. She showed up late at night, early in the morning. Reggie was on his last legs and had to say, "Look, Jack, you need some kind of help." He could barely breathe, was on oxygen, when he told her that. Cheryl stood in the background and cried and shook, fearing for Jackie's life. Not understanding how things could be so bad. During those horrible, dark days, Cheryl guiltily wished for and dreamed of Laffland.

*****

Before Cheryl went back to Sylvan Beach, rode Laffland with Sam, she wanted to talk to Jackie about it. *Did she remember? What did she remember?* A nervous feeling sloshed around in her gut when she envisioned the conversation. *What would she say? What did she want? Understanding? Shared memories? Healing? Absolution? Permission?* She wanted to know there was no connection, that the bad luck that befell her family could not be some payment for the joy and elation she felt at Laffland. She wanted to ride Laffland again, without guilt. After all, she had Sam. He was beautiful and healthy and as happy as any boy who lost his father as a baby could possibly be. That is the one thing Cheryl knew for sure: Sam was a happy boy. Nothing could change that.

"Jackie?" Cheryl said, sitting beside the comfy chair in her sister's room at Franklin House. The floral chair came from Ikea all folded up in a box and then popped up — surprise! — into a full-sized chair. They both jumped when it popped. Cheryl bought it to cheer them up. Jackie slumped in it, a faded petal in the bouquet, her old pink velour bathrobe stained and threadbare. Cheryl looked into her sister's eyes, reached for her clammy hand.

"Jack, what do you remember that is good?"

Jackie stared at her. "You know. You know what's been good. Lots of things. Booze," she laughed a little.

Cheryl smiled, pretended to change the subject. "I'm going to take Sam to Sylvan tomorrow."

Jackie's faced immediately shifted, growing darker, crimson. Cheryl dropped Jackie's hand, reacting to its sudden fiery heat.

"Jack, Jack, calm down, Calm," she soothed, rubbing the sagging pink shoulder. Cheryl's body prepared to spring from the chair, but she hung on. She desperately wanted to be strong enough for this, to bear down, bear through it, push through to the truth, hear her sister say the words, make it all come together. Instead, Jackie's breath became short and choppy; her chest bounced up and down, hyperventilating. She began gasping and pulling on Cheryl, scratching her arms and grasping at her sleeve. Cheryl pulled herself away and ran out to the hall, shouted to the nurse, "My sister! My sister! There's a problem!" And just as always, Cheryl fled the scene, unable to shake the sight of her sister's state of mind, state of life.

*****

Sam begged Cheryl about Laffland for years. Today was finally the day. Plus, she needed something, this one thing, to put her mind back in the right place, to feel happy, more than happy, perfect, for just a few moments. *Is that so wrong?* She would have said this to Jackie at one time. *It might be wrong, be very wrong.* She touched her son's smiling face, sandy hair, *just like Reggie's.* She took Sam's hand, his long, graceful fingers, *like Jackie's.* They were finally here.

Sam acted like the big grownup, handed the ticket person, this time an elderly man, the old-school ticket. Cheryl let Sam step in first, after pointing out the Pretzel logo on the side. Their mutually skinny bodies allowed extra room in the car. Cheryl first relaxed and then tensed, her mind expanded and then contracted, crowded with memories, dark ones, fearful ones. She wanted this too badly to walk away. She hoped Sam would get what she got from it. *Maybe he will feel Reggie? Maybe she will? Maybe she will at last be able to speak honestly about this, this drug, this dream? Maybe they will be able to come every week, or all the time? Maybe she could feel this warmth all the time? Maybe.*

Cheryl smiled at her son and put her arm around him. She once again formed her mother-arc of love, protection over Sam as they heaved forward, into Laffland.

THE DOOR

by Jess Lindsay

Pete was the kind of guy that was always getting into trouble. He was in my stage crew class, and I'm not sure how he managed to keep from getting expelled. Whenever the teacher wasn't around, he and Big Ben got the nail guns and fired them at each other. They were lucky that no one got hit. And for better or for worse, those two lunatics were my friends. We were all in the stage crew class together, and the three of us loved building sets for the school play.

Big Ben, easily over six feet tall and three hundred pounds, looked like a tub of lard, but the guy could lift anything. He used to get made fun of because of his glasses, but now he was the biggest guy around, so nobody dared pick on him. Pete was the exact opposite, super short and all bones, with dark hair. I was somewhere between; tall, skinny, bright red hair, and thick glasses. I never got into the same kind of trouble that they did, until the night Pete suggested we break into the high school to contact the resident ghost.

Everyone knew about Edgar. As a student, he had supposedly fallen from the catwalk and either hung himself or turned into a pancake on the stage. He was usually a friendly ghost. I didn't believe in ghosts, but Pete was really into this stuff. He loved to go hunting for ghosts at night. And Big Ben just thought it would be fun to break into the school. But Pete was really into this stuff. He loved to go hunting for ghosts at night. I agreed to go, because I was the only one of us with a car, and it was a good opportunity to get Pete to shut up about all that spooky stuff for a while. So, we slipped a small chunk of wood in the back door behind stage right and prayed that the janitor wouldn't find it.

We returned that night, around eleven, and the door was still held open by our little bit of wood. We slipped in the back, as quiet as ghosts ourselves, and walked across the dark stage. Ben carried the flashlight and Pete carried the Ouija board.

When we reached the dressing room hall off of stage left, Pete plopped to the ground, declaring that this would be as good a spot as any. I would have figured he would want to do it right on the stage, since that was supposedly where Edgar had died.

"Seriously?" Big Ben sighed and sat with his back to the exit door. The sign blared the familiar green, casting an eerie light over the hallway. I settled against the wall as Pete set up his spirit board. We all place our hands on the planchette and moved it to 'hello'.

"It feels right," Pete stated, clearly excited. "Now, we ask questions. Is anyone there?" The planchette moved to rest on the 'yes'. Big Ben chuckled.

"Did you fall to your death?" he asked. The planchette moved to 'no.'

"Do you help students finish the sets?" I asked. Once again, the little bit of plastic landed on the 'no'.

"Did you commit suicide?" Pete asked. He had always thought that Edgar fell on purpose, for some reason. But the planchette again landed on 'no.'

"Are you a guy?" Ben asked, looking very proud of himself. Another 'no'.

"Are you Edgar?" Pete continued. I felt someone trying to push the planchette back to 'yes' but it was fighting. At last, it arrived on the 'no'.

"Who pushed it to 'no'?" Ben demanded, frowning.

"I thought that was you pushing it," I teased.

"I was!" he admitted. "I was pushing it to the 'yes'!"

"Dude!" Pete gave him the dirtiest look. "You don't guide the planchette!"

"How else is it supposed to move?" Ben asked, still frowning. The planchette slid to the M, and then the E.

"Me?" Pete asked. "Who is 'me'?"

The planchette scratched out a rough phrase. Ben was no longer touching it as it moved. I A M H E R E.

"Who are you?" I demanded. I felt a chill run down my spine as the little plastic triangle moved once more across the board.

LET ME IN.

"I'm out!" Ben shouted, raising his hands in the air. I couldn't breathe as he scrambled to his feet and ran out the door. A wind rushed in, and the exit sign changed from green to a menacing red. The lights flashed. I felt my temperature rise. Panic rose with it, and I felt a desperate need to run. But I couldn't move.

"Why?" Pete asked, his eyes wide with fear. "What do you want?"

The planchette slipped from beneath our fingers, racing over the letters, pausing just long enough for us to say each letter aloud.

"L E T M E I N L E T M E I N L E T M E I
N..." It continued repeating the phrase, getting faster
and faster.

"We have to get out of here!" I cried, at last
breaking out of my frozen state.

"Wait!" Pete looked up at me, his eyes
pleading. "We have to finish, or it'll get loose!"

"It's already loose!" I replied. "I'm not sticking
around to find out what it'll do to us!" Pete hesitated,
then reached for the planchette, and I ran out the door.
Ben was long gone. I couldn't blame him. He hadn't
even seen the scary part, when the planchette moved
on its own. I climbed into my car and waited for Pete. I
felt safe outside, and I figured he would be out any
moment. I fell asleep waiting for him.

The next morning, nothing seemed to have
changed. I thought that Pete must have run home, like
Ben did, so I drove myself home as well. On Monday,
Pete wasn't at school. Big Ben and I avoided the
dressing room hall as much as we could. We never
went into the hallway alone, even though our
classmates didn't seem to notice anything. On Tuesday,
still no Pete. We never saw him again. No one did.

We thought that no one would believe us. Then
I overheard a sophomore telling her friends that the

hallway by the dressing rooms spooked her. She felt like she was being watched. And the janitor has started telling the students that he feels like there's something malicious in the hall.

We opened a door that night. And I'm afraid that whatever we let in got to Pete. Once in a while, if you're alone in the auditorium, a lone nail will fall to the stage floor. Almost like Pete is still there, up to his old tricks. Big Ben likes to think that Pete got out and is in hiding somewhere. His parents weren't exactly great at raising kids. But when I'm working on a set piece by myself, I can sometimes hear Pete's voice, calling for help.

TREK

by Nidheesh Samant

The dirt crunched under Shyam's boots as he walked along the forest trail. He led the three tourists along the moonlit path, their footsteps echoing in the silence of the forest. Shyam suddenly stopped and pointed ahead. Shyam's overseas clients now found themselves staring at an ancient banyan tree. Its antiquity was evident from its humongous size. Its aerial roots had bunched up, and matured into thick trunks themselves, indistinguishable from the original body of the tree. Shyam cleared his throat.

"This tree, my friends, is the reason for this forest's infamy. It is this very banyan tree, where the great *Vetaal* waited for travelers like yourself. He would continue haunting them for many centuries, until King Vikram finally put him to rest. It is said that since that day, this tree has never borne any leaves, cursed by the presence of the undead *Vetaal.*"

Shyam stood silently, letting his clients breathe into the dense atmosphere surrounding the tree. He could not fathom how anybody could be pleased to visit such dark, gloomy places. But the smile on his client's faces told him that they were getting their money's worth. The tall, burly man, who called himself Marc spoke in a thick accent, that Shyam could still not place, a couple of hours into the trek.

"Are you saying, this tree is still cursed?"

Shyam nodded. Marc turned to his companions – the equally tall lady Gina, and her stout and bearded brother, Yerome. He spoke to them excitedly in their native tongue. Yerome quickly took out his camera and began clicking away. Shyam sighed as he sat down on a tree stump.

The trek had been arduous for Shyam, not because he wasn't used to walking, but because he had to come up with stories and legends on the go. Their first stop on the trek had been a regular well. But, Shyam had convinced his clients about how the waters of the well inflicted horrific hallucinations upon its drinkers and were responsible for a slew of villager suicides. Shyam had then taken his clients to a perfectly normal rock and presented it to them as the worshipping stone of a demonic entity. He told them a story about a cult that worshipped the entity and convened their ceremonies at the rock. Shyam had managed to convince his clients about the vast amount of negative energy swirling around in the forest. Shyam did not really like cheating his clients, it affected his conscience. But he was in a desperate situation and could only think of the rest of the payment that was owed to him. He really needed the money.

Shyam propped up from the stump and dusted his pants. He called out to his clients.

"Let's move ahead. There is much more left to experience in this forest."

The foreigners murmured excitedly and began following Shyam. He led them deeper into the forest, leaving the banyan tree looming in the background. Marc rubbed his palms together.

"Sure is getting chilly now. What are we seeing next?"

Shyam turned around to look at his clients. All three of them were hugging themselves. Suddenly, Shyam felt it too! A chill running down his spine and spreading through his entire body. Shyam had no idea where the cold wave was coming from. He smiled at his clients.

"I have a real treat in store for you, my friends. Do you feel those chills? Well, I'm going to take you to the spot where they originate – the heart of this forest. Let's continue, yes?"

His clients nodded, clearly pleased with the idea. Shyam knew that their intrigue knew no bounds. All he had to do was throw in breadcrumbs here and there, and they would lap it all up.

The group continued heading into the heart of the woods, despite the gradually dropping temperature. The moonlight was fading now, decreasing the visibility of the trail. The trees in this area had grown in closer proximity to each other, shrinking the size of the trail. It was almost as if the forest was closing in on the group, making its presence increasingly palpable. As Shyam halted to figure out the unclear path ahead, he felt a hand on his shoulder. Shyam gasped in shock, only to realize it belonged to Marc.

"What happened?"

"It's Gina. She thinks she heard something. An animal, maybe?"

"That's impossible! There are no animals or birds in this forest. They choose to stay away from the evil energy here. It must be the rustling of leaves."

Shyam stopped mid-sentence. He had heard it too. A whooshing sound coming from an eerily close proximity. As Shyam backed up along with Marc, he heard a shrill shriek. Gina! He instinctively turned around before feeling a quick hard impact on his chin. The searing pain soon transformed into a darkness that cloaked his eyes. He felt himself losing consciousness.

*****

Shyam felt warm and cozy as he awoke. With his

half open eyes, he could make out a fire burning a few feet away. As he willed his eyes to open completely, he wished he had kept them shut. The scene playing out in front of him was worse than any nightmare he could have imagined. Shyam spotted his clients beyond the flickering campfire, or rather what was left of them. Shyam felt sick as he realized he was staring at the headless corpses of Gina and Yerome. Their bodies appeared pale, almost as if they had no blood left inside them. And yet, there was no blood on the ground. To their right, Shyam could see the unconscious Marc, several feet above the ground, tied up to a tree trunk, with the help of vines.

"Ah! You're up."

Shyam turned to the guttural voice coming from his left. He gasped, unable to speak, as he spotted the grotesque entity staring directly at him. Seven feet tall, the grey skinned anthropomorphic monster studied Shyam with its jaundiced eyes, its pointed ears twitching in mirth. In each of its hands, it held a head, one belonging to Gina, and the other to Yerome. Shyam hurled as he noticed the heads were missing the entire top area of the head. There was nothing above the forehead.

"Look pretty don't they? I will skin them later. Need to continue with my meal now. It's rare that anyone joins me for dinner. You must be the first man in centuries to do so."

Shyam continued staring in silence as the monster tossed the two heads to the side and turned to Marc. The monster's garland of bones and its belt made of intestines jiggled as it walked slowly towards its next course. It continued talking to the horrified Shyam.

"A *Brahmapurusha* like me, is blessed with eternal life. But, you have to understand, that living for so long comes with a price. I feel an insatiable hunger."

The monster fished out a hollowed skull from behind the tree and smacked its lips. It slender, long tongue moved around the set of fangs protruding from its mouth.

"There is only one way to keep away those hunger pangs."

With an incantation the Brahmapurusha stabbed Marc's stomach with its arm and upon withdrawing it, drew out a steady stream of blood that flowed cleanly into the skull goblet. As the goblet filled up, the blood stopped flowing. The monster raised the goblet to its lips and drained it in a single go. Once the monster lowered the goblet, the blood resumed flowing out of Marc's body and into the goblet. The Brahmapurusha continued consuming Marc's blood in the same way, until his body had turned as pale as his companions' bodies. Shyam squirmed. The monster cackled.

"I know it looks gruesome, but trust me, your kind taste so much better than any other animal. The best part comes next. As much as your kind loves devouring knowledge, that annoying curiosity within you, I find knowledge delicious as well."

With a lustful bellow, the Brahmapurusha ripped off Marc's head. With its sharp nails, it easily cut open the skull, to reveal the brain that lay inside. It scooped out the brain and held it in its hand, showing the wiggling mass to Shyam, before slurping it up ravenously. The Brahmapurusha tossed aside the rest of Marc's head and let out a long burp. It gleefully looked at the nauseated Shyam.

"Well, I hope you enjoyed dinner. It's now time to take care of you."

Shyam shuddered as the grey monster approached him. Time had slowed down for the petrified man. He could now clearly see the assortment of bones that was a part of the garland, their different shapes, sizes and colours. And then suddenly, in no time, the Brahmapurusha was upon him, looking down on him. With one hand, the monster picked up the shivering guide and hoisted him in the air. Shyam closed his eyes in reflex, expecting a stab in the stomach any moment now.

After what felt like eternity, Shyam had still not felt any sort of stab. He opened his eyes slowly to the see the monster looking at him with an amused expression. It placed Shyam on the ground and held out its hand to him. In the palm of his hand was a blazing red stone. Shyam blinked in disbelief. The Brahmapurusha cackled.

"A deal is a deal. You promised me a scrumptious meal and you delivered. I will keep my word to you. You can have this gem. Thanks again, for a wonderful meal. It had been ages since I had any meal of a different variety than Indian. Now, go on. Take the gem and be off on your way!"

Shyam muttered a soft 'thanks' and pocketed the gem. He hurried away from the lair of the Brahmapurusha, glad that he had gotten away with the deal he had made. He felt terrible about what he had witnessed and the fate he had led his clients to, but the priceless gem in his pocket made him feel somewhat better. Who would have known, monsters made for honest business partners?

ROSA'S BABY

by Mark Tulin

A woman's hysterical screams startled me out of sleep.

"Did you hear that?" I turned to Sherri, who was already peering out of our bedroom window.

"Yeah, sounds scary, Bill. I wonder where it's coming from?"

"I think it's our next-door neighbor, the woman who speaks Spanish."

Sherri rolled open the vertical blinds for a better view. She had excellent intuition. Judging by the screams, someone had experienced a significant tragedy, and Sherri's first instinct was our neighbor, Rosa.

"She's in so much pain," Sherri said. "It must be unbearable."

It was hard for us to imagine losing a baby, although several women where I worked had similar losses. They said that a child's death was the worst possible loss, even more than a parent or spouse.

There's a rumor that Rosa's husband ran off with the female neighbor in 3B. Rosa, who spoke in broken English and worked at a Mexican restaurant on Milpas Avenue, felt ashamed and embarrassed. Occasionally, I'd say hello when we ran into one another at the mailbox or coming from the laundry room. She seemed sweet enough, but I sensed that she was hiding something, and it was evident that she didn't want anyone to know her business.

Rosa's living room lights were on, and her front door was wide open. I could see her haunting shadow move back and forth under the courtyard's night light and hear the birds cawing above us in the trees.

With each passing moment, the screams grew more desperate. Only the most dreadful situations could elicit such wailing cries.

"Shall we call the police?" my wife asked.

I hesitated. My logical mind knew we should, but I was not the kind of person who called the police on a neighbor unless I was sure something was wrong. Even though my wife had exceptional intuition, I wanted to see for myself.

"I'm going next door, Sherri. I want to check on her before calling the cops."

"Are you sure you don't want me to go?" my wife asked, knowing that I should be taking care of myself instead of others. "Don't you get enough drama at the hospice?"

"No, Sherri, I'm fine. You're pregnant and need your rest."

I opened the front door, and immediately saw our neighbor standing in her doorway, squeezing a baby blanket against her face and sobbing. I could see several large cardboard boxes, a playpen with many Disney toys scattered in front of it, and only a couple of folding chairs in the living room. It seemed that she had just moved in, but she had been there for over a year. It was puzzling, as if she were in transition, not sure if she wanted to stay.

Overhead, a screeching crow scattered from the branches as if it were frightened. One of its feathers fell gently from the sky and landed at my feet. I saw it as a good omen and clutched it in my right hand, hoping it could anchor me through this ordeal.

"Hi, I'm Bill, your neighbor in 4C," I said, just in case she forgot my name. "Are you okay?"

She sobbed and talked in broken English. She wondered how this could happen, a new mother, a husband who left her for a slutty neighbor, and now the baby.

Her cries pierced the quiet of the 2 a.m. morning like a sharp razor.

"Is the baby alright?" I asked.

"Yes-no!" she cried hysterically. "Help— please. Don't know what to do!"

I approached her slowly, taking each step with caution. "What is it that you need from me, Rosa?"

"It not me, señor," said the caramel-complected young woman rocking herself back and forth while clutching the baby blanket. "It's *bebé*!"

Having been in crisis before, I didn't hesitate to call 911. I informed the dispatcher that the mother said something was wrong with her baby, although I wasn't sure what, and that the infant was in the house, possibly dead.

Rosa stopped crying for a moment and pointed to the inside of her house. "*Por favor*, go to *la casa* to see! In house, please."

I didn't feel comfortable, but Rosa was adamant and yanked the sleeve of my robe.

I walked carefully through the living room in my L.L. Bean bedroom slippers. The house smelled like a pot of Menudo with a strange energy hanging in the air. It was a small apartment, but it took me a long time to get through the hallway and to my ultimate destination.

"In that room, *diablo*!" yelled Rosa a few feet behind me.

Before I entered the bedroom, I could feel its spirit. It was like a dark cloud of impending doom, warning me not to look.

I turned to Rosa, who couldn't stop saying *diablo*. I didn't know what I was about to find, but my knees buckled, and I almost dropped to the ground when I looked into the crib. I had never seen anything that looked like that baby; if it was a baby. It appeared to be covered in a black shroud, almost burnt to a crisp, more like a reptile than a human infant. Whatever it was, it sure was gruesome. Although it had a charred appearance, it was alive. Its haunting blue eyes were as clear as a bell. Even worse, jagged white teeth lined its jaws and pointed horns spread from its temples.

"Si?" Rosa said. "Diablo."

"I sure as hell don't know, Rosa."

"Wasn't there, *ayer*. Not there, yesterday"

Spirits seemed to gravitate toward me, especially at the hospice, where at least one person dies per day. Even when lost souls are troubled, they confide in me about their unfinished business before they venture off somewhere into the great beyond. But I've never encountered an evil spirit as ugly and threatening as Rosa's baby.

I looked again at the baby. The thing seemed to hover slightly above the blanket as if levitating, swaying and rocking, about to pounce without a moment's notice.

I thought about running out of the room, screaming hysterically; instead, I stayed, for Rosa's sake.

"Aren't you the cutest little darling?" I lied, in an attempt to make friends with it.

I watched as the baby destroyed its rattle and responded with a choking growl. I could see its long sharp tongue, green in color, protruding from its charred lips. Believing that it would sink its devil teeth into my face, fear overcame me. I retreated quickly to the front steps, despite Rosa's plea to stay.

Shaking, I sat on the front step of my bungalow apartment, still holding the feather, looking at the ground in disbelief.

While Rosa talked out of her head in Spanish, I saw my wife waving from our window, and soon came outside in her robe and furry rabbit slippers, rubbing my shoulders and whispering that she could sense something was wrong.

"That baby in there looks awful," I told Sherri.

"What are you talking about?"

"That thing in there," pointing to Rosa's doorway, "ugliest thing I ever saw!"

"A thing? Do you mean her baby? That's what you call a thing?"

I nodded, still staring at the black feather.

"That's ridiculous, Bill. A baby is never ugly. All babies are beautiful."

Rosa and I turned to Sherri, and in unison, "Not this one!"

I continued to console Rosa while we waited for the paramedics and the police to arrive. Meanwhile, Sherri decided to take a look for herself. And it wasn't long until she came staggering out of the house, as white as a ghost, and holding her pregnant belly about to barf all over the sidewalk.

"God, you were right, Bill," she said, looking up after a few dry heaves. "It looks like the damn thing was set on fire, but its eyes were steely blue. It was cooing and barking, squirming all over the crib like it wanted to rise and bite my neck."

We both sat on the step, trying to figure out what we were going to do next.

"A tragedy like this must have a silver lining," Sherri said. "It can't possibly be all bad."

Rosa and I looked at Sherri like she was insane.

"I want my *bebé* back--not this crazy *loco* one," said Rosa. "Whoever stole my *bebé,* better bring it back."

"I'm not sure I want to know who stole her child," I whispered to Sherri.

I was exhausted, barely able to think, let alone talk. All I wanted to do was take my pregnant wife home and lock our doors and windows. Let the authorities, or, perhaps, an exorcist figure out what to do about that little barbecued demon in Rosa's apartment.

I dropped the crow's feather to the ground and took Sherri's hand. "I think we're finished here," and led Sherri and our unborn baby back to the safety of our apartment. Whatever evil spirit it was, it wasn't going to get into Sherri's womb.

Soon, a parade of people flooded Rosa's apartment— police, paramedics, reporters, and other tenants milling around in idle curiosity. But I didn't want to look out of the window. I had seen too much already and dreaded watching a little monster expel projectile vomit and twist its head in complete circles. I didn't want to see that whatever-it-was being transported by chains to the back of a police van, heading to some nutty scientist about to do some crazy experiments on it. I had enough drama for one night.

-END-

THE DEVIL DOWN IN JERSEY

by Jamie Zaccaria

It was a typical Pine Barrens landscape; the soil was sandy, the trees coniferous, and the insects and amphibians loud. There was a large, overturned tree trunk that seemed to the mark the beginning of a trail. A young woman walked toward the trunk and sat down on it. She wore hiking boots, shorts, and a tee-shirt, topped off with a baseball cap. Clearing her throat, she began speaking directly to the camera that she had set up to face her.

"My name is Mia Brown. I'm a graduate student researching the traditions and folklore of New Jersey's Pine Barrens. I'm spending this weekend camping in the Barrens to get some on-the-ground experience and hopefully interview some local folks. This video is part of my application to the Richardson Grant Program. If awarded funding from the Program, I would be able to create a comprehensive database of local folklore and history from the Pine Barrens, preserving an important part of New Jersey's culture."

The woman looked awkwardly around and then got up and walked towards the camera, turning it off.

She picked up her equipment and got inside a red truck. Starting the vehicle, she made a U-Turn back onto the gravel road. The wheels churned up dirt, kicking it into the air. Thick trees lined either side of the road.

Mia placed the camera on the dashboard, facing it towards her. She narrated to it while driving,

"The Pinelands includes over a million acres, making up 22 percent of New Jersey's landmass. This area is bigger than the Grand Canyon or Yosemite but less well-known across the country. In 1978 Congress designated it a Natural Reserve, and it was upgraded to an International Biosphere Reserve ten years later."

Swampy areas intersected the trees on either side of the road. The water was green and slimy, and insects skated on top of its oily surface. The sun shone through the windshield, illuminating smudges on the glass and creating a glare on the camera screen.

"The people who live down here are often referred to as 'Pineys' and not necessarily in a good way. Since the colonization of New Jersey, they've often been poor and discriminated against, and there were even eugenics studies in the early 1900s that condemned them. I want to make it clear that all the people I've talked to who live down here have been incredibly kind and helpful with my research."

The truck slowed down and turned off onto another road, leaving the forest behind and passing by carefully mowed fields edged by wooden fences. Mia pulled into a parking lot and turned off her car. She made her way to the building in front of her.

"We're at the Batsto Nature Center in Historic Batsto Village in Wharton State Forest, part of the Pinelands Nature Reserve and the largest state park in New Jersey. Batso was a thriving village in the mid-19th century, but it's now just a historical landmark sitting right here in the middle of the Pines."

Mia entered the building, ignored by the person with their head down at the welcome desk. Locating the entrance to an exhibit, she veered left, keeping her camera on and pointed forward.

As Mia walked through the room, she zoomed in on different objects: agricultural tools, old maps, black and white photographs. She approached a poster with a drawing of an odd-looking animal with the words "WANTED: JERSEY DEVIL" written across the top in an old-timey font. At the bottom, it offered a $250,000 reward and wanted readers to "approach with extreme caution." Narrating again, Mia began,

"Perhaps the most well-known legend of the Pine Barrens is that of the Jersey Devil. This mythological creature is said to have the head of a goat, wings of a bat, cloven hooves, and forked tail. While many people chalk it up to mere mistaken identity, others argue that the devil's existence predates white colonization. Local Native Americans, the Lenni Lenape, sometimes referred to the Barrens as 'The Place of the Dragon.'" She continued moving through the center, panning in and around educational set-ups on the soil and trees making up the region.

"The most common story goes that the Jersey Devil was born to a woman named Mrs. Leeds in the 1730's somewhere in the eastern part of the Barrens. She'd already had twelve kids and didn't want any more, so she cursed this one. And it was born a hideous creature that flew away into the night. While the story is ridiculous, that hasn't stopped dozens of people from reporting seeing the monster over the years." Turning off the camera, Mia continued leisurely through the exhibit before leaving and getting back in her car.

The next time Mia turned on the camera again, she was driving away from Batso and the Nature Center. She once again continued her narration to the device in her passenger seat,

"Even in modern times, people claim to see the Jersey Devil, or at least its leftovers. In the '20s, a taxi driver reported seeing a winged creature when he was fixing a flat tire. In 1980 a bunch of pigs were found dead right here in Wharton State Forest. Since there were no tracks or traces left behind, people blamed the creature. I want to learn why folklore, especially around this 'devil' is so prevalent in this part of the state and how that ties into the overall culture of the people of the Pine Barrens."

The pick-up turned into a clearing. The sun was setting, and the sky showed shades of pink and orange. A dirt road lined one side and thick forest patch the other. Mia walked around, searching for the best area to pitch her tent, still talking to her invisible audience.

"The soil here is sandy and acidic, making it difficult for traditional farming. The colonists who settled here were usually considered the lowest levels of society, including people who made moonshine or deserted from the army. Most lived off the land, and many still do- hunting, fishing, and harvesting fruit like cranberries. Blueberries are one of the most common crops produced in the state," she said, pointing to the bright green bushes speckled with the fruit.

Mia turned off the camera and focused on setting up her campsite. She pitched a small tent not too far from the pick-up truck, laying tarp underneath and overtop. She had a portable campfire in the truck bed, which she removed and set up. As the flames grew, Mia added one more comment to her video.

"This is my campsite for the next two nights. It's a good location because I'm pretty deep into the forest, certainly further in than most people go. I haven't seen any other campers around here either, so I shouldn't have to worry about being disturbed. Tomorrow, I'm going to be conducting some interviews with local people. But for now, I'm exhausted."

After eating a can of beans and a sandwich she had packed earlier, she put out the fire and went into her tent, falling fast asleep.

Some hours later, in the middle of the night, Mia was awakened. Reaching around in the dark tent, she grabbed her camera, turning on its night vision to record and allow her to see better. She pointed it at her face, which glowed eerily green on screen. She whispered, addressing the camera,

"I was just woken up by a horrible scream. It sounded like someone or something in incredible pain. In 1960 residents of May's Landing reported similar noises and attributed them to the Jersey Devil. But we know now that they, and probably the ones I just heard, are actually the sounds of foxes mating. Not particularly scary but definitely startling to wake up to." Shaking her head with a slight smile, Mia turned off the camera and settled back down to sleep.

The next morning the world was bright again. Mia left her campsite early to hike down one of the local trails. To her left, a stream quietly meandered by. Sunlight shone down, reflecting off the ochre-colored water. She heard birds singing from all directions, and the small plants around the edge of the streambed danced subtly in the wind as insects hopped from one to another. Once again, she picked up her camera and began narrating the world around her.

"See how the water looks reddish? That's from high iron levels. Some people call it 'cedar water.' This area is basically a massive swamp. The sandy soil produces near-pristine groundwater but makes it difficult to grow crops, which explains why the Pines was never developed into agricultural land like the rest of south Jersey."

As she made her way on foot down the forest path, the sounds of her backpack thumping against her shoulders became rhythmic. The burnt stumps of cedar, oak, and pine trees came into view.

"Forest fires are really common here and a natural part of the ecosystem," Mia said to the camera. "There are tons of animals down here too, bald eagles, tree frogs, even river otters."

Mia walked silently as the path became less obvious and more overgrown. The camera picked up sounds of her breathing and the continued noises of nature's inhabitants as she traversed deeper into the forest.

Suddenly, Mia stopped moving and swung the camera around to the right. Slightly off the path, she pointed and zoomed in on a moist soil patch. Half a dozen footprints were visible in dirt.

"Look at these!" Mia says to herself, panning the camera over each one. "See how they look hoof-like on the bottom, but then they sort of split at the top? I don't know what kind of creature would make a print like this." She investigated the area around the prints, finding no tracks coming or going amongst the shrubbery.

"In 1909, there was this crazed panic, because a bunch of people were finding signs of the devil, many of them hooved footprints that maybe even looked something like these. It was all over the state from Bordentown to Mount Holly, Burlington, Gloucester, and Woodbury. The press had a field day, especially since some of the tracks were found on roofs and other difficult to reach areas but then disappeared, leading to the belief that the creature could also fly. I don't know what made these tracks, but it would certainly be freaky to find them on my roof, especially if I only had a turn-of-the-century education."

Mia continued hiking for another hour, hoping the path would lead her towards a half-hidden home where she could interview locals. Instead, she only saw more trees.

Suddenly, a loud noise came from above, like the sound of giant wings flapping, followed by a dark shadow. Mia let out a little shriek and took off. Her foot got caught on a rock, and she fell onto her left side.

Carefully getting up, Mia brushed off the dirt on her scratched palms. She sat down on the path and clicked the camera on, sitting it down next to her, propped slightly upwards.

She pulled her left knee up to examine it, wiping away the blood flowing down her shin with a navy bandana from her backpack.

"So, this is embarrassing," she spoke to the camera, "but I spooked myself back there. I heard something in the woods, and then there was this shadow as it flew by. It looked huge, but I'm sure it was just a regular turkey vulture or something. Anyway, I freaked and tripped over a rock," Mia said sheepishly. She reached behind her and grabbed a green plant.

"This is sphagnum moss. Soldiers used it in the American Revolution for bandages. Since my first aid kit is back at the tent, I'm going to see if I can use it to stop some of the bleeding."

Mia rinsed the earthy material with water from her canteen and laid it carefully on her wound. She winced while tying the bandana around the moss to hold it in place. Hobbling, Mia stood upright and clicked off the camera, putting it away inside her bag. Turning in the opposite direction of where she was initially heading, Mia began walking.

For three hours, she had been following what she thought was the same trail, but somehow, nothing seemed familiar. She should have arrived back at her campsite some time ago, but she must have made a wrong turn somewhere. The monoculture of the forest was confusing, and she breathed deeply, trying to stay calm.

A twig snapped behind her, and she whipped her head around. Far off in the forest, there were two glowing red orbs. Mia blinked twice, hoping to clear her vision, but the certainty of what she was seeing only cemented itself in her mind. She took off running.

Half a mile later, Mia stopped. She looked around, thankfully not seeing anything alarming.

"Okay, there is definitely something weird going on out here," her voice was somewhere above a whisper, and she seemed to be gasping for breath between words. Mia took out her camera once again, finding comfort in her routine. She turned it on and shakily faced forward, speaking,

"It's already six pm, and I'm still miles from my campsite. I can't even say which direction to be honest since I got super turned around. I don't know what I just saw but something big with glowing eyes. A black bear, maybe? I don't know, but I didn't stick around to find out."

The trees seemed unusually dark and sinister against the backdrop of the setting sun. Mia was walking at a fast pace but still hobbled due to her injury. Her head turned back and forth as she inspected the treeline on either side of the path.

As her arm lowered to her side, the camera pointed behind Mia, capturing the path after her steps walked on it. It was not a well-maintained trail, barely visible amongst overgrown weeds and rocks. Each time she bounced her injured leg, the camera would rise to catch the darkening view behind Mia. Thump. Thump. Thump.

Suddenly, and unbeknownst to Mia, the trail behind her was no longer empty. A dark shape blocked out what little sunlight was left, creating a looming shadow on the camera. The skin on the back of Mia's neck prickled, and she took in a breath, slowly turning. Her eyes widened as she noticed the dark presence.

She stepped back carefully, but the sound of breaking glass made her wince. Glancing down, Mia realized her foot had landed on an old glass jug, likely used to hold moonshine, as was common in the Pines. Suddenly, two pricks of red appeared in the shadow, giving it a clear animalistic form. With horror, Mia realized they were the same pair of eyes from before.

She took off running, willing herself not to look back as a high-pitched blood-curdling scream followed her. The sky continued to darken as Mia ran faster than her injured leg should have allowed her to. She only stopped when she spotted an old fire tower in a clearing up ahead. Pausing at the base of the tower's ladder, Mia looked around. Not seeing any creature, she decided to climb up.

The rungs were wooden, and she was terrified they would give way under her weight, but thankfully they held. Mia was hoping she could get to the top and hide out up there. When she reached the shelter at the top, she banged the wooden door. It wouldn't budge.

"Damnit," Mia cursed to herself, realizing the inside of the tower was either locked or rotted shut.

She craned her neck around, hoping to see over the trees and at least figure out what direction she should go.

In the distance past a creek, but not too far off, Mia noticed what looked like a cabin. She prayed it was an occupied house rather than something abandoned. Quickly, she mentally calculated her next move. Mia would climb down the ladder and make her way through the small meadow, swim across the water, and then go through the patch of woods to get to the structure.

Taking a deep breath, Mia started making her way down the ladder. There was no sunlight left at this point, and she carefully stepped one foot down after another, hoping to stay quiet and not stumble. She hit solid ground and turned in the direction of the cabin.

Hunching over in a desperate attempt to make her appear less obvious in the meadow, Mia began quickly shuffling towards the creek. A dark shadow covered the moon's bright glow. Eventually, her eyes determined its shape, and she noticed in horror the large wings. Mia took off at a full sprint at the sound of flapping wings as the shadow grew closer.

It felt like minutes for Mia to reach the creek bed but was really no more than ten seconds. Scanning the bank, she spotted an overturned wooden canoe.

Quickly, Mia raced towards it and pulled it behind her as she backed up into the creek. The coolness of the water soaked into her feet and legs as she kept moving deeper.

Holding her breath, she slipped under the water's surface and came up underneath the canoe. There was enough space for her to float with her nose and mouth above the surface. Standing in the dark water under a dome of wood was terrifying, but Mia couldn't imagine it being less so that what was facing her outside.

Slowly she shuffled her feet across the bottom of the creek, praying that it wouldn't get deeper. She tried to ignore the feeling of slime and stone against her legs and stay as quiet as possible, moving painstakingly sluggishly as to not draw attention to herself.

Eventually, the water level receded, and Mia knew she had reached the other side. She once again slipped underwater and swam beyond the canoe. Peeking up over the surface, she didn't spot the creature anywhere. Quickly, Mia climbed out of the creek and took off running through the patch of forest that separated her and the cabin.

Her leg ached, and her lungs cried for her to stop, but Mia kept moving. Finally, she reached the structure she had seen from the fire tower. It was an old-fashioned log cabin. There were no lights on inside. She slowed as she approached the structure, looking for any signs that someone might be in there and able to help her.

Hanging around the perimeter of the decrepit building were paper lanterns. Mia approached one and looked closely at it, noticing crude drawings of a dark, winged shape that looked suspiciously like her pursuer.

She rushed to the front door and banged, only to notice that it was sealed shut with beams of wood. Glancing at the windows told her they too were closed off. Whether there was someone in there or not, they did not want Mia, or anyone else, to join them.

She darted off the porch, intending to look for another way into the cabin, or at least another hiding place, when an inhuman scream pierced the air. Mia covered her ears with her hands to mute what sounded like metal scraping against metal.

A whoosh and the creature landed 20 feet away. Mia's eyes widened. She saw now how incredibly huge and unnatural it looked. Leathery wings spread at least ten feet in either direction of a solid, hairy body. Those piercing red eyes were back, and this time directed right at her. The creature opened its long muzzle and sniffed the air.

Mia grasped for her camera, hoping to at least capture some evidence of what was going on. Too late, she realized that it was completely soaked through from her foray across the creek. Tossing the useless device aside, Mia looked around, spotting a large stick. She picked it up, brandishing it like a baseball bat. She was out of options, and this was her last stand.

The Devil screamed again, lifting off the ground, launching itself towards Mia. She swung the branch, and everything went black.

MODEL CITIZEN:
A DEADLY TALE OF BEAUTY

(Inspired by true events)

by J. Perry Carr

Liz Bath was a monster. A mammoth adversary to contend with. Known the world over as a woman to fear, her body was a weapon, and her looks could kill. She was a model after all.

Warm oil ran down her spine as a masseuse dribbled the elixir from a wooden bowl. Her statuesque figure draped over the massage table. She had a slender frame that stood more than six-feet tall. Women envied her lengthy legs, and men desired them. A behemoth in the modeling world. Nothing could stop her.

The orange glow from the candlelight accentuated her dewy skin. Tendrils of incense hung in the air, and recorded sounds of the forest filled her ears. She drew in a deep breath and let herself sink deeper into relaxation.

The masseuse kneaded her back, first in slow tender strokes, then harder, using her elbow to grind into her muscles. Liz gritted her teeth as the masseuse attempted to release weeks of tension. As the pain reached a peak, she clenched her fist, nails digging into her palm. Her eyes fluttered as she languished in the moment. She smirked in arousal.

A knock broke the serenity of the spa-like atmosphere.

"Not now," she roared, without raising her head from the table.

The masseuse stopped and pulled away. Liz narrowed her eyes and shot her a chilling glance.

"Did I tell you we were finished?"

"Sorry, ma'am." The masseuse resumed her massage, moving to her upper leg. Liz exhaled and relaxed again.

"Ma'am? It's important," her assistant's muffled voice said through the door, her knocking persistent. She had instructed Jane, her assistant, not to disturb her during her massages. This time was sacred.

"Someone better be dead." She sighed and lifted up, resting on her elbows. The masseuse backed away.

The mousey woman with chestnut hair and drab off-the-rack clothing appeared. She practically blended into the coffee-colored woodwork. Jane fidgeted with her well-worn day planner, several inches thick, with notes that stuck out at all angles.

Liz got up and patted down her flawless naked skin, wiping off the ruddy oil. She slipped on a silk robe behind an ornate abalone Qing Dynasty changing screen. She cinched her jet-black mane into a high, tight ponytail, which accentuated her prominent cheekbones and snowy complexion.

"*And*? What is so important?" She scowled at the assistant.

"Ms. Bath, a detective... A detective here to see you."

A detective? Liz raised a pointed eyebrow.

"Oh? Regarding?" She emerged from behind the screen, hands firmly planted on her hips, and stared down her timid secretary.

"A-a-a missing girl," Jane said, pushing her black-framed glasses up the bridge of her nose.

"Why do they want to talk to me? How does this involve the agency?" She tilted her head.

Jane shrugged. *Useless.*

"He's waiting in the conference room on 6." Jane pointed towards the elevator.

"Let him wait. I need a shower. I'm not presentable. I'll be down when I'm down." She flitted a dismissive hand at the assistant.

*****

Liz flung the drapes open in her penthouse living room, looking out onto the New York skyline. Harsh daylight flooded the space, and she squinted. She owned the entire building and lived in the two-floor penthouse apartment above her company, a nice perk of being the boss. Disruptions irritated her as her packed schedule allowed only limited time for herself. This put a crimp in her day.

She lingered in the apartment, taking her time showering and primping. *Make the detective wait.* Liz grew accustomed to her power and enjoyed making people squirm. Waiting for long periods aggravated them most. She liked exposing their raw nerves and seeing how they would react under pressure. It gave her vital information about their character.

Many called her a cold bitch. But if one were describing the traits of a man, they would use terms like strong, decisive, and successful. She resented the double standard, but, none-the-less, she ruled her industry, making a fortune for herself.

None of her money came from her affluent father. He died in her European homeland when she was young, and her mother followed soon thereafter. Liz floated from relative to relative until she was of age, but ruthless relations squandered her parental wealth, leaving her penniless by eighteen. Liz broke ties with everyone. She found she had a knack for business, and success came easily to her. She ventured to the United States, and little remained of her accent. An opulent upbringing groomed her for a life of rubbing elbows with New York's elite and powerful. She blended right in. Manhattan had no idea what walked amongst them.

The elevator door slid open, and Liz stepped out onto the 6th floor of the industrial chic office building. She was an imposing woman, both in stature and in spirit. Irregular triangles of black and white fabric covered her body. The contemporary, geometric dress looked more like it belonged on a Paris runway than in an office, but she wore it well with confidence. She strode down the hall towards the conference room, styled in concrete and wood. Office staff stiffened at the sight of her. Silence fell over the open floor plan as she passed.

The detective leaned in and examined the artwork on the wall. He reached out a hand to inspect the canvas as she entered.

"Don't touch that," she said.

He flinched. "You startled me. Sorry, I just..." He smiled awkwardly with a boyish charm and pointed at the painting. "Is this real?"

"It *is* a painting." She crossed her arms and shifted her weight to one hip.

"I mean, is this the original?"

Stupid cop. Clearly, he hadn't picked up on her condescension.

"Yes. A gift from a dear friend." She gazed at the piece. She adored the bold strokes and vivid colors of this particular Van Gogh. *The gnarled trees look just like our vineyard.*

"Wow. Impressive."

"Indeed." She offered her hand. "I'm Liz Bath, president and CEO of Liz Bath modeling agency. But I'm sure you were already well aware of that given your profession."

His eyes widened as she shook his hand with a firm grip.

"Indeed." He parroted her words. Perhaps he had detected her insult. "Detective Florez."

"What brings you to our agency, Detective?" She gestured for him to sit down at the large mahogany table.

"I'm following up on a case that's gone cold." He removed a photo from a manila folder and slid it across the table. The pretty young girl in the headshot stared at her. She must have been fifteen, sixteen, with a sparkle in her eyes.

"Molly Perkins has been missing for over five years," he said.

"And this involves me, how?" She pushed the image back to the detective and crossed her hands on her lap.

"There were reports that Molly came to the city to become a model." He flipped the headshot over. On the back, written in purple ink, was the word *Bath* and a phone number. His finger tapped on the digits. "This reaches the reception desk of your agency. We called and haven't been able to gather much information from your staff."

"They don't give out information to just anyone."

"The NYPD isn't just anyone, ma'am." He flipped the photo back over and shoved it across the table. "I need to know if Molly worked with you. It might help us generate a lead. Does she look familiar?"

She scoffed and smirked. "Are you joking? Do you realize how many girls come through this agency?" She flicked the photo back towards him.

"No, I don't. Enlighten me."

Liz rose and started out the door. "Are you coming?" She paused.

He grabbed the photo and followed quickly behind. She glided down the hallway past several posh offices, leading him through a maze of stylish cubicles and modern meeting rooms.

"Thousands of prospective models inundate Liz Bath every year, vying for a contract. Of those that submit headshots, we only bring in a few hundred for further review. And of those, we only hire a handful for our clients' specific needs." She waved her hand at the busy workspace.

"Girls travel here from all around the world. Some want to escape and start over and don't give us their real names. Some are runaways hiding from their past. Many of these girls want to disappear for one reason or another. Who am I to stop them?"

She strolled to an office and rapped her knuckles on the doorframe to announce her presence, though everyone already realized she was there.

"This is Shea. She can help you search through our records for this Milly girl." She gestured towards the exceedingly slender woman in couture attire seated in front of a computer. Shea nodded in agreement.

"Molly," the detective said.

"What?"

"Her name is Molly. Molly Perkins."

Did he really just correct me? Who cares what her name was? Is.

"Sure. Whatever." She rolled her eyes and walked away before he could say another word.

*****

At the elevators, Liz pushed the call button and waited to go back up to her office. The doors opened, and she got in and pushed 9.

"Ms. Bath?" An arm stuck in, forcing the steel doors to retract.

She sighed. Detective Florez stepped in.

"Done already? The receptionist can show you out." She pressed the button for 9 repeatedly. The doors closed.

"Not done yet. Still have a few more questions."

"I'm not sure what to tell you. I have no answers."

She crossed her arms and rolled her weight to one hip. The floor indicator overhead pinged as they passed the 7th floor. *How do I get rid of him?*

"Actually, I have some other photos I'd like to show you." He pulled a headshot from his folder. A young woman smiled at her innocently. "This is Julie Davidson. And this..." He pulled out another photo of a girl. The indicator binged as they passed 8. "This is Angela Washington."

"Let me guess. Missing?" she said sarcastically.

"Ma'am? Do you think this is a joke?"

The elevator sounded one last time, and the doors opened. *Finally.* Liz headed to her corner office, knowing he would follow her like a puppy. She waited to reply until they were in the closed office.

"I take my business deadly serious. That is no joke. I see what you are getting at. What you're insinuating. That somehow *my* agency is involved." She sat down behind the enormous desk. The detective opted to stand. "I don't take these unfounded accusations lightly." She pounded her index finger into the desktop. "Trying to link these girls' disappearances to my business could tarnish my reputation."

She withdrew a cigarette from a carved wooden box on her desk and lit it with a silver butane lighter. She drew in a long drag and tossed the lighter down on the desk. This line of questioning made her tense. The nicotine calmed her nerves. A cloud of smoke wafted towards the detective as she exhaled.

"Frankly, ma'am, I'm more concerned about finding these girls than your business," he said matter-of-factly. "I'd like to talk with more of your staff to see if they know anything about them."

"Very well." She waved the cigarette at him. "Talk to whoever you must."

"Thank you." He nodded, stuffing the photos back into the folder, and padded out of her office.

This was problematic. She really didn't need a detective sniffing around her agency. She leaned back in the chair and weighed her options, taking another long drag. She sat up and pushed a button on her phone.

"Get in here," she barked at the intercom.

"Yes, ma'am," the tinny voice replied through the speaker.

Within moments, Jane appeared in the doorway, straightening her skirt, which always seemed crooked.

"Close the door behind you."

Jane obliged and sat on one of the chairs facing the massive desk.

"Pull all the information we have on Molly Perkins, Julie Davidson, and Angela Washington. Photos, applications, interview briefs, client jobs. Destroy everything. I don't want a single record of them to exist. Erase them."

"Ma'am?"

"Do it. And keep that detective out of Studio C. His presence vexes me. Do whatever you can to make him leave."

Jane finished writing the instructions and shut the day planner. She nodded acknowledgement of her orders and scurried out of the office.

The phone rang.

"Yes?"

It was Carl.

"Today? *Now*?"

Carl ran her casting department. He oversaw the review of all applicants. He had been with her for years, her eyes and ears in the company. When he found a girl matching the appropriate criteria, he would call Liz to personally interview them. Today, he found a winner.

"Your timing isn't great, Carl. Okay, I'm coming."

*****

Liz took one last drag from her cigarette before throwing it onto the concrete hallway floor. She crushed the butt with her stiletto and got into the elevator. She pushed the button for the ground floor. As the elevator descended, she tried to let the stress of the detective slip away and became eager at the thought of a new young beauty. She took a deep breath. The anticipation made her giddy.

Bing. The elevator door opened, and her icy visage melted into a phony warm smile. The girl sat alone in the waiting room. *Indeed, she fit the bill.* Young, about 16, but her looks could pass for 21. Liz drew in the smell of her hair as she scooped the young woman by the elbow. She pulled her from the chair and lead her down the hallway close by her side. The girl stood nearly head-to-head with Liz. Pretty, but far from runway material, or even print modeling for that matter. Perfect.

"You must be Stacy. I'm so happy to meet you. I'm Liz." She gave the girl a one-armed half-hug as she guided her to an office.

"Hi. I, uh, thanks. Yes, I'm Stacy." The girl fidgeted in her grasp, probably wondering why the CEO held her by the arm and took a personal interest in her.

"I'd like to find out everything about you." She led Stacy to an empty office. The girl was like a doe on the opening day of hunting season. "Sit. Let's talk."

"Is this what you usually do?"

"Usually? No. But for special girls, I like to do the interview myself." Flattery typically calmed nerves.

A toothy grin filled the girl's face.

"It's just that I've never done this before. Modeling, I mean." *Obviously.* She wouldn't have made it past reception in most agencies, but Liz Bath wasn't most agencies.

"Completely fine. It's a thrill to pluck a diamond from the rough. I'm glad you came here first." Liz sat across the desk from her and took hold of the girl's hands. Her supple skin felt like velvet beneath her fingertips. She took a slow, measured breath.

"What made you choose the Liz Bath agency?" She could always use a little flattery herself.

"It's the best. Like, the best of the best, of the best, of the best."

"And you thought you were the best?" Liz cocked her head to the side.

The girl's cheeks burned crimson. "Well, I, uh, I mean, I wanted the best representation. It's not that I'm the best..." Her voice trailed off.

Liz clasped her hands hard and locked eyes with the girl.

"You are the best. If you're going to be a Bath model, the answer to that question should always be, 'Yes, I am the best'." Stacy nodded and looked down.

Liz pulled her forward on the desk.

"You can't doubt yourself. If you want to succeed in this business, hold your head high with confidence. You must believe you are the most beautiful girl in every room you enter."

Stacy smiled. Her clear blue eyes lit up her entire face.

Liz released her hands and sat back in the oversized executive chair.

"Now, tell me your story."

"My story?"

"Where are you from? What do you like to do? Family? Friends? Aspirations? Spare no details."

"There isn't much, I guess. I'm from Connecticut. Not much family left, though. I'm an only child, no brothers or sisters, and my parents passed away when I was little." Her eyes lost their sparkle and filled with sadness. "I've been living with my aunt in Bridgeport, but she got a new boyfriend who I don't like. The way he looks at me, especially when I get out of the shower." She shuddered. Liz listened intently. "I left. I don't think they'll care one bit. They might not even notice I'm gone." She fidgeted in her seat, probably questioning if she had shared too much.

"Excellent." Liz needed to qualify that statement. "It was excellent you got away from that. And why modeling?"

"My mama always told me I was pretty. So, I thought..."

"That you could make some money with your face."

Stacy laughed nervously. "Something like that."

"Alright then."

"Is that it? Did I do okay?"

Liz patted the girl's hand. "You did great. Let's get you to Hair and Makeup and have some test photos taken."

Carl waited at the office door. He smoothed his well-groomed salt and pepper beard.

"Give Stacy here the royal treatment. Then take her down to Studio C." Liz squeezed Stacy's shoulders, and the girl gave Carl a big confident smile.

Liz raised her eyebrows at Carl. "Good eye, Carl. Good eye."

He winked at Liz and led the girl away. She had a bounce in her step as she followed him down the corridor. At least the girl was happy. For now.

*****

Today turned out to be much better than Liz first thought. She grinned as she awaited the elevator, pleased with herself and her little charade. The doors slid open.

"Ms. Bath. Just person I wanted to talk to." Detective Florez stood inside.

Good God. She scowled. How quickly her mood soured. She reluctantly got in. The button for 9 already glowed. *Great.*

"You're *still* here? Didn't get what you needed?"

"Not yet. I'm heading up to meet with Jane now."

Liz pressed the door-close button forcefully several times. *Why hadn't Jane gotten rid of him yet? She had better get this job done, and fast.*

"Since I have you trapped in the elevator..."

She glanced at him sideways. "Excuse me?"

He laughed. "I mean, I have a few minutes of your *precious* time to ask you some more questions." This time he dealt out the sarcasm. She didn't enjoy being on the receiving end.

"Okay."

"Great." He pulled out a small, tattered notebook from his inside jacket pocket and clicked his pen. "Where were you the night of April tenth?"

"How should I know?" She crossed her arms. His question angered her. "You'd have to ask Jane. She carries my entire life around in that planner of hers. I don't have time to keep track of details like that. I have people for that."

"Your people aren't very forthcoming with information."

"Then they're good people, no?" She played coy.

The doors slid open at the 9th floor, and she sauntered out, away from Detective Florez. She didn't notice Jane waiting and crashed into her assistant, sending her planner flying, the contents scattered on the floor. Liz stormed past with a huff, leaving Jane to deal with the mess, both the strewn papers and the detective.

She glanced over her shoulder and saw the defective kneel beside Jane, helping the assistant pick up all the fallen pages. *How chivalrous.* She rolled her eyes.

She slumped into her office chair and pulled out a large folding mirror from her desk. As she opened it, little bright lights popped on around the perimeter of the glass. Liz looked at her features, running a finger delicately under her eye. *Desperately in need of renewal.* The excitement of the investigator put a wrinkle in her plans, and apparently on her face. A newly formed crow's foot emanated from the corner of her eye. She snapped the mirror shut and threw it back into the drawer. She didn't need a reminder of her age. Soon it wouldn't matter.

She considered the risk of going through with things with Florez still in the building. But her need erased any doubt within moments. A treatment was well overdue.

The phone on her desk sprang to life.

"Yes?" she answered. Her hard face softened. "Perfect timing. Studio C. I'll be down in a moment."

She walked to the door. Jane rushed in and almost ran into her. Again.

"Ma'am," her voice hurried and nervous, "we have a problem. A serious problem."

Liz grabbed Jane's arm.

Before she could ask what, Detective Florez burst in.

"Do you mind explaining this to me?" He held a handwritten note.

She let go of Jane, white marks already visible on the assistant's forearm. "I have no idea what that is." She answered honestly.

"Ma'am, it's—" Jane said.

"Shhh. Let the man speak."

"Apparently this is a note written by your assistant." He read aloud. "*Full delete M Perkins, J Davidson, A Washington.* Are you still going to tell me you don't know these girls?"

Jane wiped tears from her eyes and started whimpering. Florez glared with accusation.

Liz smoothed her hair and calmed her breathing. She wouldn't let him excite her.

"I merely asked my assistant to check for any records on them."

"Delete? That doesn't sound like a check. If you don't start answering me straight, I'm going to call for backup, and we'll tear this office apart. Damn your reputation."

She stepped forward to face Florez, well within his personal space, and poked her index finger against his chest.

"You will do no such thing. You will not threaten me. Unless you have more than a worthless scrap of paper, get the hell out of my building. And don't come back without a warrant."

She returned to her desk, picked up the receiver, and punched in a few buttons on the keypad. "Security?"

Florez held up his hands in surrender. "Okay, okay. No need for that. I'll go. But I will be back with that warrant."

He stormed out. Jane continued to sob to herself.

"Pull yourself together if you want to keep your job."

Jane nodded and sniffled, looking at her with red eyes.

"Now I have a job to do."

*****

Things shouldn't have gotten that heated with the detective. She made a point to fly under the radar of law enforcement. But now, she had drawn its attention. She would have to deal with that later.

Liz pushed through the stairwell door, far too impatient to wait for the elevator. The walk down would calm her mind and collect her thoughts.

She flew down the stairs, her heels clacking on each concrete step. The sound echoed down the into the depths of the building. Numbers on each landing got smaller and smaller until she came to a door labeled B. The basement. She swiped her keycard through the security strip. A red light switched to green, and the door buzzed open.

The agency's photo studios were underground, in the lower level. They found the space convenient for staged photography with no natural light pollution. Twenty-foot ceilings allowed for the creation of elaborate sets, complete with rigging for custom lighting design.

Liz also liked the privacy of the basement. While a few people worked in the studio from time to time, they didn't have shoots that often, so usually the lower level remained quiet.

But today, Studio C sprung to life. Liz entered and found Carl seated on a couch at the back. He leaned with one arm up on the sofa. He wore an impeccable ensemble from that new designer's line they previewed last fall. Carl's taste in fashion paralleled hers. Another thing she loved about him.

"She's ready for you." He extended an arm out towards the set, like an offering.

Liz stood by Carl and patted his shoulder.

"Nice work, Carl. This is a good one. I can feel it."

Long, billowing, white chiffon hung from the ceiling, tied up with white cording to create extravagant textures and folds. Complex lighting bounced and reflected off the fabric, filling the studio with a luminous glow. Liz watched the photographer work, guiding the young novice.

Stacy wore a sleeveless ivory dress. The gauzy, deep V-neck ended just above her navel. They fashioned a makeshift belt from a piece of the same cording that styled the set, giving the outfit a polished, coordinated look. She twirled around. The cloth swirled around Stacy's ankles and bare feet. The thin fabric left little to the imagination. Strands of hair fell from the loose up do and outlined her cherubic face. The makeup artist brought out the blue in her eyes with deep, smokey, eye makeup. While not gorgeous, she was lovely, innocent, and her naïve smile infectious. Liz smirked as she watched her pose for the camera.

The photographer caught sight of Liz and paused.

"Don't let me interrupt. She seems like a natural." Liz pointed towards the girl and smiled.

Stacy looked genuinely happy, having the time of her life. She spun around again and again, until she stumbled with dizziness, and giggled.

"I think we're done here. I got the shots." The photographer pulled the camera from the tripod and packed up his gear. The bright fill lights switched off and the studio dimmed.

Stacy's smile faded, and she tugged at her hair, unsure what to do as everyone shuffled around her.

"Excellent. Add these shots to my private collection." Liz shifted her attention to the girl.

"Clear the studio," Liz shouted.

Carl rounded up the last of the staff and the photographer and gave thumbs up to Liz as he swung the large metal door of the studio shut with a clang.

"Should I go with Carl?"

"No. I thought we could talk a little more."

Liz circled around the girl.

"Okay." Stacy shifted nervously and crossed one foot over the other.

"How did you like your makeover?" Liz's voice was slow and measured.

Stacy lit up. "Oh, it was so much fun. I already learned a lot." She beamed. "Like what colors go with my eyes, and how-to put-on eyeliner." She waved her arms excitedly as she talked.

"Let's take a good look at you." Liz trailed a finger down the girl's shoulder. Her movements were deliberate like a predator sizing up their prey. She clasped Stacy's hands and gracefully stretched her arms out wide, assessing the dress. "Beautiful." She eyed the girl.

Liz moved behind her.

"How is the fit?" She tugged firmly at the shoulders of the dress and cinched the fabric at the back.

"Fine, I think. It feels good."

Liz slipped her hand around the girl's waist and untied the white cord.

"Let's see how you look without the belt."

"Okay."

Liz wrapped the ends of the cord tightly around each of her hands. In a swift move, she flipped the cord over the girl's head and yanked tight against the girl's neck.

Stacy lost her footing and fell against Liz's chest.

She pulled the cording tighter.

Stacy struggled to free herself. Her fingers clawed at the cord squeezing her neck, unable to loosen the rope. She choked, gasping for air, unable to speak or scream. She turned red, and her eyes widened.

Liz remained calm. She pulled the rope firmly. She leaned back, squeezing the life from her.

Stacy kicked her feet violently. She reached her hands behind her head, trying to grab her attacker.

Liz pulled her backwards deeper into the set, never easing up on her grip.

The girl's lips went blue, and her eyes bulged, the whites staining red with broken blood vessels.

Stacy flailed her arms out. She caught a section of the white hanging chiffon, pulling it taut. A ripping sound echoed through the studio as the girl pulled the fabric.

Liz held firm, knowing the struggle would end soon. Experience and patience.

The naïve girl struggled helplessly.

Stacy's hold on the fabric loosened. The girl's hand went limp, her body followed.

Liz lowered her to the ground and dropped the cording.

The ripped chiffon, still in Stacy's hand, gave way and wafted down from the rafters, piling around the girl's dead body.

Liz straightened her dress and pulled the large studio door open.

Carl waited outside, leaning against the wall, chewing on a toothpick.

"That was quick. You didn't waste any time." He smirked.

"I'm running out of time. Make this fast. Get her processed *now*."

"During the day? Are you crazy? We have an office full of people above us." He pointed up and wrinkled his face.

"Figure it out. I can't solve all your problems. Make it happen."

He raised his hands. "Alright. I get it. Hurry. Rush. Now. Fast," he said sarcastically. He flicked his toothpick on the floor. "I'm on it." Carl disappeared inside Studio C, and the metal door swung shut.

She smoothed a few stray hairs that had freed themselves during the fray. She straightened her dress and headed back upstairs.

In the elevator, she swiped her keycard and pressed P. The penthouse. The day had exhausted her, and she needed to retreat to her sanctuary to recharge.

She hoped Carl would work fast, as she couldn't wait much longer. Her patience wore thin.

The door opened directly into the foyer of her penthouse. The grand double staircase wrapped around either side of the entryway. Lavish antiques from around the globe and across the centuries adorned the art deco apartment.

Liz stepped out of the elevator. The upper floor of the penthouse held the master suite and guest rooms. To the left, the apartment opened into a large dining room, and to the right, a spacious living room. In front of her, underneath the stairs, a corridor led to her library. She walked straight ahead.

Darkness shrouded the books. The heavy green velvet drapes blocked the afternoon sun. She lit the wick on a gilded lamp. The yellow flame filled the room with flickering shadows. Leather-bound tomes lined the shelves from floor to ceiling.

Liz removed an ornate glass bottle top from the decanter on a side table and poured herself a drink. She lifted the tumbler, giving an imaginary toast to herself.

"Egészségedre," she said. "To my health."

She swallowed the caustic liquid down in one gulp. She winced. After all these years, she still didn't like the harsh taste of liquor, but she needed it to relax.

She lounged in the leather armchair and waited for Carl, laying back, letting the liquid in her belly ease her tension. She found it difficult to rest, knowing what was coming.

*****

Almost an hour passed when Carl knocked on the wooden doorframe to announce his presence.

"Finally." She sat up, waiting for his report.

"It's ready. And *finally*? Really? Maybe if it was night, but broad daylight? This took some magic to go undetected." Carl was her long-time employee and companion. He was the only one that could talk to her this way. He kept her honest.

"I'm just eager. It's been too long since the last." They walked down the hallway together.

"I understand. It's getting harder these days. It's not just about a paper trail. Now there's an internet footprint to deal with." He pulled her hand into the crook of his elbow as they headed up the staircase.

They entered the master suite. A large round tub in the middle of the floor dominated the bathroom. The crisp white porcelain was a stark contrast to the dark ebony tiled floors and walls.

Carl had already set everything up just as she liked it. Pillar candles on every surface cast long shadows across the room.

Liz untied her tight ponytail and let her black hair spill around her shoulders. She kicked off her shoes. Carl unzipped the back of her dress, and she let the designer piece fall to the floor. She wore no undergarments. She wasn't shy about her body.

Liz stepped over the rim of the large tub. Her legs slipped into the warm liquid. She sunk down into the bath until submerged to the neck.

Carl gave a quick bow and dismissed himself from the room as Liz settled into the comfort of the bath.

Thick red blood warmed her. Liz massaged the fluid into her skin. She relaxed her head back against the porcelain and sensed the life force from the young girl's blood enter her body. The years counted backwards on her face, restoring her beauty. Fine lines around her eyes and mouth softened and faded within moments. The luster in her cheeks heightened. Her glowing skin was radiant again.

Liz sunk deeper into the bath. The blood covered first her chin, then her mouth, her nose, eyes, until she was fully immersed. She held her breath for what seemed like minutes.

A muffled voice reverberated through the liquid. *Who dared to bother me during my ritual?* She lifted her head and wiped her eyes clear with a hand.

"Jesus Christ. What the hell is going on here?"

Detective Florez stood before her with Jane.

"I couldn't stop him. He has a warrant." She made excuses.

Florez's mouth hung agape, his eyes wide.

"Ma'am. Get out of the tub." Florez drew his gun from its holster and flicked the safety. "You're under arrest."

Liz slowly rose from the bloody bath. Red painted every inch of her.

"On what charge?" She stepped out, her perfect body naked standing before Florez.

"Ms. Bath, put some clothes on." He averted his eyes from her body, looking at the floor.

"Not until you tell me the charge."

"You're taking a fucking bath in blood. Where did this come from? Whose blood is this?"

"It's pigs' blood if you must know. It's a beauty regimen I follow."

"Bullshit. There is something going on here. Maybe I'll finally get some answers from you downtown."

Liz stepped towards the detective.

"Don't move, ma'am." He pointed the gun at her, shifting his gaze up to take aim, but looked down again, uncomfortable with her nakedness.

"Well, which is it? Get clothes? Or don't move? I can't do both," she said.

Florez turned to Jane. His gun's aim drifted to the floor. "Give her a towel."

Liz stepped forward and grabbed the barrel of the detective's gun while he was distracted. Her advance caught him off guard, and he struggled to gain control of the weapon. Her strength rivaled his.

Blood dripped off her and pooled around her feet. In the struggle, Florez slipped and fell to the floor, taking her with him. Blood smeared across the tile. She gripped the gun, and he yanked it back, trying to gain the upper hand.

They wrestled for control of the gun. Neither could get any leverage as they slid in the blood. Florez wrenched the barrel towards Liz, and she fought to twist his arm away.

Bang. A shot echoed in the large bathroom.

Jane clutched her stomach. Her face wrinkled. Blood oozed out from between her fingers. She dropped down onto her feet and slumped over onto the ground.

Liz grabbed the gun from Florez and pointed the barrel underneath his chin. He held up his hands.

"Did you really think you were going to stop me?"

Liz got up, gun still pointed at the detective.

"I've crossed paths with many more cunning than you. I'm 460 years old, and it's going to take more than you to stop me."

Florez narrowed his eyes. "What are you going to do? I got a warrant. The station knows I'm here."

She lunged forward at him, and he flinched.

"You're just a scared little boy." She waved the gun in his face and flipped open his coat with the barrel. She reached into his breast pocket and ripped out the folded papers.

"A warrant. How quaint." She opened the papers with one hand, leaving a trail of bloody prints on the pages.

"Ahhh. Judge Hopkins? We go way back. 1971? 72? My youth may surprise him, but I'll make this go away. I always do."

Liz threw down the papers and advanced on Florez. She whisked him up off the ground by the neck, and he scrambled to regain his footing.

"Now the question is, what to do with you?" She cocked her head to the side. She tossed the gun across the floor and cackled with laughter.

Her demeanor changed so dramatically from the poised woman in the office to this monstrous creature. With a still flawless and beautiful body, her true horrific nature showed through bloody, matted hair and a gnarled expression. A monster lurked within.

Florez struggled beneath her grip, but the bath had strengthened and enlivened her. She dragged him to the tub and forced his body down to the edge of the porcelain.

"This is what I'll do with you." She pushed his head down to the surface of the blood. He struggled, but she didn't falter.

She leaned down, her cheek almost touching his, and whispered in his ear through gritted teeth.

"I will add your blood to my bath as I have done with thousands. Your life, your essence, will feed my soul and restore me. And who will remember you? No one."

Liz grabbed Florez by the back of the hair and yanked his head back. She raised her other hand, and in one adept stroke, sliced her long nails along across his neck. Thin red lines appeared on his flesh. Blood seeped from the wounds and flowed out in a steady stream.

She released him from her hold. He frantically pawed at his neck in a futile attempt to close the wounds. His eyes widened. But soon he relaxed and slipped forward over the lip of the bath, his blood spilling into the tub.

Liz stood and looked over at her dead assistant. *Utterly useless.* She crouched beside her and brushed the dead woman's hands away, exposing the wound. Liz stuck her fingers into the hole in Jane's sweater and deep into the gunshot wound. She withdrew her hand, covered in fresh blood, and wiped it across her own cheeks.

Liz returned to the bath and ran a hand through the liquid. Florez' blood added renewed warmth to the bath. At least it wasn't cold yet. She climbed back in and slid down. Florez' lifeless body hung over her, his blood trickled into the tub in a melodic song of drips.

Liz smiled. It had been years since she had the blood of multiple victims in one day. She hadn't felt this good in years.

Just as she settled in, a rousing cough sounded at the door. Carl leaned against the doorframe.

"Someone's been busy, I see." Carl gestured to the dead bodies.

She sighed. "Couldn't be helped." She laid back down and closed her eyes.

"Mhmmm." He sounded doubtful.

"I need you to take care of these two." She waved a dismissive, bloody hand.

"Of course."

Carl turned to leave.

"And Carl?" She sat up and leaned on her crossed arms on the edge of the tub. Red streaks poured down the side of the white porcelain.

Carl looked back. "Yes?"

"Erase them." She grinned.

*****

Epilogue

Based on a true story, *Model Citizen* is a modern retelling of the life of Elizabeth Bathory, a wealthy Hungarian woman, born in 1560. We know her from history as the most prolific female serial killer, with more than five hundred victims. Legend tells us that Elizabeth bathed in the blood of virgin girls to maintain her youth. This story imagines that Elizabeth not only preserved her youth but also lived well beyond her years, surviving to modern times. In reality, Elizabeth was tried for her crimes and imprisoned in 1611. She died in prison in 1614 at the age of 54.

ON A COLD WINTER MORNING

by Paul Mc Cabe

On a cold winter morning I found a little brother in the woods.

It was December 1998. I remember because my mum had just given birth to a stillborn little boy. Declan was supposed to be his name, after my father, but we never ended up calling him that, or anything really. In fact, we never once spoke about him. I was ten at the time and was busy getting ready for Christmas. I didn't really understand what was going on, but I saw mum cry an awful lot and dad getting quiet when he brought her home from the hospital.

I remember feeling ignored by them and that, in turn, made me draw away from the house. It became the focal point of a blistering coldness, like the eye of some menacing storm. I became afraid of the place. I feared spending any time there at all; because it meant that I had to see my mum with tears in her eyes and my dad staring into the empty hearth in the living room. So, I spent most of my days out in the woods that surrounded our yard.

The woods were not especially large but, for a small boy like me, they seemed to go on forever. They stretched out into some strange new place just beyond the ability of my feet to take me. I would often try to get to the edge but could only do so when I was with my parents. On my own, the woods played tricks on me, turned me round, and I never reached that far-off clearing that I *knew* was out there. But, to a young boy, it didn't matter all that much. As long as there were frosty branches to grasp, small animals to look for, and sounds and smells that I didn't know then I was kept busy all day. I would often go out for strolls in the morning, come back only for lunch, and head out again. I would find a suitable branch and swing it around like I was a knight and it my sword. They were my adventures.

One of those days, about a week before Christmas, I was out in the woods and I heard a sound that was unlike anything I had heard before. It was sharp and metallic, like rapping on sheet metal. There was a regular rhythm to it that set it apart from the rest of the snaps and rustles that I could hear. It echoed through the trees.

On nimble feet, I took off through the snow towards the sound. I could hear the rapping growing ever louder with each step. I held my sword out in front of me ready to slay whatever beast dared challenge me.

I came to a clearing I had never been to before, full of strange flowers. They had white petals iced gently with snow and large, black berries about the size of a marble. There was a ring of them in the small clearing and, at their centre, the source of the sound.

It was a small boy, no more than three or four years old, with blonde hair that was almost white and big, dark, puddle-black eyes. He was sitting cross-legged, in shorts and a powder blue, Power Rangers t-shirt flecked with mud. In his hand was a large dark stick topped with a strange, bulbous head. It was like a child's rattle, for whenever the boy shook it, it made a strange ringing sound like the clanging of metal horseshoes.

As soon as I saw that little boy, I felt the warmest breath of love come into me. It blanketed my insides. It felt like hands were gently and lovingly fondling every bit of me. I don't know how but this little boy with the big dark eyes was, in fact, my brother Declan come back from somewhere far away, somewhere beyond the woods. I could feel that with every bit of me. I was as sure of it as anything. *Fucking anything*, as dad would say.

Declan beckoned to me with the rattle. It made that clapping noise. I had to go to him.

He was smiling at me and I thought his teeth looked strange. They seemed like adult's teeth – big and square and grey like gravestones. I thought it looked cool, like he had fake teeth in or something, like he was wearing a Halloween costume.

I walked over to meet him.

He didn't say a word. He looked a little older than I had first thought, since he should've only been a week old. But maybe that's how babies look? He smiled and ground those slab teeth of his. He shook the rattle again and the hooves clapped again.

I reached out and Declan took my arm and gently stroked it with fingers as long and thin as straws. He smelt funny - of stale dirt and ash. Granny's special home with all her friends smelt the same.

The hooves clapped again. And again.

I smiled at Declan and looked in the black of his big eyes.

I felt a sudden lick of warmth at the soles of my feet – a jolt of pain.

My insides went car-crash wild.

The hooves clapped again, and I felt myself falling as the ground opened up beneath me. Declan fell, too, pulling me down with him. He smiled at me and in my little brother's eyes I saw flesh blistering in fire and a constellation of stolen babes. All of them burning. Like kindling.

END

STAGNANT

by Dean MacAllister

The automatic doors at the entrance to Darwin Airport opened silently. Mr Dennis Graves was hit by a wall of heat and humidity he had never before experienced. He wheeled his bag over to the taxi rank, wiping his forehead with a handkerchief, already perspiring. The stifling air created the sensation of breathing warm soup. Panting, he waved at a man leaning against a taxi.

"Hey mate!" The smiling driver approached him and grabbed the handle of his bag. "Where ya headed?"

Mr Graves produced a piece of paper from his shirt pocket and handed it to the driver. The man unfolded the paper, reading it. Frowning, he let go of the bag.

"Are you sure this is it?" he asked, looking him up and down. "You know where that is? That's out bush, in Arnhem Land. Not exactly a tourist area. You probably aren't gonna be welcome there, either."

"Look, can you take me there, or not?"

"I can, but it's ages away and I'll have to drive back and it'll be dark by then and-"

"Money isn't an issue," Mr Graves stated firmly.

The driver stared at him for a while, a concerned look on his face.

"I hope you know what you're doing," he mumbled. He grabbed the handle of the bag and dragged it towards car.

Mr Graves got into the back of the taxi and was relieved to find the air-conditioning had been left on. The car rocked as the driver climbed in.

"Okay! Here we go. My name's Fred. Get comfortable, this is going to be a long drive. Maybe around five hours or so. What was your name?"

"I'm Dennis."

"Nice to meet you, Dennis." Fred put his indicator on and pulled out. After a couple of turns they were out on the open road. "Is this your first time in Australia? You're a Brit, yeah?"

"Yes, it is and, yes, I am."

"Hah! Long flight, ay?"

Mr Graves simply grunted, staring out at the red desert sand along the sides of the highway.

"So, I take it you're travelling alone?" Fred asked.

Mr Graves sighed. He slowly turned his head to look at the creature sitting beside him. Its black, empty eyes stared back at him. Water trickled from its limp hair down its pale blue flesh. Its jaw hung loose, long, viscous strands of saliva dripping from the sides of its toothless gape. His nostrils filled with the smell of brine and rotten fish, the smell of a seaside market on a hot day. He felt bile rise up in his throat and swallowed it down with difficulty. He closed his eyes, took a deep breath and went back to staring out the window.

"I wish I was, Fred. I really wish I was."

*****

Mr Graves woke up from the shaking of the car on the dirt road and rubbed his eyes. Outside, the night crept in and the lack of streetlights made it difficult to determine where they were.

"Welcome back, mate. You were out like a light. We're pretty much there. About an hour out of Gunbalanya, on that road you wanted. Do you have a specific address?"

The headlights reflected off some shirts up ahead. Three local men were walking down the side of the road.

"Can you just stop here?"

"What, in the middle of the road?"

"We'll ask these men."

Before Fred could stop him, Mr Graves had the window down and was calling them over. They approached the car with a mixture of suspicion and curiosity in their eyes.

"Whadaya want, white fella?" one of them asked.

"Any of you chaps know an Uncle Benny?"

The three of them laughed and one of them tapped the side of his head, the international symbol for crazy.

"That's not a good sign," Fred said under his breath, "Let's go back into town and see if we can find you somewhere to stay, yeah? I don't trust these guys."

"How much do I owe you?" He produced a large fold of bills.

"Jeez Dennis! I dunno what it's like where ya come from, but it's not a good idea flashing cash like that! It ain't safe, mate."

Mr Graves stuffed a wad of the money into his hand.

"That's way too much!" Fred protested, but his passenger was already out of the vehicle and grabbing the bag out of the back.

Mr Graves waved at the taxi driver, who sat with a conflicted frown. Reluctantly Fred waved back and turned the car around. It stopped suddenly and the driver signalled him to return to the vehicle.

"Listen, this is my card. I don't feel right leaving you out in the middle of nowhere. Call me if you need any help. Don't do anything stupid out here, okay?"

He accepted the card with a nod. The taxi drove away.

Mr Graves turned to the men. "So, I take it you know where he lives?"

"Why do you wanna know, old man?" the tallest of them asked.

"I have business with him."

"Business with Uncle Benny?" The three of them laughed. "Then you've got crazy business."

"Fifty dollars. I'll give you fifty dollars each if you show me to where he lives."

The trio stopped laughing and stepped forward. In the dull light of the moon Mr Graves could tell by their faces they were suddenly interested.

"Fifty each? Sounds like a deal, old man." A hand was extended, and Dennis shook it.

Mr Graves dragged his bag along behind him, stumbling on the dirt path. The wheels caught on rocks and twigs, but he kept pace with them as best he could. After what seemed like an hour, the men stopped and turned to him.

"See that light over there?" the tallest man asked, pointing. A tiny dot of orange danced behind a few trees in the near distance. "That's Uncle Benny. We can't take ya no further. We aren't allowed over there. Neither are you, but ya can give it a go. He's none too friendly and's got death on him. He speaks English not bad, but he prolly just tell ya to leave."

Mr Graves pulled out three yellow notes from his pocket and paid the men.

"Cheers, old fella!"

Before he could thank them, they had already vanished into the scrub as if they were never there. The night suddenly seemed darker and colder than before. All trace of the day's heat disappeared. The sheen of sweat on his body gave him shivers and a feeling of hopelessness washed over him. In the distance a dingo let out a sad and lonely howl. Here he was, on the other side of the globe, in a place that wasn't even on the map, so close to his destination; but fear was turning his legs into stone.

"C'mon Dennis," he muttered, "This is why you came here. You've already done the hardest part. Just one foot in front of the other."

He took a few steps and found himself gathering speed. He crashed along, pulling his luggage towards the light. The bag flipped over, but he didn't stop, dragging it face-down through the scrub. Something with small legs ran by his feet and something else without feet slithered by, but he didn't stop until he was standing in the small, lit clearing.

He doubled over, trying to catch his breath.

An aged man sat on a log on the other side of the flames, smoking a cigarette and running his hand through his long, white beard. He looked up but didn't seem surprised.

Mr. Graves studied him. He wore a dark shirt, a leather hat and worn-out jeans. Nothing about him stood out except for the deep bags etched under his old, sad eyes. He looked like a man that hadn't slept for years.

Mr Graves realised that he'd been standing there for a while, staring without even speaking a word.

"Hello," he said, a little too loudly. He cleared his throat. "Are you Uncle Benny?"

The man continued to smoke in silence.

"Right, well, my name is Dennis Graves and I have travelled a very long way to meet you. You see, someone wrote a story about you and something you said and I was searching the internet-"

"What's in the bag?" the old man asked.

"Everything. Everything I have left. It's yours if you want it. Or I can get you anything-"

The man pointed at another log close to the fire. Mr Graves dropped the bag and crossed over to the log, sitting down.

"… I can get you anything you want. You just name it, Mr Benny."

"Uncle."

"Sorry?"

"Uncle Benny. There's no 'Mr Benny' around 'ere," the man said.

"Right. Uncle Benny, I umm, I have a problem that I think only you could help me with."

"You want to know what it is."

Mr Graves paused. "Uh, yes! Yes, I do."

"Is it here?"

He looked beside him. Barely a foot away it sat, leaning towards him. Wide-eyed, it soundlessly mouthed words at him, a foul stench emitting from its lips.

"Don't look at it!" Uncle Benny shouted.

Mr Graves spun around, surprised.

"Why not? What will it do?"

Uncle Benny flicked his cigarette into the campfire and stared at him.

"My people, my mob, Mr Graves, we're what you'd call 'nomads.' We need to go walkabout. We need to keep movin', explorin', learnin'. We tell stories and we have dreams. You know what I'm talkin' about?"

Mr Graves gave a small nod. When he had read about Uncle Benny, he had tried to research the Aboriginals of Australia, but with hundreds of different native tribes and languages he hadn't gotten very far. Besides their use of boomerangs, spears and dot paintings he knew very little about them.

"I'm gonna tell you a dream that my ancestors told me through my grandfather. It's an important dream and if you interrupt me I'm not gonna finish. Get it?"

Again, Mr Graves nodded.

"When I was young, my grandfather sat me down and told me about the spirits. He told me that people have 'em. He told me that the animals have 'em. He even told me that streams and mountains have 'em. This is what my mob have always believed. But he gave me a warnin'. He told me that not all spirits were good spirits. He told me that the world was made with opposites, each one needin' the other. He said the sky needs the ground. The sun needs the moon. The birds need the fish. And the livin' need the dead. Without one, there could not be the other.

He told me that people a long time ago started to forget their place. They started to see the world as theirs to keep and use as they wanted. Man forgot that he was just another link in nature. They lost their way and climbed up the mountain, forcin' all animals and rocks and trees and rivers to serve them. They took what they wanted, built what they wanted, ate what they wanted and drank what they wanted. They forgot what they came from. They forgot what they were."

The fire popped and sparks rose into the night sky.

"All the other spirits watched on and became jealous," Uncle Benny continued. "But they were afraid of the men, who would break and burn the trees, steal the rocks, eat the animals and keep their skins and feathers. But there were other spirits that weren't afraid of men. You see, men thought they were special. They thought they had no equal, or opposite. But they were just land spirits. They were only a half of a whole. They forgot about the water spirits."

Mr Graves' eyes opened wide.

"My grandfather told me that when we are born on land our other half is born in the sea. This half used to walk about aimlessly, but after a while they began to notice us. Their hearts became jealous. They saw that we enjoyed the warmth of the sun and that everythin' on land bowed to us and they grew unhappy. They got tired of the fish and the shells and the coral. They wanted what we had. So, one day they set out."

"To where?" Mr Graves blurted, instantly regretting his interruption.

Uncle Benny gave him a look but continued.

"They all began their treks. They started their long journeys to find their other halves. The thing is, it's hard and slow to walk under water. It takes a very long time to get anywhere and the people on land are always travellin'. Every time we move to another place, they have to change direction. But they keep on walkin', never stoppin', with only one thought in their mind: reachin' their other half. That's why my mob, we have to keep movin'. We have to walkabout. Otherwise, our water spirit might find us."

Mr Graves shrieked.

"It's touching me!" He could feel its wet skin pressed against his arm. "What can I do? I'll give you anything!" he moaned.

"There's nothin' you can give me that'll help," Uncle Benny said, staring at the ground with a sad look on his face. "I'm sorry."

"So, I travelled here for no reason?"

"You travelled for a reason. You just travelled too late. Shoulda' done it when you were younger."

"Help me, please!"

"Help you?! And who's gonna help me?"

Mr Graves' mouth opened, but then shut without saying a word.

"The thing is, Mr Graves, we are old men. No one listens to old men. I tried tellin' the kids in the area. I tried warnin' 'em, but they just laughed at me. They call me 'Crazy Uncle Benny.' They run past me, afraid. But I can't blame 'em. I can't get angry at them for not listening to an old man, 'cause I was one of them. I was just another dumb kid that wouldn't listen to my grandfather when he warned me. He told me to walkabout. He told me to travel, to meet other people.

"But I was lazy, ya know? I was happy 'ere. I learned English from my local mates, swam in the local stream, kissed the local girls. I had my books to read. I didn't wanna go nowhere, either. Just like you. I just laid back and became stagnant. Just like you. Now my water spirit has found me. Just like you. Bloody hell man, my water spirit is even sittin' next to yours! And you come to *me* askin' for help? What am I supposed to do for you? I can't even help myself!"

Tears began to run down Dennis' face and once they started, they could not be stopped.

"I can't live like this. How can I live pretending he isn't touching me?"

"Nah, I can't imagine ya could. Not that ya have long to go now. You been starin' at it too long, invitin' it closer. Sorry I couldn't help. I would if I could, ya know, but I'm guessin' I won't be long behind you."

Mr Graves pulled out his wallet and opened it. In the clear pocket, next to his driving licence, a smiling family stared back at him. He traced his finger around their faces. A solitary tear landed on the photo.

"So, what's going to happen to me?" he asked. "Is it going to hurt?"

Uncle Benny picked up a nearby stick and threw it into the fire. He produced another cigarette, lighting it. He blew the smoke up towards the stars.

"The way I understand it, we're all just moths in a jar. He just wants your container. I'm guessin' he's just gonna take the lid off and set you free."

Mr Graves gathered himself and took a deep breath. When he was ready, he turned to face the spirit. Its eyes grew larger and its mouth stretched into a gruesome smile. Slowly it grabbed his shoulders and brought its face close to his. He couldn't look away. He sensed himself sinking into its eyes. Then he felt himself falling.

LA LLORONA

by Lesley Morrison

The day I left winter in Calgary and arrived in Puerto Vallarta was a day of noise: the rumble of tires over pavement on my late, too-fast drive to the airport, the roar of the plane, the noisy echoing airport at my destination, even the roar of wind through the open window of the taxi. We sped north along the coast through villages of poverty abounding, along tiny fields and orchards, past thick jungle from which pillars of smoke rose. When the taxi stopped in front of the hotel, no respite: there was the final and unrelenting roar of the breakers crashing on the beach.

The proprietress of the hotel Casa del Sol was Maria, a large motherly woman who spoke English with a heavy accent. After the arrangements were made, she took me to the suite I had booked on the ground floor with a private patio just a few steps from the beach.

The suite was spacious and clean, with black and white tiled floors, a gas stove top, and fridge. The main area had a table with four wicker chairs and a padded L-shaped bench seat along the wall. The kitchen was equipped with a large set of stainless-steel cookware. There was a basket of rolls and fresh fruit on the counter.

Later, with a rum and lime juice, I sat on my patio and watched the sun set, the smoky pink horizon turning to smoky umber, the water changing from blue to gunmetal gray. The pelicans fished in earnest now, skimming low along the rolling breakers. I sat out until it was dark. The tide was high, almost up to the palm trees that bordered the porch, the sea an invisible roaring giant beyond the surge of froth that slid smoothly over the sand into the pale nimbus of the porch light.

The first night I didn't sleep but learned the sounds of the night: the whine of the fridge, the drip of the tap, heard in the sudden silences between the crashing breakers.

In the morning, I returned to the patio, still shaded by the hotel, and ate a bowl of fruit salad made from perfectly ripe pineapple, mango, and passion fruit. Fishing boats were lined up in a row out in the bay. Stabilizer arms extended, weighted for balance, they poised expectantly against the skyline. Squinting up, I could see the black outlines of gulls and frigate birds soaring in slow formation against the depthless blue sky.

A small crew of men worked around the hotel, effecting renovations with shovels and cement mixed in wheel barrels. They greeted me cheerfully and asked polite halting questions about Canada.

"There are many mountains?"

"Yes, we have many tall mountains." I made vague upward motions. Then I remembered a postcard I had with an address on it and fetched it to show them.

"Ah, snow; cold there," they repeated, clustered around me, and we all nodded emphatically, staring at the unfriendly peaks of the Rockies.

They looked young to me, but Maria said they all had families of their own. I wondered what they thought of me, a woman alone in a vacation place of families and couples. I had some hope that I might not stand out; my hair was long and dark, and my skin had an olive cast.

The days became routine. I walked into town past a garbage-lined slough where a pure white egret made its home, past disparate sights, an immaculate villa next to an empty garbage-strewn lot, a beautifully landscaped hotel designed for the tourists, while across the street, small shacks with no glass in the windows.

There was a large white adobe church with
people often about; one day a bride and groom plus
entourage descended the steps as I walked by. I bought
buns and cheese and ground coffee to keep in my
room. I looked around the small open shops with dirt
floors, ducking through tunnels of hanging blankets
and T-shirts. I tried to ignore the poverty and the
resulting guilt I felt—how could they help but resent
us, even as they depended on us to come and spend our
money? I dined on fresh sea bass and unfamiliar
Mexican dishes; the menus had little similarity to their
Canadian counterparts.

Back at the Casa del Sol, I sat on the beach
under the shade of a palm tree and read paperbacks
from a free exchange at an American-style coffee shop.
Or I lay back on my beach mat, shading my eyes and
watching the frigates wheel high above me, their broad
wings spread in a constant, effortless glide.
Occasionally, native vendors came by, holding out
boards covered with cheap jewelry, or handfuls of
shirts on hangars. I smiled and shook my head, or
pretended to be asleep. One old man with a limp was
particularly persistent, and I finally bought a crudely
carved horse just to be rid of him.

At night, I wondered why I was here. By day, I
achieved my goal, which was to exist, unthinking, but

as night fell and the tormenting voices in my head began again, I would take a pill and wait for sleep to come.

I slept restlessly and had strange dreams fueled by the crashing waves. In my room, with the tide high, it was like being onboard a boat. When I dreamed of Angie, lying awake in the night was unbearable. I would get up and make tea, wrapped in my robe, then stand outside on the patio facing the salty wind. Some nights I would see an elusive black and white bird the size of a small chicken tiptoe along the edge of the porch light, one eye fixed on me. It was companionship of a sort, like the gecko that frequented my kitchen. Later I learned that this bird was a black-crowned night heron, a nocturnal species of short-legged heron that walks the beach by night, feeding on small mollusks.

I began to take my lunch and walk along the beach in the late morning. I walked with the sea at one side, an unending line of habitation on the other: elaborate beach houses, motels and restaurants that eventually transformed into shacks and abandoned outdoor cafes and small cement ruins while the beach grew garbage-strewn and scabrous. Few tourists came this far. I would stop and swim if the water was calm or go wading if the waves were too big. Afterwards I sat and ate lunch, while the sea birds cried poignantly above the wind. Then I would slowly make my way back to the hotel.

One day, as I approached, I could see people clustered at the edge of the sea and running figures. A sense of alarm came over me. Arms waved and voices cried out. I looked out into the sea and saw a swimmer's head on the crest of a wave. As the wave rolled beneath him, a surfboard with a limp figure on it appeared, sliding over the wave's top. Slowly, the swimmer maneuvered the board into shore. Four or five men were waiting chest deep to help. They pulled the board up onto the sand and rolled the person off, then all I could see was a line of huddled backs as they crouched around the board. I heard Maria's voice, and turned to see her standing in the beach entrance, her broad face worried. I didn't want to get in the way, so I went to my room. As I unlocked the door, I heard the approach of a siren.

The next day at the coffee shop, I heard the rest of the story from Guy, the American expat shop owner. The sea had been rough; two swimming teenagers had gotten into trouble. A tourist staying at the hotel had taken out a board for one, and Hector, one of the hotel workers, had gone after the other. The tourist had come back with one boy, and the second boy had made it back on his own, but Hector had not come back. The tourist had gone out again and found him. The ambulance took him to the hospital, but there wasn't the right kind of equipment in the ambulance, and he had died. He left behind three young children and a wife.

Maria came to my room later and apologized for the event. She explained that it was especially upsetting as Hector had been a cousin. She didn't know why he hadn't taken a life preserver. Now his wife had three small children to raise.

"Can I do anything to help?" I asked her.

"There is a collection. Some of the guests have contributed," she told me. I signed several traveler's checks and gave them to her. I wondered if there was more I could do.

The next day, as I passed the hotel office, I saw a group of people talking to Maria. Something about them made me realize they must be Hector's family. A young woman with a ravaged face would be the wife. There were several children, an old man, probably their grandfather, and another woman who looked like a sister.

Maria called my name and gestured. As I approached, she explained something in Spanish, and their faces turned to me.

"They want to thank you," she said. The grandfather nodded slightly. I wondered if he was the old man on the beach; he looked like him, but I wasn't quite sure. Their dark eyes were sad, but not grateful.

That was fine with me. The children stared, a little girl and two boys, one older, one younger. Something in the girl's face held me. She was about four, Angie's age, barefoot and dressed in a white cotton shift. I knelt down, smiled at them, and held out my hand.

"Hola," I said. The boys continued to stare, but the girl put out her dimpled hand and touched the tips of my fingers. Her lips moved in a whispered, "Hola."

"What is your name?" I asked. She said nothing, but Maria answered: "Daniela."

In the days that followed, I watched the remaining workers surreptitiously, trying to remember Hector by his absence. One had a mustache, one a mustache and a goatee, two were clean-shaven, all had dark hair and pleasant smiles, all were of similar height. If I could have somehow seen Hector again, I was sure I would remember him. I wondered about his family and how they were managing.

The death preyed on my mind. The sea became

an enemy to me, and I no longer swam. It was large and powerful, obviously dangerous. To be killed by the sea was a tragedy, but not a mystery.

Now the drowning was mixed up in my dreams, and sometimes it would be Angie's small body on the board. These dreams turned me into someone different. Now when I woke in the night, I walked along the beach in the dark, crying, the waves streaming around my legs, not caring what happened to me. But somehow, I would turn and arrive back at my room as dawn touched the sky's edge.

There were several drownings during that time. In the coffee shop the tourists looked grim and made remarks about the lack of safety procedures and equipment. "They should have lifeguards all along these beaches," said one. "Why don't they post signs when the sea is rough?" asked another. I said nothing because I understood. The sea was too powerful. The people who lived next to it saw it as I did, an inevitable force that took victims when it chose.

Maria came to my room one morning. "There is a rumor in the town," she said. "They say that La Llorona walks the beach at night, crying for her dead children."

"La Llorona?"

"She is an old legend, the crying woman. They say she has a white gown and long black hair that blows in the wind. The people are afraid, though the priest tells them there are no ghosts."

"Poor ghost," I said. My hair was tied back by day, but at night I left it loose. Maria gave me a look but said nothing more.

"Maria," I said, "would you take me to see your cousin's wife tomorrow?"

*****

They lived on the outskirts of the town, inland. They had a small farm with pineapple trees and some garden vegetables. When we arrived, we were ushered in by the young mother, introduced to me as Yolanda. The house was small and dark, but clean. The grandfather sat stoically at a wooden table, performing ablutions with a pipe. I had not seen the old beach vendor with the carvings for days; I was almost sure it was him. If I could see him walk, I would know. Yolanda served us coffee. I heard the voices of children outside. "They are milking the goat," said Maria.

When everyone was seated there was an awkward silence.

"Maria was telling me of a legend—a ghost

woman who cries," I said, to make conversation before I tried to explain why I had come.

"La Llorona," said Maria.

The name was repeated all around, with nods. The grandfather spoke in Spanish, slowly and at length, punctuating his phrases with hawking noises. I was sorry that I'd brought it up.

When he was finished, Maria said, "He tells that there was a woman long ago who was very beautiful, and of a son of a rich man from the city who visited her town. They fell in love and were married and had two children, but then one day he left her and went back to the city. She went loco, crazy, and she wanted to punish him for leaving. So, one night, she threw their children into the arroyo and they drowned. The next day, when she realized what she had done, she became so overcome with guilt that she drowned herself. So now, when the arroyos are filled with water, she walks along and cries for her lost children. This is an old legend that has been passed down from generation to generation."

"How sad," I said.

There was another awkward pause.

"I was wondering if I could help somehow with the education of the children," I said. "It will be hard for you to support them on your own."

Maria spoke in Spanish. Then the grandfather asked a question, his voice querulous.

"He asks why an American tourist would want to do such a thing," translated Maria.

"Canadian," I said. He shrugged.

"Tell them I lost my own child," I said. "I was sorry about her husband, and I want to help these children who have been touched with death as well."

Yolanda nodded after Maria told her. Then she spoke swiftly and at some length.

Maria said, "She says she is sorry about your child. She says there is never enough money, but somehow, they have always managed. It will be harder now without Hector's income, but her sister's family will help harvest the fruit and vegetables. She doesn't know what you could do; the children will not go to school, because they will help at home and at the bodega. She says if you want to give money, she will not stop you."

"But if she had the money to send them to a good school it wouldn't cost her anything. It would be such a help later, when they could get good jobs and send money home." I paused, fearing I could not make her understand.

At that moment, the three children tumbled into the doorway and stopped short, staring. I got up to greet them and was rewarded with a shy smile from Daniela. I bent to smooth her rumpled hair, stifling a sudden urge to sweep her into my arms. In the silence that followed, I realized why I had come. The idea that had been growing inside me pushed its way to the surface, and I could not stop the words that spilled out of my mouth.

"What if one of the children, Daniela, came and stayed with me for a while and went to school in Canada? I'm sure I could arrange it. She could learn English, and study to be a teacher. She could come back and really be a help to the family, to the community. It would be easier for Yolanda with just the boys to look after, and I would still help with money."

Maria looked at me, then translated rather hesitantly. Upon hearing her words, Yolanda spoke more rapidly yet, her hands waving. The grandfather stared, his frown deepening.

I put up my hand to stop Yolanda's outpouring. "Just think about it for a while," I told them. "Tell her to think of the children and their future. This is a chance for them all. I'll go now."

I paused in the doorway and turned. "Gracias," I told Yolanda. I forced myself to smile at the old man.

Maria came to my room the next day and said that Yolanda was upset at the idea of her children going anywhere, but she had promised to think about it. "But, would it be allowed, señora?" she asked.

"It could be arranged over time," I said. I would call my lawyer and ask him to find out about the options. I was energized by the idea of setting the plan in motion. It was almost a shock to feel this way after so long.

*****

I had still heard nothing from Yolanda by the second day. I was getting anxious. Had Maria just been polite? Maybe Yolanda had no intention of even thinking about my proposition.

I was in the town when I saw Daniela, standing alone on a sidewalk, waiting to cross the street. I knelt down beside her. "Where's mama?" I asked. She shook her head, and her face started to screw up. The coffee shop was next door.

"Come and have an ice cream." I took her hand and led her into the shop. I explained to Guy that it was

Hector's daughter and that I had found her alone on the street.

"I can let her aunt know she's here," he offered. "She works at the bodega."

"I'll take her home. I know where she lives."

We walked along the street, hand in hand, finishing our ice cream cones, loitering in front of the displays of cheap jewelry. The feel of the small hand in my own turned me back into the person I had been before. It was such a simple thing.

I heard a high-pitched cry and turned to see the aunt running towards me. The child was snatched away, picked up, and hugged, thin legs dangling. Then the aunt turned her attention to me and spoke angrily in rapid Spanish. Others gathered, staring. Daniela's eyes were wide with alarm.

I suddenly felt angry, too. What right did she have to scare the child that way? I threw up my hands in a gesture of defeat and walked away.

The following day, I was sitting in the coffee shop when the old man came in. He spoke briefly with Guy in Spanish. Afterwards, Guy came over to my table, looking embarrassed. "He says to tell you that there are many versions of the legend. In one, La Llorona is an evil spirit who takes children who do not belong to her."

Later, in my room, I lay on the bed, coiled protectively around the hard knot in my stomach that had pulsed to life upon hearing Guy's words, tumorous, filling with dark blood. What gave him the right to speak to me like that, to use some old story in such a hurtful way when I was only trying to help? Waves of resentment spread through me, in concert with the surging breakers outside. Now I just wanted to get away from them all, to leave this place and never come back. First thing tomorrow I would move up my ticket.

*****

I woke at 3 a.m. The room was flat, two-dimensional, in shades of black and darkest blue. Outside was real, the darkness humming with energy. I stood on the porch and loosed my hair, feeling the fingers of the wind stir through it. I started down the beach, then turned and walked up the path next to the swollen arroyo, towards the town. When I reached the main road, I kept to the shadows, away from the dim streetlights. The fragrance of the bougainvillea rose into the night, thick and intoxicating, tinged by the smell of decay from the egret's slough. Ahead, the white adobe church glowed faintly, drawing me. The knot in my stomach cast threadlike tentacles out, scudding along veins and arterials, growing larger, fed by dark blood. I crossed the road and entered the church.

I paused in the entranceway. Inside, dim shafts of light from the high narrow windows to my right fell across the pews and altar, across the tapestries on the opposite wall. Dark shapes on the tapestries looked like hooded figures. All was quietly surreal, the air heavy with meaning. As I watched, dust motes hanging within the shafts of light began to move, then rise and fall in eddies, forming intricate ever-changing patterns. I watched, unable to move, while chills chased up and down my spine. Here and there the movement in the air began to solidify, thickening into corporeal substance; then there were glimpses of firm, unblemished flesh, plump, rounded limbs and rippling fabric that swirled in unseen currents. A breathless chord of music swelled, making the air quiver. Sweet laughter echoed, faint as a memory.

As I watched, spellbound, small angelic figures swam like supple fish through the air, diving, weaving, encircling one another, their little round faces perfect, lips parted in laughter, showing their tiny pearly teeth. Their eyes shone like black buttons, devoid of anything human.

I watched them feint and dodge, their dimpled bodies as graceful in their games as a flock of birds that moves as a single organism.

As they tumbled to and fro, from one side of the church to the other, I noticed movement on the wall with the hangings. Shadows shifted within the heavy fabric each time the cherubs drew near. I stared, and the shapes grew clearer, tall figures who pressed upon the surface of the tapestry. I felt the knot in my stomach pulse. Each time the cherubs brushed the wall, the figures became more substantial. Now I could see red eyes like glowing coals. The curtain began to swell and ripple as they strained against it. Somehow, I understood that they were being nourished as the cherubs brushed by. Soon they would be strong enough to break free. The cherubim played on, unaware.

I heard a soft howling like a distant wind as the cherubs drew near the tapestry once again. I felt sudden sharp glee, and realized I wanted the cherubs to be taken—corrupted and engulfed. I understood the desire of the trapped creatures. I could help bring them to life. I took several stumbling steps and reached for the wall.

Then a presence filled the church, vaster and more timeless than the cherubim or the creatures in the tapestry. It contemplated me. It would only wait. I froze, a wave of shame rushing through me, then turned and ran from the church.

As dawn began to color the sky, I found myself far down the beach, sitting with my arms wrapped around my knees, rocking. Where had I been? The church must have been a dream. I had wandered along the arroyo, hearing my own voice independent of me, moaning like an animal.

Angie; my Angie. It was my fault. I had said that. He had said that. We'd blamed each other; we'd blamed ourselves. Our marriage was finished; it had already been broken. But my secret, my shame, was far deeper. How could any mother admit that she had done such a thing? A mother who had left her child alone downstairs, had thought that the door to the back yard was locked, the yard with the path to the latched gate, the gate Angie had almost learned to open, the gate that led to the pool, the pool with the deadly still waters. He was supposed to look after her, supposed to watch her, and she knew he would forget; and she wanted to prove what a failure he was, to hurt him for what he'd done, not to the child, but to her: the last hurtful words he'd flung and caused the rage and resentment to expand that black knot in her stomach to bursting.

But she didn't really know he could not understand her, did she, as she called to him that Angie was downstairs and that she was going out, and he answered, something, she didn't hear what, but she didn't wait for him to come down. And she had assumed he'd heard her, assumed the back door was locked; she hadn't remembered forgetting to lock it again after she set the plant outside to drain because she'd over-watered it. She hadn't known what would happen; how could she have known?

But somehow, she had.

*****

I was leaving the next day. I walked into town one last time to have dinner. The weather had finally turned overcast. I passed over the bridge and looked for the egret. It was there in its usual spot, alone, snow-white bird in a stinking slough, waterlogged garbage lining the banks. I walked on, avoiding the rusted grates. A thin dog stood on the median, tearing at some garbage in dire concentration, ribs delicately outlined. I passed through the markets, past the dark tunnels of hanging clothes, the glimpses into dirt-floored tent shops where children played under the tables. Tonight, the eyes that met mine seemed hostile. No murmured holás, just a dark gaze and a turning away.

People were everywhere, crowding the sidewalks and streets, buying food from the street vendors. People were lined up in front of the church. Many foreheads had dark smears on them. It was Ash Wednesday.

A small truck drove by again and again, blaring some announcement. Someone bumped into me as I passed, making me stumble. Through the crowd ahead I saw the old man, limping, coming straight towards me. His eyes held me. I paused, unable to move, as he approached. We faced one another, the crowd parting around us. He lifted the lid on the satchel he carried and produced a carving of a small figure, a child perhaps. He held it out to me in some obsequious parody, then his lip curled in a sneer of triumph. I turned and pushed my way through the crowd, back to the hotel.

And now I was in the taxi, speeding towards the airport, finally inland, away from the roar of the sea, leaving a part of myself in the place I would never see again. She had fed upon me, and I upon her, so now the two of us were no longer mere human and myth, but two half-shadows doomed to haunt the sidelines of the living, mourning what we had lost and could never have again.

*****

La Llorona walks the beach at night, crying, leaving soft bare footprints that are washed clean by the surging waves. Her gown and her long dark hair stream in the wind. Only the black crowned night heron marks her passing, one nervous eye affixed.

A WOMAN BY CANDLELIGHT

by Jason Brown

Peals of feminine laughter rose in the candlelight. The edge of scandalized hysteria told the Earl that his ribald joke had hit its mark.

"What else was I to do?!" he exclaimed, delightedly. "It was a bad marriage. The voluptuary and the valetudinarian. We were ill-fated. Ill-matched."

"I perceive that *you* were the voluptuary, my lord?" The girl smiled at him from the middle of a table.

"Of course," he returned her smile. "I am ever devoted to the pursuit of *Epicurean* pleasures!" His voice was melted chocolate dripping onto her senses.

"And your late wife was the valetudinarian?"

"Alas!" he sighed, almost sincerely. "Jealously would she guard her health against all threats; both real and imagined."

"A rare enough concern in the mind of a peasant girl!" interjected their companion from the far side, sipping her wine.

"Do you truly believe that I, of all people, would have married a mere peasant?!"

The girl's wineglass hovered at her lips as she stared at him, suddenly uncertain of her place.

"Forgive me, my lord. I didn't mean to imply…"

He raised his own glass and drank slowly, deliberately; holding her gaze above the rim till he was satisfied.

"Hers was one of those old Gaelic families who lost their foothold after our Norman ancestors crossed the Irish Sea with Strongbow."

The girl did not seem reassured.

"As her father went to great pains to remind me at the wedding feast!"

All three women at the table laughed at this and the tension dissipated.

The Earl replenished his crystal wineglass and he held the bottle before his nearest companion. His new wife placed her delicate hand over her own half-full glass and smiled demurely. "Not for me, husband. I want a clear head. I intend to remember this night for the rest of my life." A flicker of wickedness widened that smile for a heartbeat and the Earl chuckled.

He took in the faces of the three women: each one a darker shade of desire than the last. His new bride was not the only one who would remember this night for the rest of her life. He dipped his glass in salute to the company, drew it to his lips, then drank long and deep, draining it utterly. Sighing with satisfaction, he placed it back on the table with a deliberately elegant flourish.

The girl at the far end was saying something. "Isn't it extraordinary?!" He couldn't remember her name, or if she was the friend or the friend's sister. "Did she really shut herself away in the turret room?"

"Who?!" the Earl wasn't quite sure what was being asked. Perhaps he should stop drinking before he was too drunk for the delights ahead.

"Your first wife! Did she truly shut herself away? Or was that just malicious village gossip?"

"Yes. She did. Shut herself away in the turret room and slowly starved herself to death."

"Extraordinary! Some people are absolutely beyond the pale, are they not?!"

The room's many pools of shadow undulated as the candles guttered silently.

"Indeed they are!" cried the Earl and his companions whooped with laughter once more.

"Indeed! they are!" The words came from the doorway, borne on a voice harsh and brittle with scorn.

The laughter was struck down. The shadows darkened perceptibly.

The new mistress of the manor opened her mouth to challenge this interloper, but the sight of the stranger killed the words in her throat. The woman's feet made no sound as she moved towards the table. Every eye, but the Earl's, followed her leaden, deliberate movements. She stretched her long pale arm over the table and raised the bottle.

"An indifferent vintage," she said curtly, dismissively. "You're as parsimonious with your second wife as you were with the first."

She laid the bottle on the table before the girl, then took her chin in a pale hand and raised the face to meet her terrified gaze.

"So, this is she." The stranger traced the line of the girl's jaw, then slowly drew her fingernails along the sallow skin of the exposed neck. "Very beautiful. Very…willing, I'm sure."

A sudden gesture of the fingers caused the girl to gasp. She clamped a hand to her neck. She stared in shock at her husband. Her eyes widened. Blood began to gurgle from between her fingers. She tried to say something. Her eyelids fluttered. She swayed gently in her chair, then toppled over like a felled tree, hitting the floor with a meaty thud.

"And what are these?" The stranger moved to the girl seated in the next chair. "Companions? Friends?!"

Standing behind the chair, the stranger took the girl's chin in an iron grip and, admiringly, stroked her russet hair with the other hand. "I wish I'd had companions. I wish I'd had friends to warn me of what was to come."

A quick twist and the neck snapped like a dry branch in the forest. The girl's body slumped forward onto the table, knocking over her glass and spreading a deep red stain across the wedding-white tablecloth.

The stranger turned her gaze to the third girl. In the delighted laughter and knowing talk, she'd seemed so confident and worldly. Now she was a trembling weeping child.

"Please, please don't…" the words were overtaken by shuddering moans as she began to cry.

The stranger picked up the toppled wineglass and snapped it in two. She contemplated the long, broken stem for a moment; then pressed the sharpened point to the girl's quivering bosom and pushed it into her heart. A last pathetic whimper escaped her mouth before she fell silent forever.

The stranger moved quietly to the chair at the foot of the table and sat to face her husband.

Thrown by the light from several candles, the shadows strained and crept through the room, as though trying to escape the presence of this pale wraith. The Earl now saw her properly for the first time since the day of her hasty and unceremonious burial. There could be no doubt, this was his dead wife sitting opposite him at the dining table. In life, her hair had been a field of golden rape shaking in a summer breeze. Her eyes had danced with a verdant iridescence. Now, in death, her hair was dull yellow; streaked with mud. The eyes were pale grey; pale and dead.

When her father had given his daughter to the Earl in marriage, the first thing he'd noticed about the girl was her lips. He'd thought them ripe strawberries, full and longing to be tasted. Her lips were no longer ripe or full. They were blanched; drawn back in a thin, cold smile. She wore the same plain white shift in which she'd been buried; spattered with an ugly cascade of grass stains and caked earth. Her hands were also caked with dried earth and several of her fingernails were broken.

It was curious that, as he sat there staring at this apparition, the Earl did not feel fear. Apprehension, perhaps? An edge of excitement, certainly. But there was something else; something deeper and more thrilling.

"You look…changed. Beautiful, but changed!"

Her smile remained fixed. Steady. And very unnerving.

"You should know better. For a man who was always deeply fascinated by what lies beneath the skin, you should know better. What was it that your father used to tell you? That sage advice from his days on the turf."

"Never judge a horse, or a woman, by candlelight."

"Yes. That was it."

He felt as though he'd just lost a point in some subtle game they were playing. The ground seemed to shift beneath his feet. He decided to go on the offensive.

"It is customary that, when a person starves herself to death, she has the good manners to remain dead." He tried to keep his voice even. "But then, your lot never had much in the way of good manners!" If he'd hoped that the insult would move her in some way, he was disappointed. Her cold smile remained in place; her filthy hands spread out on the ruined tablecloth.

"What else was I to do? You kept me locked up in that turret room."

"I visited you every day."

"Yes. You visited. Every day. To feed me. And to bleed me."

He thought he saw a flicker of emotion as she said that.

"A man must have a pastime. An interest, beyond the quotidian mundanity, to indulge in from time to time. And who better to indulge me in my interests than my own wife? You were my property after all. Your father gave you to me." He smiled his own cold, thin smile as he warmed to his subject. "When I think of how that uncouth old man reveled in the wealth and status our marriage conferred upon him, it leaves an unpleasant taste in my mouth."

"My father is no longer in a position to enjoy the riches you bought me with." Her voice dripped with venom.

"Did you…?" He threw a cursory glance at the three corpses lying between them—then looked her directly in the eyes. Slowly, she tilted her head to the side and the new angle made her smile a crescent of naked malice. It was difficult to reconcile that smile with his memory of the forlorn young woman who sat at the window of the turret room every day, staring out across the hills as though she was waiting for a rescue which she knew would never come. Even more difficult to see that smile on the face which had once so passively resigned itself to the daily bloodletting he'd subjected her to. How quickly she'd faded from a beautiful and vital woman to the pale, nacreous image on a tapestry left too long in the sun! But this thing which sat before him now was just short of being truly grotesque. She was familiar and strange; her presence shaped the shadows around her. *She* was now the thing that darkness fled from. The Earl should be fleeing, screaming, something. Instead, he just sat there; fascinated beyond all thought of self-preservation.

"Why did you come back?"

"What night is tonight?"

The Earl glanced pointedly to the body at his feet. "It *was* to be my second wedding night!" he replied in a mocking, singsong tone. He raised his eyes and held her cold steady gaze once more. "Now, it is merely All Hallow's."

"To my people, it is Samhain!"

The Earl forced a snort of derisive laughter down his nose. "You Gaels and your pagan superstitions!"

She rose from the chair, rounded the edge of the table and, deftly stepping over the bodies on the floor, was at his side before he could react. She leaned over him; her stinking dew-drenched hair hanging from her head: and placed one hand on his face. Her hand was not merely cold; it was marble, nothing would ever warm that hand again. A tall, thin candle flame was reflected in her dead eyes. Or maybe it wasn't a candle; perhaps it was the reflection of the cold fire which now animated her corpse.

"No mere superstition. I am right before you."

His heart was a crazed tiger desperate to escape his ribcage and his breathing quickened as the air around him thinned to nothing. The dull ache of an erection pressed against his satin pantaloons.

"I've never wanted you more!"

Her cold smile became a cruel grimace. She moved her face closer to his; their noses almost touching.

"I never wanted you at all."

She kissed him. Her cold lips seemed to stick to his. He grabbed her free hand and pulled it down to his crotch, willing her to relieve his growing need. Instead, she ripped it free of his grasp and embraced his head with both hands. Her strength was astonishing, inhuman. She wrenched free of the kiss, the thin flame in her eyes was now a triumphant blaze. Twisting his hair round her fingers, she pulled his head to one side exposing his neck. Then she pounced on him, her teeth tearing into his flesh. The candles guttered and the shadows danced, terrified and exultant in the same moment. And then they gathered round the Earl, blotting out the room and the table and the bodies and the candlelight and even the dead woman who had returned to him; the shadows draped over everything. And then…stillness.

*****

A monochrome landscape opened up before her. Walking the lonely contours of undulating silver hills; frozen waves in a timeless, deathless sea: the red thirst had paled to nothing for the time being. They called to her: the gentle hillside, the solitary tree and the unsettled earth of her now porous grave: whispering of a rest she knew would be fleeting. And when the thirst rose once more; when the need became undeniable: she would rise to another Samhain midnight. Drawn on by an ungovernable desire, she would walk abroad once again. But she would remain a woman. A woman beyond the hungry earth of the grave. A woman beyond the shattered chains of an impermanent death. A woman caressed by moonlight.

<u>END</u>

JOROGUMO

by Sarah Jane Huntington

Some people believe that before the time of the Titans and even earlier than the Immortals. The Ancient Ones existed.

The Ancients became responsible for a great many crimes, many acts of depravity, cruelty and death.

Ballads were sung and stories were told around campfires. They were kept alive and well in myth and folklore. Each Ancient had a thousand faces and a thousand stories. Generation after generation held the knowledge and warnings close, until our modern day dawned.

Humankind has forgotten all about their true beginnings and this worked greatly in the Ancients favour. One will never defeat what one doesn't believe exists.

They hide freely among us, feeding from our fears. Impossibilities happen.

One such Ancient is Jorogumo.

June 11th, 2020

Mikito yawned widely as he stretched, his joints popped and argued with him as his spine creaked wearily.

"I'm getting too old for this," he told no one in particular. Only one face in the quiet room of six looked up at him. One of his fellow suicide rangers, the newest fresh-faced addition to the twice-yearly voluntary team.

Mikito shrugged and squinted, he examined the map that lay spread out in front of him.

Aokigahara national park. Sometimes referred to as suicide forest, with good reason. Aokigahara is the place many choose as their place to die. His job is to search and locate the reported missing, radio for assistance, then the heart wrenching task of transporting the bodies. Just like he does every year and has done for the last fifteen of them. His radio didn't always work in some of the dead zones of the vast forest and mountains, but Mikito remembered locations and he remembered people.

He recalled every face lost, missing or found deceased by their own hand. Right from the day all those years ago, when he'd carried his own brother's remains out from the mouth of the fateful forest. Dead by his own hand.

"Two Brits gone missing, late to check in by three days." An older weatherworn ranger told him. He passed over a photograph of a happy couple, "In your grid."

Mikito nodded solemnly. He recalled them both well, a sweet, polite, happy couple. A tall man and a pretty, fair-haired lady. Both had been excited to be hiking and seemed deep in love.

"Ah, yes. My grid." Mikito bowed and said a silent prayer. He hoped the nice couple were alive and only lost, maybe delayed by the beauty around them. He didn't think they were the suicidal type. He expected to see them arrive back with big smiles.

He shook his head sadly, *You never can tell.*

June 6th

Anna watched a tiny bird as it hopped along a thin branch and grinned widely.

I love this place, she thought. Her limbs were tired, and her joints hurt but she felt great. Her mind was clear, and for the first time in months, she felt she could breathe properly. She swallowed two painkillers and started the water boiling for the last of the coffee.

"Morning." Jack climbed out of their tent and dropped a kiss on her blonde head.

"Hey, no!" She laughed, "I'm all sweaty and yuk."

Jack pulled a disgusted face and Anna stuck her tongue out at him in return. The pair had spent seven days hiking in Aokigahara forest and both had enjoyed every single wonderful moment. The incredible views and caves to explore, the trails and the shy wildlife. The silence, peace, and solitude have been just what Anna needed. Jack was more than happy to get away from Tokyo too, although he came for the hiking. For him it was a chance to prove that at forty, he could still cut it.

Despite all the well-known horror stories, they hadn't come across a single dead body. Only the remains of two camps, both empty but with belongings still lying around. Jack noted the locations, ready to give them to the ranger they'd met and talked to on the way in. They'd passed a group of hikers who were on their way back down to the entrance four days ago. The exhausted group had happily given them tea bags, bows, and friendly handshakes.

"Two more days." Jack reminded her. Anna snapped out of her daydreams.

"I know," she sighed and stood up to rummage in her backpack. Anna pulled out a packet of porridge, "We should come back next year, or again this year, or we could just stay!" She laughed, "Gosh, I do love it here."

Jack rolled his eyes, "I was thinking of hiking in Poland or Sweden for…" He stopped and stared at the treeline in bewilderment.

Anna followed his gaze and saw a small face peeking out from behind a thick tree.

"Someone's there." Jack spoke quietly. They hadn't seen another person since they passed that group. Only serious hikers ventured as far as they had.

"Hello?" Anna called out. "Are you okay?" She turned to question Jack, "someone must be lost?"

"Must be." He answered.

Anna saw long black hair swinging gently in the slight breeze and a small delicate hand resting on the bark of the tree. She heard a high-pitched childish giggle and frowned. *If she's lost, why is she laughing? Is that a child?* Anna's maternal instinct kicked in as she walked towards the tree with her hands held in the air as a peace gesture.

"We can help you if you're lost. Hello? Kon-nichiwa." She tried a Japanese greeting last and kicked herself for barely knowing the language.

A figure calmly stepped out smiling and Anna saw the stranger was a woman. A beautiful, young, Japanese woman, wearing a plain white but muddy dress and worn black boots.

"Lost," the woman told her and giggled softly.

Anna held out her hand in sympathy and friendship. *She must have wandered off from a group,* she thought, *They can't be far away.*

Jack joined her and held out a mug of steaming coffee for the woman. She took it gratefully and wrapped both slender hands around the warmth.

"You better come and sit down." Jack told her and pointed to their camp. "Come and sit?" The woman took Anna's hand and allowed herself to be led to their campsite. She sat on a log and sipped her drink happily while she watched them.

"Shit," Jack said puzzled, "Now what do we do?"

"The radio, try the base station, or we can look for her group? She can't be alone out here and we're two days' hike from the bottom, aren't we?"

Jack fetched his pack and fiddled with the small handheld radio they were given. The radio failed to tune. They were warned about dead zones by the suicide ranger. The sound of static filled the air. The woman jumped up, her mug falling to the ground as her eyes filled with wild panic.

"It's okay," Jack soothed her, quickly and switched the radio off, "It's harmless." He risked a glance at Anna who watched the scene with narrowed eyes.

"How does she not know what that is?" She whispered.

Jack shrugged; he wasn't sure himself. The woman sat back down and blinked rapidly. She wrapped her arms around herself and rubbed her arms. "She's cold, hang on."

Anna heads into the tent, looking for a sweater. *Somethings wrong here, this all feels too weird. Where is her group?*

"One minute, wait." She heard Jack say. He ducked awkwardly into the tent to join her.

"Okay, I'm spooked." He told Anna. She breathed a sigh of relief, glad it wasn't just her who found the newcomer suspicious.

"I'm thinking," Anna whispered, "Lets pack, but listen. She's either lost and dehydrated, or she's come here to kill herself, or we're going to be attacked, or robbed, or something; and she's the scout."

Jack closed his eyes, "I don't like any of those ideas, but the last one seems a bit dramatic."

He began to roll up his sleeping back and fold his belongings. Anna peered out of the tent and reached to drag the packs inside, she saw the woman sitting quite serenely as she examined the pack of porridge.

"Probably. Her manner is, well, it's odd," she whispered.

Jack nodded and filled his pack, "She must be dehydrated, I guess. We'll help her look for her group. Or do you want to head back down?"

Anna paused. If they headed back down to the entrance of the forest, they wouldn't make it in a day. They'd have to spend the night with her. The idea that sends a spike of cold terror down her spine and she shivered.

"Help her look." She decided. "Quick as we can, we'll find them and we'll leave."

Jack agreed, "Okay. This is still weird, but she looks harmless."

As soon as they had their things packed. The trio set off.

"Friends," the woman told them and pointed into the thick deep woodland off the slight trail.

Jack had noted the groups position and had taken to carrying their compass again, stopping to chart their progress on his map. The compass had started to spin relentlessly on occasion over the last few days, before it settled down to show its proper directions again. The ranger told them that might happen, a magnetic effect from some of the massive boulders dotted around.

"Is it working?" Anna asked. Jack gave her a thumbs up.

She was afraid of them becoming lost. They only had enough supplies left to last them until the next evening, when they should be checking in at the base. Anna watched the woman in front lead the way on an overgrown trail, she seemed to know the forest very well. She stepped over fallen logs and avoided low branches gracefully.

Anna had given her a thick green sweater to wear and the stranger pulled at the stitching, unravelling the wool as she walked.

"Friend. See." The woman spoke in her musical voice and stopped.

Anna craned her neck to see around her, expecting to see a small camp and a group of relieved and friendly faces.

Instead, a decomposing body lay abandoned in a clearing, surrounded by a circle of dense bushes.

A small tent still stood at the side of the almost mummified half naked body. Its grey skin pulled tightly across its skull and its body looked as if it had collapsed in on itself.

Anna struggled to comprehend what it was she was seeing. Her legs weakened as her heartbeat raged inside her ears. She was vaguely aware of Jack catching up to them and turned to vomit.

"Friend," the woman announced proudly once more. She grinned widely and crouched down beside the body. A rush of flies took to the air in fury. A fat spider slowly crawled out of an eye socket as Anna fell to her knees in shock.

"But.." Anna stuttered.

"We need to go now." She heard Jack tell her but still, she couldn't move. "Quickly." She felt her arm being yanked forcefully back.

She's gone mad. Anna thought, *She's been out here a long time and she's gone mad. What do we do?*

Anna tried to stand on rubbery legs and failed. She stopped to take a deep breath, gulping down a lungful of air.

The beautiful woman began to jerk and jolt wildly, her head snapped back painfully. She fell forward on all fours as her mouth stretched impossibly wide. She hissed as her hands ripped at her sweater and dress, tearing her clothes open. Two exposed small bare breasts and smooth skin began to shrink as coarse hairs sprouted up in their place. Her abdomen bloated rapidly. Two thick hairy legs tore outwards from her hips. The sounds of crunching and popping filled the air as the woman groaned, her breathing frantic.

Jack pulled Anna backwards as her bladder gave out in fright. Her spine hit a log as her mind froze in complete terror. Jack stopped pulling her and ran.

A rush of spiders erupted from the stomach of the dead body as long fangs began to grow from the spider woman's mouth.

Anna heard screaming and realised it was her. Her vision clouded and she blacked out as the spiders engulfed her body. Scuttling into her open mouth, swarming down her ears, and hurrying up her nose.

The woman was no longer a woman. She reared up on four legs, while the front four stretched and cracked. Torn clothing fluttered like ribbons to the ground. Multiple black eyes blinked in synchronicity as the car-sized monstrosity began to slowly move. Lithe and muscular. An ancient and terrifying sight. She shot a thick web that cocooned Anna alive. Eight long legs stepped calmly over her.

The spider woman felt a pang of fierce hunger. She ran after Jack. The forest vibrated beneath her eight feet.

Jack jumped over branches and twigs, saliva sprayed from his mouth as he frantically sprinted, looking for any trail. He ran at a furious speed, half sobbing in horror.

I'm so sorry Anna, he thought. His heart beat an angry rhythm as bitter bile rose up in his throat. *What was that thing?*

Jack stopped and leant against a tree. He dropped his pack on the ground and bent forward heaving. "Anna." He whispered aloud and sobbed. He wiped his face on his shirt. "Anna" he mumbled again. But he had no intention of going back.

Jack quickly checked his compass, but it spun around in furious circles. He threw it to the ground and stamped on it. *We all walked left, I'll go right.*

Jack took three long deep breaths and ran. *I can make it. I can make it.* His mind chanted. He ran in long heavy strides. *There! The trail! I'll get help.*

He almost laughed as he broke through the treeline in a frantic jump.

"HELP." He shouted. His legs picked up speed. His mind praying someone might be close enough to hear. His feet pounded the ground as he darted past trees and bushes. He jumped a fallen branch and ducked under another. Pure survival instinct propelled him.

I'll run all the way, I'll get help. He chanted, repeating it to himself.

Jack saw a sudden flash of white. He collided with a tree, hitting his head.

As blood dripped down his face, he stared down in shock. *A sheet?* He shook his head groggily.

I can't move. Why can't I move? Finding his body bound tightly, he moved his throbbing head to look around. A rustling sound came from above him. Jack saw an impossibly large spider making its way towards him from high in a tree. A canopy of white spread out behind it.

It's a web, I'm in a web. Was his last coherent thought before his mind snapped entirely.

The huge spider dropped down gently and came creeping towards him, followed closely by an army of a thousand much smaller ones.

Jack saw himself grotesquely reflected in its many eyes. He screamed in horror, then in agony as she reached him.

June 20th

Mikito stood quietly and mourned. He had become used to death over the years but still, he mourns those that chose to pass and sheds a tear.

"Bodies?" A fellow suicide ranger asked him.

Mikito sadly shook his head. All he's found is the British pair's belongings and a few bones. The national park has animals which feast on the dead, a greatly disturbing thought.

"Job never gets easier. They must have been very sad." His companion stopped a moment to join Mikito in mourning.

The pretty blonde lady and the tall man. The happy ones. Or so Mikito thought.

That's how he decided to remember them both, as happy. He never guessed that of all the people who chose to visit Aokigahara, they would be the kind of people to be suicidal. "You can't always tell." One of the rangers once told him.

No, you never can tell.

YAMA UBA AND THE HIGANBANA

by L.F. Falconer

*In the early times of 19th century Japan, Moriko
left the sanctuary of Aoyagi's garden...*

Like small torches, yellowing claws upon
Moriko's fingertips burned as she pushed her way
through the tangled wisteria. The longer the claws
grew, the more painful they became. Her heart
thundered beneath the thinning skin of a sagging
breast, pounding, threatening to rip its way through.
Only the bloody swaddling of the infant pressed
against it kept the heart captive. The stony earth cut her
naked feet. Jagged, broken limbs caught her pale blue
kimono as if to strip it from the abomination hidden
beneath, for what right had such a monster as she to
wear it? There had been a day not so long ago when
she had borne the same delicate beauty as the garment
itself. A time before the hunger had driven her to
madness.

Moriko stopped to catch her breath, panting amid
the tangled vines, the rancid perfume of the fading
blossoms masking the scintillating odor of the blood
she wore. Drawing the infant from her protective

embrace, she stared down at the delectable face that peeked through the silk folds. The smooth, unblemished cheeks. Bright eyes. A shock of jet-black hair.

A dribble of drool slipped over Moriko's trembling bottom lip, staining itself with blood as it slid across the greasy gray flesh of her chin. It hung like a pendulum before breaking free, spattering the child's cheek. Moriko lifted the infant closer to her face and clenched her teeth. Peeling the swaddling back, she exposed the child's head fully in the dim forest light. The infant gazed up at her and with a cherubic chortle, smiled. Moriko opened her mouth. Two rows of razor-sharp teeth smiled at the baby in return. From the pit of her soul, the ravenous hunger bellied up. Newborn flesh would taste so sweet. So sweet.

A katana sharp pang cut through her torso. Shimmering with tears, her carnelian eyes welled. She leaned her head back, her eyes clamped shut. A mournful wail squealed and slithered through the bramble.

Had not the child's mother been satisfaction enough? The sweetness of Yuki's blood still nestled in her nostrils; small chunks of her flesh lingered between

Moriko's teeth. Smacking her lips, Moriko stared at Yuki's child once more. Yuki had been a friend long before she had become a feast.

Wrenching back her gnawing hunger, Moriko clutched the child back against her sallow bosom and pushed onward through the vines, deep within the Sea of Trees on the western flank of Fujiyama.

It had been boredom alone which had led her to stray from the protection of Aoygai's garden...a year ago? More? Less? Time in the mortal realm passed differently than it did for the Yōsei. Moriko was certain it must have been years, yet it felt as if only a day or two had passed since she had wended her way through the wisteria hedge to explore the forest surrounds. She'd had every intention of returning to Aoyagi's garden before it was too late. But within the thick, beguiling stands of the hemlock firs, the hollies, cypress, oaks and cherry trees, she'd soon lost her way. The night had fallen swiftly and locked her into darkness. Alone with the voles and the bats, deep within Moriko's aching bones, the Yōsei curse began.

The woodcutter, Eiji, had come upon Moriko the following morning. His good heart insisted the lost girl return with him to his home, a humble hut at the base of Fujiyama beside an icy stream, clean and welcoming. There, she was tended by Yuki, Eiji's smiling wife, expectant with child. The two young women became fast friends and Yuki bade Moriko live with them, to help ease Yuki's lonely existence within the woods and to aid with the birth and raising of the child.

Moriko knew she should have refused. She was cursed. It was in her aching bones. Her itching skin. Her fading color. Her growing hunger. No longer did she even recognize her bent and twisted shadow, or her gnarled hands, so cold and unfeeling. She was becoming a stranger to her own heart. Becoming Yama Uba … a monster…And she would soon present Eiji and Yuki grave danger. Yet the goodness Mother Aoyagi had instilled within Moriko's mortal soul was powerful, and the girl believed she could stave off the hunger and control the curse.

She was wrong.

When Yuki's child emerged, so too, did Moriko's repressed hunger. The more the hunger grew, the swifter Moriko withered and aged. Believing Moriko to be ill, Yuki offered herbs and tea to no avail. Moriko continued to deteriorate while struggling to deny the change. Fighting to reject its inevitability.

Yet Eiji knew. Moriko could see the knowledge of her secret reflected within his eyes. Within his disdain. Within his pungent fear.

One day, leaving his axe behind lest it invoke Moriko's hesitation, he bade her accompany him up the mountainside and into the forest where he had found her. Once deeply ensconced within those woods, he begged her to return to her own place within the Sea of Trees. He made it clear that should she dare return to his hut, he would not hesitate to raise his axe against her.

Enraged, Moriko dug her yellowing talons into Eiji's throat and sunk her sharp teeth into his flesh, satisfying at last the frenzied hunger which had been building inside her. When the woodcutter was no more, she followed the path back down Fujiyama to his hut, where Yuki and her daughter awaited Eiji's return.

Distraught by the sight of her husband's blood upon Moriko's blue kimono, Yuki sought the protection of her husband's axe. But the powerful Yama Uba overwhelmed the new mother and soon, she, too, was devoured.

In the depths of Moriko's soul, the curse of the Yama Uba battled with the blessings of Mother

Aoyagi. A scream of remorse tore from Moriko's throat. She snatched the orphaned child of Yuki and Eiji to her shrunken breast and began to run. Shambling up the stony hillside, she did not stop until she finally located the wisteria bramble she had lost sight of so long ago.

Now deep within the Sea of Trees, she broke through the vines at last, entering a hidden glade. Amid towering stands of bamboo, the leaves shimmered in sparkling emerald. She recognized the familiar filigreed katsura leaves in shades of scarlet and gold, the mounds of fuchsia and vivid blue hydrangeas brightening the dense, dark shadows.

She was almost home. Though home it was no longer. Having left it behind, she could never return. Yet she must return. Not for herself. For the child.

Across the glade, in the distance, stood a garden older than time. Gleaming with a silvery sheen within a shaft of golden sunlight, a tall, graceful willow beckoned, lithe with draping boughs. Like a string of pearls upon the grassy sward, a ring of velvety enoki caps encircled the tree. Stands of azaleas, hydrangeas, tiger lilies, and peonies graced the surrounding lawn, cloven by a gurgling dancing brook.

Unable to control the salivation seeping between her hot and bloody lips, Moriko stumbled forward, coming to a stop at the rim of the mushroom perimeter, repelled by mad terror. She still had a choice. This, she did not have to do. She could move on, return to the deep forest and live a long, lonely life as Yama Uba, satisfying her all-consuming hunger with the muscle and blood of mortal men.

Blue sky shattered amid the sharp willow leaves, falling like spears of lightning into pools upon the grass. Each sunlit shaft impaled her spirit, driving in with fiery pangs. Every babble of the brook screamed into her ears.

Moriko glared down into the eyes of the choice morsel cradled within her aching, arthritic arms. The child's flesh could ease her pain. There were many mortals in the world, each one a tonic. Yet the child had not been born to serve her needs. Did it not deserve a life of its own? There were many more lives she could choose. Yet how delicious this nascent flesh, more so because it had been born through love. It was wrong to eat it, yet so satisfying if she did.

Conceding at last to her own needs, Moriko keened and took a sharp step of retreat, turning her back to the mushroom encircled willow tree. Once more, she brought the child close to her gore-laden lips. The rapture in her heart sparked shudders in brutal waves, rocking her like a tsunami. Grasping onto her last shred of humanity, she took a deep, coarse breath, wheeled around and forced herself to step over the mushrooms, into the ring.

Swift as a Samurai's sword, an erupting inferno engulfed her from the inside out. She gasped her mortal shock. Her legs liquified and she collapsed, nearly crushing the child beneath her. Managing to find enough strength to pull the baby free, she quivered beside it on the grass, shaking feverishly. Her hand, spotted and curled with age, crept and settled restlessly atop the infant sheltered within its silk swaddling, darkly stained with its mother's blood.

"Aoyagi, please." The rattle of death girdled Moriko's voice. "Mama …" Her words faded and died upon her lifeless lips.

Accompanied only by the soft swish of the glistening willow leaves, the baby's quiet coos danced through the lingering silence. Within the long, passing moments, the coos slowly morphed into mewls, then into a squall, shattering the quietude. From the verdant blades crawled a tiny orchid mantis. Spreading its lavender and ivory wings in full splendor, it flew onto the stained silk and brushed its spiny, purple forelegs against the child's spittle-specked cheek.

Like drops of morning dew, tears of sorrow crept from the willow leaves above and dripped onto the grass. The branches rustled. Argent leaves shimmered in the broken sunlight. The bronzed bark on the trunk wavered ephemerally. Through a glimmering murmuration upon the bark, a majestic wood fairy emerged, draped in moss and leaves. Tawny silken hair, the same shade as her skin, swept the grass as she bent to remove the Yama Uba's dead hand from the wailing infant.

The tiny mantis reared up, raising its forelegs in a karate stance.

Her wooden voice softly blending with the rustling of the leaves, the tall, wood fairy spoke. "Valiant Hana." She plucked the mantis from the swaddling and carefully placed it upon her own shoulder. "Arigatou gozaimasu. Your valor shall be rewarded."

Cradling the baby then in her thin, brown arms, Aoyagi brushed the bloody spittle from the child's cheek. The infant sniffled and grew calm.

"My daughter," the wood fairy whispered. "You are safe from harm. I am Aoyagi and shall be your mother guardian. And you, most precious child, shall be known as my Takara, for as long as it shall be."

With a kiss to the baby's forehead, Aoyagi sealed the child's fate to her protective bond. Shielding the infant against her breast, the wood fairy then knelt to the earth. Lovingly, she brushed her free hand, from head to foot, over the cooling corpse of the old Yama Uba, at one time also a child of her heart. A child left abandoned in the garden whom the wood fairy had adopted. A child taken into her home in the enchanted realm, blessed as long as she remained within it. Cursed if she departed. Destined to die if she attempted to return.

"Rest well, my sweet Moriko." Aoyagi's tears fell as gentle raindrops upon Moriko's lifeless bosom.

Like snowmelt, the aged and mottled cadaver in the pale blue kimono withered into the grass. The green blades hummed, and the ring of platinum mushrooms swayed as if dancing in the wind. Aoyagi arose and vanished back into the viscous willow bark, ushering the infant and the mantis into the realm of the Yōsei—the secret land of Fairies, where the child would be blessed as long as she remained. Doomed to become Yama Uba if she ever departed Aoyagi's realm.

And in the spring, from the rich, volcanic soil where Moriko had lain, a stately higanbana sprouted from the earth. A single spider lily stained as red as mortal blood.

BLACK SHUCK

by Kevin Patrick McCann

"Off out for a walk?"

Jean nodded, "Too nice a day to stay inside," and it was. The sun shone, the sky was clear and there was a crisp tang in the air. She smiled at the hotel receptionist who smiled back.

"Will you be wanting lunch?"

Jean thought about it for a moment. "Oh yes, I'll not be going far; probably just a stroll up onto one of the fells."

The receptionist smiled again and then said, "Give me a time you'll be back by." She paused at the sight of Jean's sudden frown. "Health and Safety Rule," she explained. "If you say you'll be back by say twelve and aren't and still aren't by one, the Search and Rescue'll be out looking for you."

Jane felt her stomach swoop. "Why's that? Isn't it safe?"

"Oh, safe enough," said the receptionist, "as long as you stick to the paths. It's just we do get heavy frets."

"Frets?"

"Mist; it can come down very sudden. If that should happen just stay put. Some folk have tried making their way back in them and got lost or had a fall." She looked Jean up and down, took in the walking boots, jeans, bright orange anorak and woollen hat before adding, "Have you got anything to snack on just in case."

Jean nodded, "I'll swing by the village shop." She smiled again (it'd been years and she was enjoying the feel of it) and added, "Thanks for reminding me and do you know, I should have remembered that. When I was girl, me and my Dad used to come up here for days out and we always did that…" For what she thought was only a few seconds (it was closer to a minute), she fell silent. The receptionist waited patiently until she spoke again. "We used to have pub lunches in…the Old Dog I think it was called."

"The Black Dog you mean. That's just down the road from here. If you go out the main gate and turn left it's about two miles."

It was a perfect morning and as Jean walked, she pondered. She'd forgotten about the frets but then, well, all she remembered from her days out here as a girl was clear skies and perfect days like this one. But that's the way you always remember the past: blue skies, perfect Summers, all lies, all of it like snow at Christmas and they all lived happily ever after.

She remembered lying on her bedroom floor, ear pressed to the carpet, listening to the nightly arguments, the muffled curses; she remembered the cold silent mornings (no smiling faces at their breakfast table) and the day she took one of Dad's razor blades and drew a pattern on her arm with it. It hadn't hurt at first (the blade was very sharp) and the blood had smeared dry quick enough; the cuts weren't very deep after all.

She knew there must have been a fuss, but it was blank again after that. She remembered a day out up here. There must have been more but now they all blurred and blended into one. It was a day like this, and it had just been the two of them; just her and Dad. They'd walked up onto the fells but couldn't have gone too high as she was only…how old was she then? Eight? Ten? And then it's blank again.

The Black Dog was smaller than she remembered but then that was always the way when you went back. The past was always small and ordinary… just like the present…and the future would just get smaller. She called in and ordered a glass of mineral water. The place was nice enough and the barmaid had pretended to be interested when Jean told her she'd come here as a child. She was like an extra in some low budget horror movie: knew her lines but couldn't act her way out of a wet paper bag.

On her way in, she'd spotted a gate in the wall at the far end of the pub car park and just beyond that a path that wandering up towards a low fell, so asked the barmaid where it ended.

"A small tarn called Shuck's Pool. It's only a short step, not too steep and well worth it."

Jean nodded. "I'm due back at The Eagle for lunch at one." She glanced at her watch, "And it's half-eleven now. Do you think I've time?"

The barmaid frowned, "You'd be pushed," she said then added, "We do lunches here. I can ring them for you if you like. Tell 'em you're having lunch here."

Jean smiled. "Would you mind?"

"Not at all; what time will we expect you back?"

Jean thought about it again then said, "Two at the latest."

Jean finished the last of her drink and bought a cheese sandwich wrapped in cling film, "In case I get peckish," and as she turned to go suddenly paused and said, "Shuck? That name rings a bell."

The barmaid laughed, "It's just some old story. Black Shuck's supposed to be a phantom hound haunts the fells. The tarn's where he's supposed to drink."

"Why would a phantom need to drink?"

The barmaid laughed again, "Exactly," she said and for a moment, Jean was tempted to stay for another drink. It was nice to just be here and *shoot the breeze*.

She suddenly remembered her Dad used to say that; put on a fake American accent to make her laugh. Or they'd go into some café, just the two of them, it always seemed to be just the two of them, and (winking) ask the waitress for, "Cup of cawfee 'n' ham on rye," and the waitress always laughed and said, "Sure thing Marlowe and then lean in and say, "Yon a case?" then look at Jean and say, "Who's de broad?"

"You okay?"

The barmaid's voice snapped her out of her daydream. "Sorry," she said, "Just a memory of me Dad." She smiled apologetically, "He only died a while back and I'm still a bit raw."

The barmaid reached out and gently got hold of her hand. "Do you feel like talking?"

Jean shook her head. It was well meant, she knew that, but talking didn't help. Her Dad always said that. Talk changes nothing; it's just so much useless blather.

The barmaid had been right. It was a very gentle slope. *Fol-de ree* Her Dad used to sing that…*I love to go a wandering along the mountainside*…never at home though. Suddenly she could hear Mum's sharp voice shouting, "Stop that!" and he would.

But then one day she was gone. Jean got home from school and Dad had told her Mum was gone, run off with another bloke, and they'd never mentioned her again. So after that it was just the two of them. She'd left school at sixteen and went straight into a job stacking shelves at the local supermarket. She still carried on living at home. "Good of you," he'd say, "staying here to take care of your old Dad."

She'd had the odd boyfriend. Nothing serious though. And besides which, Dad hadn't liked any of them. So, they faded too. She was content enough and went from shelves to check-out to Junior Manager. Her Dad had taken early retirement but then one day she'd got home and he'd said, "Who are you?" then later on tried to pretend it was a joke.

"Course I know who you are," he'd said. "You're my Jane."

Jane was her Mum's name, but she'd let it go. Now, it all clicked together like some giant jig-saw: the way he'd lose his thread when they were talking; forgetting people's names. All the other little things she'd chosen to ignore.

But they had his pension, the mortgage was paid off so she could afford to go part time. Neither of them talked about it and she was glad for that. At first, it wasn't so bad. He didn't really need much looking after, just keep him fed and company. But then it got worse, much worse. In the end, it was social workers, artificial sympathy, hugs, hand holding, and vague promises of help that never materialised.

He'd look at her sometimes and tap the side of his head with his index finger and say, "Going backwards…this…going backwards."

One day she'd got back from work (short-shift, only ten til two) and found the sandwiches she'd left for his lunch untouched. The TV was on in the living-room but he wasn't there. She called out, No reply. She went upstairs and saw the bathroom door was shut. She knocked. "Dad, you in there? You all right?"

No reply so she tried the door. Unlocked. She went in. He was sitting in the bath. Fully clothed. The water was red. A coppery smell. His eyes half-open. A note propped up on the cistern.

> *Not fair on you.*
>
> *I'm off.*
>
> *Sorry.*
>
> *Love Dad*
>
> *X*

It was only a gentle slope, but she was already out of breath. No...not out of breath: not able to breathe. She stood very still, closed her eyes, counted backwards from ten, felt her breath coming back. She opened her eyes and thought *maybe leave it to-day* but then she could hear Dad's voice saying *come on our Jean pick up your feet not far now* so carried on.

And it wasn't much further. She reached the crest and found herself looking down into a bowl-shaped depression encircling a small tarn edged with reeds. There was a gentle breeze that set the reeds muttering to themselves (*Dad did that*) and furrowed the tarn's brow.

She looked back. The pub and car park were much further off than they could have possibly been. She looked ahead and the horizon tilted. She felt herself falling: damp turf rushed up to meet her, she was rolling down a gentle slope, sharp reeds pricked her cheeks, dried fronds tickled her forehead. *Wake up, our Jean, time for school.* And she just wanted to sleep.

She woke up suddenly. It was cold. Dad was shouting. Dad was dead. It was cold. She sat up and looked around. Thick cold mist. She stood up and looked around. She could see maybe a couple of yards in any direction. The silence was so complete she spoke aloud, "Hello," to make sure she hadn't gone deaf.

"Stay put" that girl at the hotel had said. "If a fret comes in, stay put." She looked at her watch. It had stopped. She shuddered and thought *God Almighty but it's cold* and decided that at least she could climb back out of this depression. Once she reached the lip there might be less mist.

But there wasn't and it was just as cold. Her jeans had turned a shade darker with the damp they'd absorbed, and she'd forgotten her gloves. She looked down. Close cropped grass but no sign of the path. If she could at least find that she'd be able to get back down on her own. It wasn't a steep climb, so it'd be an easy descent. Might be hours yet before Search and Rescue turned up and it really was too cold to hang around.

If she stuck close to the edge of the depression and followed it round, she'd be bound to find the path. Had to. She took small steps, treading carefully, and for a split second had an image in her mind's eye of a chicken picking its way through a minefield. The close-cropped turf now silvering with dew was patched with rabbit droppings but there was still no sign.

Then there was: a path of bare soil lower than the turf on either side of it. Visibility was still down to a couple of yards, but she could see the path clearly enough so if she trod carefully, took her time, it'd be okay.

She made a start, and it was easy going. The path was wide but after a while she realised it wasn't sloping down and then it curved to the left. She stopped. *This is wrong. If I turn round and go back...* which is as far as she got. Ahead of her, still blurred by the mist, was a dark shape, wide at the base and tapering towards the top. *Probably a cairn.* But it changed shape again and began getting bigger. As it padded through the mist, she could see it was a huge dog about the size of a calf, thick black coat pearled with dew, long tongue lolling out of its half-open mouth. It stopped a few feet away. Its paws weren't on the path but above it and level with the turf on either side.

It moved closer, so close she could swear she could see herself reflected in its eyes. She couldn't move. *Look away!* she thought, *Don't stare at it direct, it'll see that as a challenge.* She tried lowering her head but as soon as she moved, the dog growled and moved even closer. She could feel an icy cold breeze that was its exhaled breath dancing round her legs. She took a step backwards and then tried lowering her head again. The dog stayed silent and unmoving. She had the urge to turn and run but fought it down. She was terrified but her mind was clear. For months she'd had difficulty concentrating on anything. Words on the page no longer went in; TV was the world looked at through a plate glass window; conversation was just so much pointless blather.

She took another step back and thought, *Mr. Holmes they were the footprints of a gigantic hound!* She took another step back and thought, *It's not real. None of this is real. I'm going mad; you coming? That's what Dad used to say.*

The mist surged like a tide coming in and enveloped the dog and when it receded a few seconds later, the dog was gone. Jean turned and looked behind her. She was almost back to where she'd started from. She glanced back down the path. The dog was still gone so she turned and ran back onto the turf. Her legs were shaking but her mind stayed clear. *It wasn't real. It looked like Black Shuck but it can't hurt me cos it's not real...*

She turned and began slowly walking back along the lip of the depression. She heard a growl ahead of her and the dog came padding out of the mist. It stopped a few feet away and bared its teeth in a snarl. She took a step backwards and the dog became translucent, transparent and was gone. She heard a growl behind her and spun round. It was there now and still baring its teeth.

Her legs gave way and she crumpled to the ground. The turf was wet underneath her and, suddenly, she began to cry. Slowly at first, just her eyes overflowing and hot tears of frustration streaming down her cheeks. She hadn't cried in years not even when her Dad...not even then.

The grief came now, thick and fast, shaking her body the way a terrier shakes a rat. Her hands clawed at the turf. She fell onto her side, brought her knees up under her chin and lay there, foetal, blinded, sobbing.

"Eh come on now, our Jean, don't take on so."

It was Dad. His voice. Crystal clear. She froze mid-sob, opened her eyes. The dog was close now. Right by her. It lay down next to her, stretched its neck and licked her face; not wet though; dry and warm. The dog moved sideways, closer, close enough to feel its warmth pressing against her. She curved her arm over empty air and thought, *Maybe I'm dead...when I had that fall...*

"Don't be so bloody morbid! Now go to sleep like a good girl."

"Yes, Dad," she said quietly and shut her eyes.

She woke up suddenly from a dreamless sleep, her favourite kind. A sharp shrill noise, it was a whistle and then a voice shouting, "Jean, can you hear us?"

She sat up and shouted back, "I'm here!"

The mist had lifted and now she could see three men coming up the path towards her. They were all dressed in bright orange waterproofs and the one in the lead shouted, "Stay put. Have you injured yourself?"

"No," she shouted back standing up. "I'm fine."

The men reached her. One of them had a flask of hot, sweet tea and handed her a mug with the words, "Get that down you. Warm you up." Followed by, "Have you got no gloves?"

"Forgot them," said Jean, "but I'm fine. Feel," and reached out and pressed the back of her hand against his face.

The man frowned. "You're warm as toast," he said and then pressed the back of his hand againgst her forehead. "No temperature though." He smiled, "You must have a passionate nature." He paused then added, "Colin by the way."

And as they walked back down, he said "The barmaid at The Black Dog phoned and told us you were well overdue. Get caught in the fret did you?"

Jean nodded.

"I'm glad you had the sense to stay put then. You'd be surprised how many folk don't." He paused again and when Jean merely smiled added, "So did you see Black Shuck then?"

She didn't answer and after a minute's silence he said, "You're very quiet. You all right?"

She smiled, "I'm fine. Never better in fact."

LEGEND OF THE JOGAMMA

by Shashi Kadapa

The child dressed in neem leaves, face smeared with turmeric and vermillion powder, cowries' necklaces swung around her neck, screamed a warning. The old zamindar (landlord) lurched towards her, stiff with anticipation and slapped her. She picked up a sickle and again shouted a warning. She blindly slashed across the throat spouting jets of blood. Then she ran crying and shouting along the temple wall and jumped into the river below. She turned her face at Sanjana as she jumped, and the young face changed to the apparition in her dreams.

It begins

Sanjana jerked awake as something scratched the window. She shone her torch and the face of an old woman with matted hair, face smeared with haldi (turmeric) and vermillion powder stared at her. The bloodshot eyes pierced at her fiercely. A flash of lighting lit the night, and the face was gone. Sanjana shouted and her parents rushed in.

Her father switched on the light to find Sanjana looking through the window.

"I saw the face again. It was right there outside the window."

Her father opened the window letting in the wet forest breeze in.

"Sanjana, there is nothing outside. Look."

The silent dark forest stared back at them. The trees waved in the approaching storm. It was ominous and foreboding and the branches danced flirting with the winds.

"Sanjana", said her mother, "you are imagining things. Do you want me to sleep in here with you?"

The night passed without any untoward event. Sanjana could not sleep as she recalled the face that had appeared in her dreams many times.

The visions started after she had gone to the forbidden graveyard behind the ancient Yellamma temple at Saundatti, a town in Dharwad district, India. She was a history student at the Karnatak College in Dharwad and had gone on a college excursion.

Worried, her parents took her to their family doctor.

Dr. Acharya Bhaskar Rao, physician and a family friend was also a scholar in the history of South India and Karnataka State, the culture, gods and goddesses, and the lore. Sanjana spoke of her dreams and the face.

He stared at Sanjana pensively, then reached to a bookshelf and pulled out an album, turned the pages and showed her a picture. It resembled the apparition that she had seen in her dreams and in the window.

"Yes. Looks like her. Who and what is this?"

"This is a picture of a jogamma, devadasi. Dev means god and dasi means servant. The jogammas are married to goddess Renuka and some of them are forced to serve as prostitutes in the temple."

"What is a jogamma?"

"Let me tell you the fable."

Fable of the Jogamma

The doctor began. "The lore begins in Bhagavata Purana much before the Mahabharata epic. Renuka was the wife of sage Jamdagni and they had five sons and lived on the banks of the River Malaprabha that flows by Yakama Hill, where you went for an excursion. The sage demanded absolute piety from his wife. To please her husband, Renuka tied a cobra into a Shimbi, the roll of cloth that women place on their head to carry pots and baskets. Then using her devotion, she made a pot from sand and carried water in it to her ashram."

The doctor continued. "One day, Renuka saw cavorting gandharvas and apsaras, male and female heavenly beings. She felt a tinge of wistfulness and imagined that she was in place of the apsaras. Her vow of chastity broke. The cobra slithered off her head and the sand pot crumbled drenching her in water."

The doctor paused to have a sip of water and then continued. "Sage Jamdagni was incensed at his wife's infidelity and ordered his sons to behead her. All except Rishi Parashurama, the sixth avatar of Vishnu refused. Parshurambeheaded her with his axe. Pleased, the sage granted him a boon and Parushurama asked that his mother be brought back to life. Renuka became revered as goddess Yellamaa and settled in the forests of Saundatti hills. She attracts women and men devotees. Women become jogamma and men are eunuchs, called jogappa. They abhor violence and will never harm you as such acts would be against the tenets of Renuka Devi. The temple was built in pre-historic times and modified by successive kings."

"This is a myth, a fable. What has that to do with me?"

"There was a case that I read about in government archives during research. About 100 years back, a young village girl, Kamala, was forced to become a jogamma. On her first night, when she was to sleep with a man, the girl killed him and committed suicide in the Malaprabha River. Her old guardian died some years later and was buried in the forest in an unmarked grave. Legend says that the old guardian who was a jogamma haunts the forests seeking a young girl who she will claim as her ward."

Sanjana sat quietly. The doctor asked, "Did you disturb any grave or try to unearth anything in the forest?"

She hesitated for a moment then blurted, "Yes. Behind the temple ruins by the river was a very old graveyard. I found an idol and put it in my backpack. Here it is."

She pulled out a small statue, grey with grime and dust.

The doctor studied it and said, "It is the idol of Devi Yelamma and is made of panch-dhatu, five metals. You should have let it be where it was."

"What can I do now? Should I go and put it back?"

"Do not do that. The forest and the hills are full of duṣṭaśaktigaḷuevil spirits, daityas, and unfulfilled beings. They will possess you."

Sanjana was 19, an age of rebellion and curiosity.

"Evil spirits? I would like to know more."

Sighing, the doctor rummaged in his cupboard and pulled out an old cloth bound book. "This book describes all the ancient evil spirits. You may want to read about them."

They went back and Sanjana spent the day reading the book and examined sketches drawn many decades back.

*****

After a couple of days, the papers reported the suicide of the Doctor. The doctor had smeared haldi and vermillion on his body, and pictures of jogamma and Yellamma were littered in the room.

The whole community was shocked. No foul play was suspected, and the case was closed.

Sanjana wondered. Did he die because he spoke to me about the jogamma? Will my father and mother be next? Why do I get these visions?

Anger, outrage, and worry filled her, and she was determined to find out more.

*****

She received a parcel the next day. The doctor had couriered it before his suicide. She opened it and saw a number of typed pages and read the cover page.

It said, "Sanjana, I have tried to visualize and recreate the story of Kamala. The story will help you to understand the situation you face."

Late 1800s

She read the story. The village of Chulki in Dharwad district had not seen rains since three years and the panchayat, village community elders, sat under the banyan tree, discussing their predicament.

"Goddess Yellamma must be very angry. We have not carried out the varas, rituals, since four years ago. That is why she has withheld held rains and water."

One of them spoke. "We have to dedicate a girl to Yellamma Devi who shows signs of divinity."

None was willing to give up his daughter as a devadasi. They eyed young Kamala of the lower Kuruba caste grazing sheep.

The sarpanch, village head, beckoned an old jogini Shantawwa and whispered in her ears. The old crone removed some sap from a datura plant, mixed it with dirt and approached the girl who smiled back.

Patting her head lovingly the crone smeared the sap in the child's hair entangling the strands into a mat.

Then started shouting. "Look Kamala hair is turning into jatha (matted hair). Devi Yellamma has selected her as an offering." Then she prostrated at the child's feet.

According to superstitions, when the devi selects a child to be her servant, the first sign is matted hair.

Other sarpanch members fell at her feet and started shouting in loud voices.

"Jogamma, Jogamma prakataaadalu (Jogamma has appeared)."

The news spread and the parents came running, the poor father was reluctant to force his child to become a devadasi. But poverty is evil, it is powerful, it bends even the fierce pride and love of a father, and he reluctantly agreed to give up his daughter.

Shantawwa was appointed as her guardian until the child attained puberty.

Kamala becomes a Jogamma

They prepared her as an offering.

At the temple, Shantawwa and other retired joginis stripped her and placed garlands of flowers, tied bevu (neem) leaves around her chest and waist. Haldi and vermillion powder was smeared on her body. The dholak drum kept hammering a rapid beat and an old woman played the ek-tara, a single string gourd instrument, singing songs of praise to the deity.

Camphor pellets and incense sticks were lit and she was led to the seven sacred ponds for a bath. Then she was led inside the temple sanctum. That was the last her parent saw of her. She and Shantawwa were placed in a small common room that they shared with other girls of her age.

*****

Kamala was still a child, but the landlords and the upper caste people watched her lasciviously, waiting for her to gain puberty and grow.

Kamala would often remember her village, the open farms, the forest, herding sheep, her parents and siblings, and cry in Shantawwa's arms.

As per traditions, jogammas are married to the deity and not allowed to wed. Shantawwa adopted the child as her own, looking at her as the source of income in the future. She felt guilty at the deceit she had used on the child.

She often reasoned to herself. How could I refuse the order of the sarpanch? I would be forced to beg. Now I am old, I am forced to bring another girl into this profession.

Kamala sometimes stood on the temple ramparts and looked into the green waters of the river. She was not allowed outside.

Often Kamala would see older girls dressed up in finery led out accompanied by drums and songs. The girls would return the next morning, crying and bleeding with pain and held down while seniors administered bhang to sedate them.

Kamala kills the zamindar

The day came when Kamala attained puberty, and she was readied for her first night. Hefty gifts in grains, fruits and gold were offered by the rich landlords to deflower the virgin.

Kamala was decked up, sedated, and sent along with the crying Shantawwa.

"Kamala. You have to go into that room and do what the rich man inside asks. Just lie down quietly and it will be over in a few minutes."

The middle aged drunk zamindar with a massive pot belly took the girl into a special room in the temple complex. An oil lamp fluttered dimly, casting ominous dark shadows across the room.

The drugs had worn off and Kamala stood shivering with fear.

Kamala screamed and he slapped her sending her reeling into a corner. He advanced, hand raised to strike again.

Farm implements were stored in the corner. Kamala picked up a sickle and stood glaring at him.

"Stay away from me. I will kill you."

Laughing, he lurched at her.

Desperation and fear goaded her. She slashed blindly cutting his member and his throat.

Bleeding and choking, the zamindar stumbled back and Kamala opened the door and bolted as the shocked temple workers watched.

She ran through the door and jumped into the river. Her body never floated to the surface and the villagers said that the river claimed her.

Shantawwa was inconsolable and lost her mind. She wandered around the temple and the villages searching for her ward. She died some years later and was buried in the forest along with an idol of the Devi. The evil landlord was buried in the graveyard near the forest edge. There are myths that he holds Kamala's soul captive forever.

The British Government that ruled India in those days stepped in and banned the devadasi system. However, it continued furtively.

Sanjana is infested

Sanjana had started humming the chant of "Udho, Udho, tai Yellamma (hail greetings mother Yelamma)." The jogammas recited this chant in the temple and when they went seeking alms.

Some of the strands in her hair had matted. No amount of shampoo and oil could untangle the knots. She tried cutting them off, but the scissors slid off.

One morning, she heard the doorbell ring. An old Jogamma stood at the door seeking alms. She held a bamboo basket with a small idol of Yellamma.

The crone kept chanting her mantra and extending her jholgi bag, asking for alms. Sanjana filled a vessel with rice grains and poured it in the bag. Blessing her, the crone smeared a pinch of haldi on Sanjana's forehead.

Feeling dizzy, Sanjana cried out and fell in a swoon. Her parents rushed in, gathered her and put her on the bed. She kept muttering incoherently about jogamma and Devi Yellamma.

A compelling force spoke to her.

"Baaa (come), we are waiting. It is time. Release us."

Sanjana goes the temple

Sanjana brooded but kept quiet. She got up early next morning and took a sickle from her father's tool shed. She left a note on her pillow, packed the sickle and the idol into her backpack, and set off to Yellamma Gudda hill to return the idol to the grave.

The temple was chockfull due to the full moon, she managed to get a quick darshan of Yellamma, and then set off to the forest.

She used the map from her previous excursion and thought she knew the spot where she had picked up the idol. She wandered around, finally found the path to the grave, and arrived as dusk set in.

*****

The full moon cast a pale, yellow light, and Sanjana was frightened. Her legs ached from the walk and she was hungry and was beginning to regret her decision to come alone and at night.

Countless forest insects chirped with bats and owls flying overhead silently. The path was rough. She remembered that the path went up a hill and then sloped down to meet the river.

The path twisted and turned, and she saw shadows closing in. She ran up the path and stood panting beside a small stream that flowed into the river.

The shadows reached out to grab her. She stumbled and fell into the stream bed that was slick with mud and water. Sliding, she grasped at the branches and creepers, tearing them off as she slipped along the crooked stream bed. It turned sharply at one corner and her momentum threw her into a tumble on the bushes.

She got up and stood petrified with horror as she looked at the creature that towered above her. In the moonlight, she saw the large head, horns, and teeth that glistened in a snarl. It smelled of stale water and rotting flesh and it tried to grab her. Even in panic, her mind recalled that this was the malevolent, flesh eating daitya, demon Daka.

Ducking, she ran, stumbling, with the creature grabbing at her hair. Branches crowded her and roots clung at her feet. The ground moved and shifted. She saw cobras rearing with hoods ready to strike.

She ran along the path until she saw the stone pillars that marked the entrance to the graveyard. A mist blew in, covering the place and choking her with a nameless fear. It clogged her senses and she coughed.

Running on, she tripped and fell. The idol tumbled out of her backpack and the creatures backed off hissing and growling. Sanjana picked it up and held it in her hands. It glowed, working as a talisman to ward off the daityas. The demons shrank back when they saw the idol.

Danavas, lower forms of Daka, floated in the night, crowding her to make the idol fall. Her grip was loosening on the idol and she knew that she would drop it any instant. Daka and its minions waited.

Where was the grave? It had a small marker that she had kicked…Where…. yes, there it was, the fallen marker …, there was a hole in the ground from where she had lifted it.

She fell near the hole and brought up the idol. The idol was now glowing fiercely and becoming warm. She pulled out her sickle and left her bag. Her face suffused in the warm light and lit up the demons.

Sanjana pushed the idol to the mouth of the hole. A voice seemed to resonate through the night. Do not leave the idol. The demons will possess your atma soul.

She dropped the idol into the hole and the evil spirits closed in grabbing at her legs and stabbed her. She flayed weakly at the beings with her sickle and felt her life ebbing away.

Something moved in the hole and a hand reached out and dragged her inside the shrouding blackness.

Into the grave of the Jogamma

Sanjana was semi-conscious, incoherent, and hazy as she was pulled by a *devina ghali* wind devil through a labyrinth of tunnels. After some time, the motion stopped and she opened her eyes groggily.

The grim face of the jogamma of her dreams stared at her silhouetted by other beings. In panic, Sanjana tried to get up but firm hands held her.

The crone said, "Hudugi, girl, do not struggle. We are jogammas and will not harm you."

"Who are you? What is this place? Why am I here?"

"I am the soul of Shantawwa. You must have heard about me."

"Oh, but you died more than 200 years ago!"

"Yes hudugi. You and we all are in pretyoni, the nether world where the soul resides after death."

"Death? Am I dead? But I can see and speak with you."

"Yes. Your soul is speaking to mine."

Sanjana began to cry, just sobs with no tears.

The crone rested her arm on her shoulder. "After death, pretyoni, is the stage where the soul resides for 10 days. On the 10th day, the antyeshthi karma is performed, where the atma enters the realm of the pitriyoni."

Sanjana could not make any sense of this and stared blankly at the woman or her soul.

The crone continued. "The son of the deceased has to immerse the ashes of the dead, at the mouth of Vaitārāṇinadi River. The river flows from the underworld hell of Naraka into the River Malaprabha. Crows are the guardian, and they will carry the soul. Once the offerings are immersed, the soul is liberated and it will enter heaven or hell, depending on the karma. I and a thousand other joginis are trapped in this nether world. We want you to immerse our ashes."

"Why don't you immerse the offerings in the river yourself? Who has trapped you?"

"The evil landlord that Kamala killed. He has formed an alliance with the demon Daka. They guard the dwar, the gate out of the pretyoni spirit realm that leads to the mouth of Vaitārāṇi river."

"Even in this world you are very well informed. Why did you kill the doctor?"

"We are non-violent. It was Daka and other evil spirits."

"What has this to do with me?"

"Hudugi, you upset Kālbhairav, the keeper of time, when you picked the idol. You were pulled into this vortex."

"What can I do to escape?"

"You will have to kill Daka and escape from this world. The king of crows will accompany you and you can give us salvation."

"What? Kill the daitya!"

"Yes. If you set our souls free, then a thousand jogammas and our Devi will bless you and give back your life."

"Why don't you kill it yourself and set me free?"

"We are non-violent and cannot hurt anyone. Kamala killed the zamindar in fright."

"How can I alone fight the demons? I do not have the strength."

"We have been vested with limited divine powers and will give them to you. You will not become invincible and will feel pain, but you can fight. If you show true faith, strength and courage, Sage

Parshurama will come to your help. However, inner courage and strength of character are vital. Do not let us down."

Sanjana felt angry, resented the evil Daka and the zamindar who had imprisoned these women. She was young and an activist in her previous life. Anger boiled through her at the fate of these helpless devotees.

"Amma. I give you my word. I will fight these evil spirits and free you."

As if on cue, the mass of jogammas bowed down with their palms folded in a namaskar. A black crow sat on a rock and cawed in response.

"Dhanyavada, thanks. We are waiting for more than 200 years for a champion to free us. Hudugi, you can use your sickle. I will bless it. Are you ready?"

Sanjana pondered for a moment. How can I fight these demons? What if I fail these women? Well, she reasoned to herself. She was already dead, so what more could happen?

"All right I will do it." She held out her sickle and stood ready.

The jogammas applied turmeric on her face, put a garland of cowries around her neck, stood in a circle, and chanted the holy mantra of Devi Renuka.

Sanjana felt a surge of energy and power and felt the sickle vibrate. She started walking along the river to the yonder with the crow as her guide.

Innumerable fires and flashes from lava flows shed light in subterranean world.

The crow led her through caves of boiling hot, acidic streams that bubbled, sending out toxic vapors. With her powers, she stepped through them unhurt.

Sanjana fights the Gaṇḍabheruṇḍa

As she walked, a huge bird swooped down on her and grabbed her by the waist in its talons. The crow cawed a warning, but the bird held her tight and flew through the tunnels, twisting and turning as it flew up rocks and crevices.

It was the dreaded evil alter ego of Gaṇḍabheruṇḍa, the twin headed Garuda, vehicle of God Vishnu. While Garuda was worshipped as a god, this was the evil side.

It craned its two necks down trying to eat her with hooked beaks braced with sharp teeth. It finally settled down on an escarpment and turned towards her, the head moving sideways like an owl as it judged the distance. The crow dove at the creature pecking it on the side and the belly.

The Gaṇḍabheruṇḍa pecked with one beak and tried to catch the crow with the other. Sanjana wriggled, slashed out with her sickle, and rolled out of the talons. She leaped aside, the beak hit a rock that shattered, and pieces fell into the chasm below.

The bird jumped and tried to cut her in its giant talons. She swung the sickle, severing one toe. The bird squealed in pain and rushed at her, wings fluttering, and pecking with both beaks in painful fury.

Sanjana ducked the first charge, went underneath, and swiped at its throat, bringing out fountains of sticky green ooze. The bird thrashed and backed off hopping to the edge of the rock. Alas, it moved too fast and tumbled into the chasm where it disappeared. Sanjana and the crow sidled into a crevice to watch for the bird.

After a few minutes, she got up looking askance at the river that flowed far below. How was she to get down?

The crow flew along, helping her find easy handholds, and rock-strewn paths. Finally, they were just above the river that flowed close to the precipice on which she stood. She had to swim to the bank on the other side across the ravine.

Fight with the makara, crocodile

The river flowed silently but with a deadly force, the undercurrents moving in many different directions. Sanjana felt that she would be torn apart as she swam through the currents.

Something caught her legs in a firm grip, huge jaws twisting her leg and dragging her into the water. The crow cawed over them.

It was a monstrous makara, a crocodile mad with hunger.

Her footing unstable, Sanjana fell into the water and was dragged beneath. Her powers allowed her to breath underwater and she turned around to see the bloodshot eyes of the crocodile.

It grasped her by the leg and dragged her deep into the river. It opened its mouth to get a good bite. As the crocodile started opening its mouth, she kicked the jaws with full force and freed her leg.

She dove under the beast and slashed the soft underbelly.

Hurt and stunned, the crocodile turned over and swung its massive tail. The tail caught her and she was flung out of the water and landed on the bank. The crocodile then charged, scampering swiftly from the water, jaws wide open.

Behind her was the bank that led to an open expanse. Sanjana bolted, jumping over the rocks and putting the beast behind her. She could see a circle of light ahead.

Fight with Daka

The crow sat on rock some distance away from the light. It cocked its head towards the light and cawed. Sanjana guessed that this was the gateway to the outside world and Daka would be on guard. This was the last fight, a test of her courage, and she would be against demons with timeless experience in battles.

The thing was huge with four arms and stood roaring in fury at this invasion of its lair. The evil landlord and the daitya had merged and stood on the rocks. One arm held a mace, the other a spiked chain, and another a sword. The fourth held a struggling girl, presumably Kamala.

A large number of jogammas knelt chained behind the creature. Daityas and danavas tortured them, pushing red hot spikes across their bodies, violating them in all possible ways.

It roared, "Ha hudugi, come and join my harem. You are mine for all eternity."

Adrenaline coursed through Sanjana, the sight angering her. "Eternity? You worry about the next few minutes after which your soul will go headless to Naraka."

Angered, the creature hurled the long, spiked chain that shattered rocks tearing deep furrows on the ground. Sanjana ducked and the spikes tore at her back. She had to get close underneath the creature. Its long reach would certainly cripple and enslave her.

As it raised the chain to strike again, she ducked and scurried, hiding behind a rock. The chain changed direction and smashed the rock, exposing her. She ran fast under the legs and slashed with her sickle, cutting deep gashes on the legs.

The creature roared with pain, jumped a few paces and brought the mace with full power on her head. She lifted her sickle to block. The force of the blow made her cry in pain and pummeled her into the ground.

"Ha, hudugi, ready to give up. I do not want to dismember you. Surrender like all those girls behind me."

"Never!" She jumped up and slashed with her sickle into his chest, drawing out green goo.

Hurt and surprised, the daitya slashed with his sword across her stomach. As she doubled down in pain, it rushed in flailing the mace and sword.

Sanjana rolled aside as the weapons broke the rocks. She quickly held his arm and jumped on his head and hacked with her weapon. It dropped the mace and reached with the free hand. She slid and hung on his neck near the putrid face and slashed at this throat.

Dropping the girl from his fourth arm, the daitya grabbed at Sanjana, catching her legs. He dangled her in front, gloating and laughing.

"Aha, Hudugi. I got you. My underlings are waiting. When they start torturing you, you will beg for mercy."

Sanjana cut and slashed at the fingers severing the digits and it leaped back very angry and thundering.

The battle continued with each striking furious blow on the other.

But this was an unequal battle. Sanjana was tiring, for while the jogammas had blessed her with power, there was a limit. Yet, she fought back with her sickle until she lost her grip on the weapon. When that was gone, she picked up rocks to fight the beast.

If the fight had taken place in the upper world, paeans would be written about her bravery. But this was patal loka, there was none to witness her bravery, except the terrified captives.

At one point, she stood spent and unable to raise her arms. She felt sad that as the last hope of the jogammas, she had failed them.

The creature struck her, and she fell, unable to move. It placed a massive foot on her chest roaring and snarling its victory. It raised its sword to behead and send her soul for all eternity into naraka.

A flash of light and thunder sounded. Through hazy eyes, Sanjana could make out a fiery sage in a dhoti and top knot and with an axe standing over her. The diatya shrunk back cowering in terror.

"Daka. You have tortured enough souls of my mother Renuka Devi's devotees. I Parshurama, will end this terror you have brought."

It was the great sage Parshurama of ancient lore, invincible, and with great powers over all beings of the three worlds. As Shantawwa had promised, he came to the rescue when Sanjana fought bravely.

The sage flashed his axe sending the daityas head tumbling into the darkness of naraka. The he looked down at the fallen girl and spoke in Kannada language.

"Dhairyaśāli yōdha huḍugi, nim'ma śauryadinda nānu prabhāvitanāgiddēne. Nanage varavannu kēḷi. (Brave warrior girl, I am impressed by your valor. Ask me a boon)."

Sanjana felt a surge of energy, all her wounds healed. She prostrated in front of the sage and prayed.

"Nannannu ish ṣivār āśīrvadisi, jōgam'marige mōkṣa nīḍi nannannu biḍugaḍe māḍi" (Bless me rishivar, give salvation to the jogammas and release me)."

" Āddarinda irali. Tatastu (So be it. Thatasthu)."

The sage disappeared in a flash and the gateway opened. She quickly scrambled and grabbed the prized sickle.

Souls of the thousand jogammas were swept through the waters to the outside world.

Sanjana swooned and was carried by the river outside and she drifted to the riverbank.

Escape and salvation

Dawn was breaking as Sanjana stirred, still groggy. Events of the past few hours were hazy. Did she really experience them? Was it a fantasy? Who would believe her if she told people that she had fought and vanquished a fierce demon of the underworld?

Well, at least she still had the sickle.

She saw her father and a search party running at her.

"Sanjana. Why did you come here alone? Foolish girl. Are you all right?"

Through bleary eyes, she glanced across the Malaprabha River.

The souls of a thousand jogammas shimmered on the water. They raised their hand in blessings and bowed down in a deep namaskar thanking her for releasing them and then disappeared into the forest.

"I am fine, great, never felt better."

--END--

UNDER YOUR FEET

by Sergio "ente per ente" PALUMBO

edited by Michele DUTCHER

Someone once said that hard times could make you bitter or make you more compassionate. And for the duration of such bad circumstances, people around you should have always supported you, or so they were supposed to. Did they really?

The island of Agathonisi, about 10 miles off the Turkish coast with a population of only 200 people, was presently facing an invasion by hundreds of immigrants. This event was largely ignored, however, as it was the big islands situated nearby that really got all the media attention day by day.

With the island's highest point being only 686 feet, and a combined land area of 5,598 square miles - which included the uninhabited islets of Gláros, Kounéli, Nerá, and Psathonísio- the municipality was home to two villages, both inland. The first one, whose Greek name was translated as 'Big Village', was prettier than the second one named 'Small Village'. There was also the island's only port - a settlement consisting of a few hotels and not much more, except for shops for tourists. But it wasn't only that which made the place distinctive these days.

Throughout its history, the island had never been of much importance: having been shortly occupied by the Kingdom of Italy during the early 1900s, it was handed back to Greece from Italy in 1947. Then, not many things happened, undoubtedly, until the present times.

During the past few months, however, the island was becoming important, as a very useful passageway, or a forced key point, and its real place in history was only now in the making. Night and day hundreds of men, women and children coming from the Middle East, arrived on the narrow shores of the island. The locals were sympathetic to their sufferings and gave them food, water and clothing, but there were no facilities to provide for such large numbers.

With one guard and two assistants to watch the coast - who were only trained to register the coming and departure of boats - all that the islanders could do was blow their whistles to keep these newcomers off the main town beach. There were no public restrooms, so it was not surprising that the immigrants relieved themselves wherever they could. The island's doctor, because of the current economic restraints of Greece, had left a few months earlier so there was nobody to deal with health checks or any medical problems.

It was common to find needy people from abroad drying out their clothes on any fence they spotted. They ate in the open, and collected their belongings along the streets, waiting for the right moment to leave that place, so they could continue their desperate journey northward - to the much richer countries of Europe. Many of the locals complained that the tourists were being scared off, so the major source of income of the island was in danger. At times, they even made fires - which had once sparked a forest fire that took many hours and help from outside the island to extinguish.

Only a few news-people had noticed that the tiny Greek island of Agathonisi was really sinking under the myriad of immigrants coming in by boat illegally during the last three weeks from the Turkish coast. Without support from Europe, overstretched local authorities could only rely upon a few teams of local volunteers to prevent disasters and humanitarian issues. Moreover, as increasing numbers of people continued to arrive, the island was getting deeper and deeper into trouble. Beyond that, the local population was becoming angry about the trash scattered everywhere, like very old blankets, plastic bottles, and boxes on the ground. The few newcomers who found a way to escape the policemen - and continue their journey, eventually - left behind old blankets and such before moving on.

Being overwhelmed by poor and desperate immigrants that arrived on their coast every single day, with no end in sight, there was a certainty among the shop-owners that the tourist season was already over this year - even though it was only July. *But there was something else that the authorities were even more afraid of*, though no one spoke about this, and no media had ever covered. At least not so far. And to keep those strange facts concealed, and unbeknownst to the rest of the population at home and abroad, a man had already been sent to do his job. He had been appointed for protecting the secret of the place itself, and of the island's sewers...

Kleisthenes Anthis had black hair that fell around his ears and dull-looking eyes. His clothes were either a little too loose or a little too tight, although he considered himself to be skinny, undoubtedly; nothing ever really fit him correctly. Only the worn-out work uniforms he wore when he was on duty looked good on him. He thought this was probably because he was used to spending most of his time underneath the street level, while making reports or fixing something in the sewage system somewhere, commonly on the smallest islands. Actually, he was also in charge of another task, *much stranger and less known* - a secret he had to keep to himself, according to the rules of the Central Office in Athens and given the importance of the job itself. This other duty was exactly why he had been sent here, not just to accomplish an easy repair task that any other common worker from his company might do.

Kleisthenes was 46 years old, stood nearly six-and-a-half feet tall, had all of his hair shaved off, and two vivid chestnut eyes on a seemingly severe face. He believed he knew far more about the weird and unwholesome than could possibly be good for him. But, having reached this age, there was no chance he was going to change occupations any time soon. He definitely would not be looking around for a new job while Greece was in such terrible economic trouble – as was true for most of the other countries of this part of the world. Without mentioning the bad climate change, the ecological degradation, and the effects on human health of the recent great and unprecedented environmental disasters that Africa and South America were still experiencing. Those inhabitants would soon move from in search of some more livable place, be it in North America or in old Europe, *if these areas might still be reputed good enough nowadays…*

Several work activities commonly brought workers like him into contact with sewage and sewage products, and that meant trouble many times, but his peculiar duties made him face a completely different set of problems. After all, his job was especially meant to protect society, even if what was being protected was a secret and not living people. Of course, in doing so, he and the others like him did a great service which helped common citizens to have a better life. The service he provided also allowed the average person on the street to be more at ease and without worries on their mind night and day, and he liked to think of it this way.

It was certainly better to allow the rest of the population of his country think that they lived in a world that they had freely shaped to meet their needs and will, staying at the top of the food chain – on top of all the other known creatures - instead of knowing they resided in places that frequently bordered with darkness and other unspeakable truths, never to be publicly revealed to everyone. Perhaps you would agree as well, maybe, if you were aware of exactly what we were discussing? Perhaps it would be hard to say, as you can't figure out what's the matter so far, undoubtedly.

As the middle-aged man passed three people who were easily recognizable as immigrants because of their worn-out clothes and their facial features, a thought crossed his mind. A strange image hit his fancy while he was staring at them: these refugees were roaming the streets like little shadows that tried to move while remaining unseen. Or so they seemed through his eyes. Strange to say, that way of depicting them was not much different from how he considered what he himself had been sent here to investigate. It was the same way as those creatures who - according to the few who had reputed to have spotted them or laid their eyes on such faint figures - might be considered to be shy, hidden shades that preferred to walk in complete darkness. And for many reasons...

Kleisthenes immediately moved away from those men who were part of the many groups of really desperate immigrants that Turkey simply – and plainly - took the opportunity to get rid of, as if it was just putting out some trash that it didn't care about. For that country, it didn't matter if such people died at sea, or elsewhere, as long as they had left the shore at night and got away from its boundaries, never to return. And never to be heard from again, of course.

The man loved to walk along the beach, well, not directly on it, but along the street that ran next to it:

he had always enjoyed that scenery. The particles coming up from the coast, picked up by the wind, made almost everything in the vicinity a sand color, like a bread-crust-coating that hid tiles and parts of the shrubs. The short-sleeved, white shirt he was wearing let his complexion get a darker skin tone finally, which didn't happen often, given the fact he usually worked underground. Well, today, he went on duty when the sun set, so he had most of the day free to enjoy the scenery and have a good time - maybe even sip a famous zesty *kítro* liquor after lunch.

*****

After eating, the man spent some time relaxing at a small though dignified, Neo-Classical mansion, which had been restored and converted into a restaurant. Located beneath a fruit tree full of mottled drupes and situated next to the center of town, the sunroom had a few outside tables and looked very comfortable and tasteful without being extravagant. That spot seemed perfectly suited to any tourist's needs, and openly invited you to remain there while enjoying your stay. It specialized in seafood and traditional dishes and served a reasonable selection of standard meals and other favorites like *tomatá keftedes*. The man had savored the courses and had been greatly impressed with the job the kitchen had done. Now he just wanted to take a few minutes more to better assimilate what he had happily eaten. He had forced himself to stop gobbling with difficulty, given the tastiness of the food.

As Kleisthenes sleepily dozed in a post-meal nap, a strange message reached him. It appeared on the display of his small, battered satellite tablet that was part of his equipment from work. The poor condition of their present economy and the scarcity of funding for personnel like him didn't let public servants have better devices. The text was not too clear, but it ended this way: 'Call back the Central Office immediately for further details." That was exactly what Kleisthenes did.

"What is the matter now?" the man asked himself. "A change of plan maybe?" According to the instructions he had previously received, he had been sent here just for a common cover-up. Actually, the situation had been a little different from previous tasks he had easily accomplished, as the presence of many immigrants on the island itself, and what that migration had brought along, had made the situation a bit more delicate. And more important, too.

There had always been a few cases regarding a solitary *Eurynomus* that happened to visit, or take up residence in, the sewage system of the islands in that area, but the sum of food it consumed had never been much of a problem, truth to be told. That netherworld demon's tastes in food left a lot to be desired, as an *Eurynomus* usually fed off the rotting skin of dead animals, – or, rarely, of human corpses. So, the creature left nothing behind him but the bony remains of the deceased. Such a legendary being was also reputed to have a second mouth so it could eat huge amounts at a fast speed. Kleisthenes could have confirmed that such hearsay was true, if he had been allowed to speak publicly about it. But he wasn't allowed to do so, the same as anyone else who did this job – whether on an island or on the mainland.

In the past, because of the ancient legends about such creatures and the fear that they might be found in Greek caves and tombs, some villages were reputed to have changed their funerary customs accordingly to prevent their deceased loved ones from becoming food. Many churches would only cremate corpses to better protect and honor their dead. But those scary legends from a time gone by were now only that: *legends no one believed in anymore*. And that non-belief was profitable for many good reasons: to keep the tourists visiting the country all-year-round; to prevent citizens from being scared and openly calling for a strong, though very expensive, action from the government; and to escape some troublesome questions that might consequently arise very soon about the monsters of the darkness, both from ancient times and from the present. These were monsters that still lurked around urban areas, especially at night, benefiting from the darkness and the caves the stretched beneath the surface of a city.

There had always been spotty discoveries of bodily remains, especially of animals - although human remains had been found at times as well. These remnants appeared to be strangely skinless which had occasionally drawn somebody's unwanted attention. It was all consistent with the typical behavior of an *Eurynomus* that had chosen a particular site - be it a sewage system, some caves, or an underground tunnel. This usually happened on an island, as such monster seemed to prefer islands instead of the mainland, the same as many tourists did, after all. It would preferably choose such territory as his main hunting ground because the isolation fit in perfectly with its need for secrecy as it ate the skins of the dead to survive and led its unholy life. It was not much more than that. Most of the time, it was not difficult to deal with such situations for someone experienced like him. This was due to the long-lasting relationships the Central Office had with the local policemen, and the secrecy involved in all of his tasks, anyway.

But this situation was different, taking into account the continuous arrival of so many immigrants on a daily basis, and their staying here under some very unhealthy conditions which, unfortunately, also caused illnesses and fatalities. These new arrivals made everything progressively more difficult. In fact, the number of corpses left on the streets for hours before someone discovered them and took the dead away, or the passing of some old newcomer who had been in hiding unbeknownst to anyone else, posed a serious problem. So many abandoned dead was a clear, strong call for those creatures which then brushed aside their reclusive behavior and became more daring. Such aggressive moves meant increased danger for the local population. All of this might result in an undesired disclosure of everything that had always been attentively kept secret, given their usual practice of going out at night and keeping completely out of sight.

There were now too many hungry, ill, and desperate newcomers which led to too many dead men lying about on the island. Therefore, there were too many chances of a wild *Eurynomus* being spotted somewhere by someone. Some locals might also be attacked or harmed in the process, and that wouldn't be good. Besides, too many corpses that were half-eaten or skinless would cause trouble: they might attract the attention of the media and, finally, even become a matter too big and insidious to deal with quietly.

Simply put, it was okay to let any damn *Eurynomus* be free to do what he had always done and eat the skin of a few corpses so they could live; but this had to occur without anyone else knowing about it and without causing problems. The main office's policy was as simple as that.

When Kleisthenes contacted Dauid, his bearded superior at the office, the words he heard left him very surprised, and worried. In fact, his orders seemed to have changed now and not for the best, resulting in trouble for him. He feared that there would be problems *whether he followed the orders, or whether he didn't execute what he was told…*

"Your duty has changed," the voice from the other side of the phone was explaining. "You not only need to resolve the issue soon and cover the matter, but you also need to catch one of those monsters and bring it back to our offices, using whatever methods you think are best…"

"What? Can you repeat, please, sir?" he cried out in a really incredulous tone. "How…why?"

"There are some people here that want to have one of these creatures at their disposal - to study it, or just collect it, I don't know. Why they want it shouldn't concern us at all. It's all included in the secret part of the last economic agreement our government recently, and forcibly, signed in order to get the funding from Germany, Finland and the other major European countries to save us all from bankruptcy. I can't tell you any more than that. That's enough said on the topic. Anyway, they may ask us eventually to find and capture some of the other legendary, mythic beings that still reside in Greece – *and we know that there are many of them nowadays, even though the citizens are not commonly aware of those*…- and simply hand them over to their representatives, so they can do their own experiments in their laboratories. And our government can't oppose such requests, as a matter of fact," Dauid explained.

"I see…" the man whispered, with a dejected expression that made his face appear partly weird and partly funny in the reflection on the tiny display of the device. He continued in a trembling voice. "Certainly, I'll do my best, but I don't think I could…"

"You have to," the superior cut it short. It seemed clear that he didn't want to hear objections to his orders from that moment on.

"Yes, sir, I'll try…" Kleisthenes stated, and then immediately ended the call. As soon as he was alone, and with his thoughts that already started to trouble his worried mind, he understood that he had been asked to accomplish an exceedingly difficult task, and he wasn't sure he could complete it. It was one thing to cover-up all that had to be kept concealed as was customary under such circumstances throughout the whole country. But it was another matter to take and detain – if that might be the right term to use - one of those creatures. He really didn't know if it was something he could do. *Such an attempt might endanger his health, or even his life.*

*****

Another night began, and Kleisthenes had changed his clothes for the difficult work to be done. And for what might come out of it.

As he sadly thought again of what he had been told by his superior, he watched a few videos showing recent media footage covering the present trouble with the immigrants on the Greek islands. It didn't take him long before he got tired of it all. The man switched off the TV applet as the credits of the last video-news rolled. He had already had enough of all those images about desperate people coming from abroad, and the health dangers the locals and those newcomers were facing on many Greek islands. There was no news, of course, about the lethal danger he himself was going to face soon, underneath the streets, in those sewers, as all of that was meant to remain secret – not only for the time being but also in the future.

He had been thinking deeply for the previous two days, looking for a way to get out of that situation, but with no viable solutions. *'Thing is, I don't know what else to do,'* the man told himself, very regretfully. *'And I can't think of a good excuse for not doing my job.'* He wished that a very bad downpour could occur this evening, filling the roads and stopping most of the activity on the island - so he might have a real excuse to postpone the duty he had been given. Besides, no *Eurynomus* went out when a storm came. Such creatures were said to be able to smell the rain coming, over the beaches, through the wind. But bad weather during that season, on such small island, was so unlikely that he thought would never happen. And then, even if it did, nothing could prevent him from accomplishing his task the next evening, so rain tonight wouldn't make much of a difference actually.

The man poured a glass of water and swished it around in his mouth before spitting it all out. He still had a very bad aftertaste inside. He also wondered if the small *ovelistírio* shop up the road, that served meat on a stick, was open now. Maybe he would be a well-advised to stop and eat something there - or perhaps he could stop at a local *kafeneía* before leaving the small hotel where he was staying. *Or maybe not*, he reconsidered immediately after, *I don't want to upset my stomach, other than having that terrible who-knows-what flavor in my mouth, and that strange smell in my nose...*

*****

Clothing choices, when you went underground, especially for exploring sewers like that, depended greatly on the type of site you were going to enter. Some facts to think about were cave temperatures in the area; how long the trip was supposed to be; and what type of trip it was. A good rule of thumb, according to Kleisthenes, was that a member of a three-person party would stay warmer in the same clothing than they would in a larger group, as larger groups generally moved more slowly and paused more frequently, so they also generated less body heat through activity. In his case, as he was alone, he obviously preferred to have on his worn-out though favorite uniform that kept him dry and comfortable. He took a plastic trash bag stored in his helmet or a blanket in his pack, as he usually did, to provide an extra safety. A pair of gloves and sturdy chestnut boots completed his usual outfit.

As soon as Kleisthenes got to the place where he would start his underground walk, he began removing the manhole cover so as to shimmy down. It was already about 11:30 PM, which was the best time to go into the sewers. In his right hand he had a small metallic *klouví* that was a metal cage which was meant to contain the creature he was going to take soon, supposedly the size of a predatory bird. He also carried a dark dustsheet that he planned on putting all around the cage once he had completed his very difficult task, to prevent any inopportune looks from anyone else in the streets before he brought it to the designated site.

The temperature had slightly dropped at night, but it was still warm and made him visibly sweat. There was a vibrant wind that helped him to breathe better, though it didn't let the man feel more comfortable as he bustled about the manhole to get underground. He easily went down the first duct of those sewers, under the light of his hands-free helmet mounted headlamp, and put the cover back in place again over his head, leaving the entry point closed behind him.

His mind was full of many worries, as he

wasn't sure about exactly what tools to use to capture one of those legendary beings. What he did most of the time was try to find and quickly remove all the skinless corpses he stumbled onto, so as to keep that matter secret, long and short of it. He hoped that he wouldn't get into bloody fights tonight. He knew he was no good at fighting, but he also knew he had to expect the unexpected if he dared to go down into the sewers actually looking for such a hungry monster.

Moving as silently as he could, he gave a glance back the way he'd come in. He made his way unchallenged down into a large room with an entrance to another very long tunnel stretched into the distance. There he stopped. An unending trickling somewhere behind him indicated a lesser leakage not far from his position. The sewage system on the small island wasn't very big, or very old, truth to be told, but it let him easily see the possible dangers of foolishly going too deeply at full speed, undoubtedly. Looking ahead intently, he swallowed hard and decided to proceed.

Following the main tunnel proved to be easy and the clatter of stones under his feet sounded like strange gunshots in the stillness. In that secluded area underneath the town, no faint luminosity coming from the streetlights ever filtered through from overhead. It was strange to think that, when he was a child, he had never dared to enter an empty Venetian-style house in his neighborhood in Athens that was covered with carved stone ornamentation and supposedly full of ghosts, because he was too afraid. His friends, on the other hand, went into the house by the woods during the weekends to have fun, and also have a laugh at whoever might be easily scared. Now that he had grown older, life had brought him to a much more unusual and more troublesome activity.

With each passing moment, he was getting closer and closer to the site he was looking for. It was as though he had crossed over into a completely different world that was very far away from the one of the humans. And he had to be wary if he didn't want to get lost at one branch point or another. As he studied his surroundings, he couldn't shake the sense that the place was studying him as well. Though Kleisthenes thought that maybe he had just gone down too many sewers very similar to that one, and this had begun having some effect on him. The ground in front of him was strewn with old leaves and empty beer bottles, and a damaged doorway at the far end of the tunnel led deeper into the sewage system. The unbelievably poor maintenance of that area both disappointed and upset a professional like him.

His eyes scanned the area, spotting a peculiar

shape nearby, and he knew that there was no possibility of mistaking what it was. The man stepped through the doorway. The air was palpably colder on the other side, smelling of ashes, spilled beer and trash everywhere. He held his flashlight like a weapon because it was endowed with a high-impact plastic body. He also adjusted the headlamp on his helmet for a better view.

There was a body lying on the ground, half washed by the ever-present liquid in the sewers. Its lack of movement and the overall dark complexion under the illumination of his lights made it clear that it was lifeless now. A corpse that some *Eurynomus* probably brought here, recently, to feed upon. How could he doubt it?

As the man moved forwards, a noise from the farthest end of the tunnel was heard, and he moved the light accordingly to meet whatever might be the cause of it. A second of awkward silence passed while Kleisthenes readied himself for what was coming. And then he saw it: an *Eurynomus!* Its size was not bigger than a medium buzzard, and its mouth was still busy devouring the skin of the corpse he had just noticed. Its meal probably consisted of an immigrant from the Middle East that might have come to the island in the last few days before sadly dying alone in the end. It had been found and brought here, wherever the body might have laid when he died. And now, the unnatural feeding process was underway, before his own eyes.

The fact that the monster wasn't distracted by him being there could only mean that it hadn't spotted him yet, or that it happened to be so hungry that he didn't care if any living human was around at present. Food was all that mattered to that creature, and nothing else was of any importance, unless it interfered with in some way.

The legendary being's coloration was like that of a meat-eating fly: commonly depicted as a small creature endowed with large deep eyes and showing its long teeth in a gesture of derision, with black-blue skin and wearing a coat of fox fur that covered its back. It undoubtedly was a deceiving freeloader from the lower world that feasted on dead pickings. That was certainly a very disagreeable show of cruel manners; some bloody acts you wouldn't like to watch in a place like this, surrounded by dim lights, especially at night and alone underground. But the man had to do it. That was why he went down there after the sun had gone down. Night was when an *Eurynomus* usually preyed upon the corpses of the dead immigrants. And this one was used to bringing its targets to a specific site before eating the skin and moving away again, unseen and silent.

Actually, having found it was already a piece of good luck for the clever Kleisthenes. He was going to act immediately before anyone else might, by chance, come around and see that bad sight. Not that he expected any other human to walk this duct underneath street level any time soon.

Though, there was something worse than that: he had to prevent it from feeding at any time in the open, up there. After all, a single body of a deceased individual turning up skinless was strange enough, especially if somebody found it and started investigating - *but a huge heap of recent corpses without skin all assembled together in one place would be much more unbelievable and was bound to attract too many undesired interests*... - if they were ever spotted. This wasn't ever going to happen, at least not as long as Kleisthenes was appointed to such a task, as he took to heart how important his job was.

The creature moved its eyes towards Kleisthenes - maybe curious about the strong luminosity of the flashlight or because of the smell of a living man - and turned its whole attention towards him. At that moment, something happened. Under the unsettling look of that fierce though unnatural beast, the man almost gave a start. Then, unexpectedly, the light of his headlamp, along with his main flashlight, diminished noticeably, swiftly making the area he could see around him smaller and smaller. It was just as if the world was disappearing and he might end up being caught in the middle of the increasing darkness.

Damn it! What was going on? Without wasting time, he went for his secondary lamp, a smaller searchlight dangling at his belt. He knew he couldn't let things stay that way, with no visibility at all, but the other source of illumination, once activated, didn't last for long either.

As soon as all the light was gone, the man remained in that overpowering blackness, listening to the beat of his heart. The whole place was silent, though he didn't think it would stay that way for very long. All he could hear was the whisper of air in the tunnel and the noise of his breathing. It must have been past midnight by now, but it didn't matter to him. What did count was what could be occurring soon...

Something had made all of his lights - the headlamp, the flashlight, and the secondary one he always brought along with him in case of malfunctions - stop operating suddenly. That had not just happened by chance, and he had spotted one of those beings just a moment before. So, could one of those creatures have unexplainably developed the ability to damage or drain energy from the batteries of his lamps from a considerable distance? That thought was unsettling.

Was the creature in close proximity now and did that increasing closeness simply make things worse? Who knows? This was an unprecedented occurrence, though it still wasn't something he couldn't mentally get a handle on. A monster like that lived in dark places and preferred to attack when there was no light around. Could that creature have evolved that useful power over the course of the time, unbeknownst to all humans like him? All of this together added much to the man's increasing worries. He cursed his bad luck. It might also be that the three lights had just died because of other problems, despite such a circumstance being very unlikely; but he didn't think it was just by chance that he had ended up in full darkness now.

Hidden by the oppressing blackness, his hands clutched anxiously at his uniform, though touching himself or his equipment didn't give him any relief, nor make him feel safer. He knew sewers and could move in the dark, so, usually snuck out of a tunnel like this and never managed to get caught, even when things were at their worse. That was how he had previously survived his difficult tasks in the sewers and had done his best work, until today. The present situation looked very different, and more unpredictable, so he really was afraid and doubted that he would escape with his life.

There was only one other source of light he might turn to, it was really short-lived, but nothing else came to his mind. He took out of his uniform the resin light sticks that were part of his disposable equipment. They didn't make a lot of light, but thy were the cheap means that their government let them have nowadays. And the illumination that shone out was very brilliant at first!

He activated a light stick and pointed it at the creature. It shielded its eyes, letting him gain a better position, but he saw, much to his disbelief, that it wasn't just a single *Eurynomus*. **There were two of them**, and they both seemed to be very hungry, both anxious and eager to get to another human skin, be it of a corpse, or even of a living being with blood still flowing in his body!

"What the...damn it!" Those monsters weren't supposed to ever work and go hunting together. *Was it possible that the unusual presence of so many people on that small island, and the subsequent deaths of many ill and elderly immigrants, might have attracted several creatures like that at the same time, given the great amount of targets available?*

This was something that the man would never have expected, and he considered that he had probably underestimated the problem – the same as his superior, undoubtedly - putting him in deadly peril.

Kleisthenes was commonly able to handle one of those monsters, preventing the creature from attacking him as he dealt with stealing a corpse and try to hide it. When he had started out tonight, he assumed the same thing was going to happen, but two of them were too much. An *Eurynomus* moved faster than a young, well-trained, and experienced man, so the task of capturing one of them – as he had been ordered to do - would have been difficult enough. How could he do that with two of them?

He stood up, vehemently rising to his feet. He kept throwing other light sticks and started running to the exit. He was unsure if he could really reach it, though what else could he do now but try?

He raced out of that place and both creatures followed. He was out of breath, in pain, and becoming desperate. In an extreme, desperate gesture, he tried something he hoped he would never have to turn to it, as he was unsure it might work. He tried it only because he had no other options at his disposal now. A tired Kleisthenes took a little jar out of the pocket of his worn-out uniform. He opened the top of it, taking the sticky liquid substance found inside, and covering all the skin of his face, his neck, and his shaved head with the gel.

As soon as he got part of his body covered in the smelly substance, he noticed that the two coming monsters were slowing down, until they completely stopped and didn't try to approach any closer. Then, they started to retreat and disappeared in the farthest recesses of the sewers that no light seemed to be able to reach. He had done it just in time! The man almost couldn't believe it.

He knew, and legend had it, that such beings preferred to feed on corpses where they would strip the skin away, and they were said to rarely attack a living man. But they had grown accustomed to the living, obviously, and would go for a normal man if opportunity arose.

What he had tried had proven to be efficacious. As his nose smelled the sticky substance on his gloves, head, and face, he thought that it was really true, after all: *just like no child in the world, nor a single teenager, had ever liked to eat vegetables willingly, so there was no legendary monster - that just loved meat - which would ever like to feed on them.* And that was exactly what such liquid taken out of the jar was made of: *sieved greenery!*

As Kleisthenes was recovering from the deep fear that had enveloped him until a moment ago, and was coming to his senses, he sadly considered that things had not exactly gone as he had wanted. He had failed to apprehend one of those beings tonight and there would be consequences for it all. His superior would receive a complaint from some rich North-European big shot. Consequently, he would also soon be blamed, but he had been able to save his own life in the end. At lest that wasn't bad. And it had happened just thanks to that veggie substance kept in the jar, wasn't it unbelievable…?

Who knows, maybe he would try to eat more vegetables at lunch and dinner, an exhausted Kleisthenes considered. As far as he saw, that was a very healthy way to live and it also helped you to remain alive, luckily. Perhaps you would agree with Kleisthenes as a matter of fact. After all, 'luck had to trample under your feet all reason, sense, and understanding'. *Or was it merely faith which Martin Luther referred to in such a very old quote, anyway*?

THE AMAZON PROJECT

by Bernardo Villela

Mauro Silva couldn't imagine why he was summoned to his boss's office, but he went without delay. The door, with the old-fashioned frosted glass that read "MARK JONES, VICE PRESIDENT," was open.

"Silva, this is about the Amazon Project. You speak the language, right?" Jones was referring to Portuguese. Mauro Silva had worked for Fulcrum Paper for nearly eight years and he knew that if Jones remembered he could speak "The Language" that was enough of a win, what language was irrelevant.

Fulcrum had been facing issues with their Brazilian logging operation: arson and the suspicious deaths of some workers onsite, suspected murders.

"Our man on the ground quit. São Paulo is no help. Americans and Europeans go so rarely they think they can do what they want. All I got was some nonsense. What is that?" Jones asked, indicating an email. "Bull-tits? Boy-Tits?"

Mauro recognized the word.

"Boitatá, a local superstition. I'll get to the bottom of it."

That was the only answer he could give. Whether or not it was truthful, Mauro didn't know. Sure, he could speak Portuguese, but he couldn't speak their language, he came from a different world.

Reticence aside, Mauro left the following day on a nearly twenty-four-hour trip: Dallas to Houston to São Paulo to Manaus to a riverboat. It was only on the short cross-state jaunt that he relaxed and read a story. The length of the trip stripped his nerves raw. He feared not just for his safety if unsavory elements were actually threatening the work, but also failure. Fulcrum wasn't agro business, clearing these trees to create pasture, the biggest deforestation offender by far. So why was their operation targeted?

All along the Amazon River, Mauro was serenaded by cicadas with a far more grating, far less percussive call than he was used to. It added to his unease. On arrival at the worksite, he met with Jefferson — the new local foreman and like many Brazilians, his forename was a US president's surname — who showed them the burnt ruins. Ecoterrorists would be inclined to sabotage to company's equipment, Mauro thought, not raze all these trees.

Alternatives didn't seem to make any more sense, Mauro then asked: "Where are the nearest natives?"

"Indians? Close, but not that close. And why would they do this?"

Exactly.

The crew was brand-new, but they knew what happened to the last workers. It was hard to motivate them. Mauro had to figuratively crack the whip, an unfortunate echo of the past: he, a white man, threatening the livelihood of Black and mestizo workers.

These aren't slaves, but how free are they? They don't want to cut down the trees, but they want to feed their families, and the trees won't feed their families.

Mauro had never had to make such a choice, but he had made a choice. He had another job offer that aligned more with his convictions, but the money was better at Fulcrum Paper.

Mauro went by Maury at home. He didn't mind the Maury Povich jokes, nor the thought of being married to Connie Chung. In the office he was Silva and felt like as much of an outsider as he felt here.

Yet, during his first full day on the job overseeing the site, things went well. They didn't offer the laborers overtime but would work them more hours the first few days to make up for lost time.

The sun was setting when he called an end to the first day. Many acres had been cleared and he only felt ambivalence. He didn't have a family to feed, but he did have a job to keep.

As the men were packing up and leaving, Mauro looked over at the tree-line where their work would start tomorrow. Throughout the day, when he'd had a minute, he'd ask people what they heard about the fires and the alleged murders. Either they didn't know, or they weren't saying. Mauro wasn't surprised. And his real job was to get production back on track, not play Sherlock.

A sliver of orange and yellow light remained in the sky, but an indigo darkness was rapidly falling over the worksite. He was snapped out of his reverie by a cacophony of the rainforest's nocturnal chorus of birds, insects, and primates hailing the arrival of something large. And it came, slithering out from between the trunks was a massive snake.

It had the large scales of a green anaconda and the diamantine head of a boa constrictor but was larger than both by far in girth and length. Its skin was yellow with dark orange markings shaped like leopard spots.

All along its length the snake combusted. Its serpentine form now a contiguous chain of fireballs that approached Mauro and the men trying to get home.

What Mauro dismissed as a local superstition, the boitatá, now came his way at an unnatural speed.

The boitatá's sinuous motion amazed Mauro, it was far too effortless given its size. Passing the stack of felled lumber, its tail touched it. Under normal circumstances the flame would smolder for a time before catching and spreading, but even its fire was supernatural and scaled the lumber rapidly and spread across creating an impromptu bonfire.

Mauro started running. He's always been fast. He used to play soccer and still ran on his lunch break. He was sure that reaching the truck meant that he was safe.

The burning smell intensified, and pain shot through his body. He'd been set alight! Mauro dropped and rolled. The conflagration snuffed. He coughed. When his eyes opened, he saw fangs surrounded by fire darting at his face. He was hypnotized by the snake, its lambent glow lit his face, and immobilized him. Within him his breath caught, nerves electrified his body stiffened. The snake's head engulfed his existence. Benumbed, heat and venom plunged him into darkness.

*****

When the owls, nightjars, and bellbirds had quieted and the sun rose on the worksite Mauro's neck had been mauled, his body moved aside by the skeleton crew that still had to work to survive while they could. Through the underbrush a large groove that followed the boitatá's path could be seen. Most who would see it outside this community would not understand it or believe what it was if you tried to tell them.

As they were getting started the youngest worker on the site was worried.

"Jefferson, what do we do?" he indicated Mauro.

"The Americans will find out soon enough. Cut down the trees while you can, you gotta eat, don't you?"

KINEPIKWA

by Andrew M. Bowen

The tired old man lay down on his bed and blinked his bad eye. At times, he thought he would go insane from the pain of its neuralgia. Of course, dealing with the Army of the Tennessee could also drive any man insane.

"Bragg? How could the man be so pusillanimous?" Jefferson Davis reflected. Chickamauga was the only battle in which the Confederates fielded a larger army, only the efforts of General George H. Thomas prevented utter destruction of the Union forces, and Braxton Bragg refused to follow up what could have, should have been the greatest, the most glorious Confederate victory of the war. However, Bragg certainly had some bunglers beneath him. *"Not Leonidas, though. As much as he argues with Bragg, I cannot believe he would conspire against his superior. I've known him nearly 40 years, ever since our West Point days."*

The president closed his eyes and massaged his temples. Who could replace Bragg? That popinjay Beauregard? *"I can't trust him."* Joe Johnston? Davis didn't trust him either. Despite their friendship, he wasn't sure if Leonidas Polk, "The Fighting Bishop," would be quite up to snuff. *"God help the Confederacy, Bragg may be our only hope. If only he would fight."*

"The Great White Father is having troubles."

Jefferson Davis sat up in astonishment because the door was supposed to be locked. He saw, standing two feet away from his bed, a Choctaw woman garbed in a beaded headband and blouse, breeches, and moccasins made of deerskin. A medicine bag hung at her side.

"How did you get in here? What do you want?" Davis began to lose his efficient temper. He didn't want to deal with uninvited guests, especially when he was trying to deal with the aftermath of Chickamauga, especially when they were of an inferior race.

"Things do not go well for the Johnny Rebs, do they, Great White Father?"

David was struck temporarily speechless at the woman's temerity. He sprang up even though he did not want to offer violence to her. He noticed she wasn't smiling.

"My friend, if you have entered this room for no other purpose than to comment upon our country's misfortunes, please leave. I should have the guards eject you." He wondered where they were.

"Marse Robert was beaten at Gettysburg. He is now fighting along the Rapidan, and it doesn't seem likely he'll advance again. Vicksburg is lost. Knoxville is lost. Corinth is lost. Memphis is lost. New Orleans is lost."

"I am well aware of our reverses, and I am quite confident we will ultimately prevail. We will win our freedom, madam. We will be independent. Now I ask you to leave. I must think about a speech I have to make in Atlanta.

"Politicians do not like to hear it, Great White Father, but there are more important things than speeches." She smiled for the first time. "The Confederacy's approaching defeat for one."

"There you are in error. We have the will. We have the finest troops in the world. We will not be beaten."

"The Johnny Rebs just lost their best chance to defeat the Yankees. You cannot get supplies from across the Occochappo, the great waters you call Mississippi. Only two ports are left, Mobile and Wilmington. The Great White Fathers and Mothers of Europe do not seem likely to intervene. Many in the

Confederate Congress regard you with as much kindness as they regard the Yankees." She glimpsed the rage on Davis' face. "As pleasurable as it might be, I did not come here just to taunt the Great White Father. I offer a path that will lead to victory."

Davis studied the woman's face and wondered if she were mad. However, there was something in those eyes, and he had to admit her analysis of the Confederacy's fortunes held too much truth. She appeared to be more astute than most members of the Confederate Congress, not that that was any great trick. "All right, madam. For the nonce, I will accept that you are not mocking me. What is your name, and how to you propose to help our nation?"

"My name is Shadow Owl, and I am a medicine woman of the Choctaw. I intend to help the Johnny Rebs by giving them their greatest weapon."

Thinking about Joe Johnston and P.T.G. Beauregard and the poor morale of the Army of the Tennessee had put Davis in a testy mood. "You do this out of the goodness of your heart, no doubt?"

"By no means. We want the Confederacy to cede us, all of the first nations, Oklahoma as our own. We are willing to let your people have Arizona and New Mexico in exchange for a free hand with the other lands west of the Occochappo. We forfeit all claims east of the river.

"The nations will also forfeit any claims against the Confederacy for the property some of us held before we were driven west."

Davis stared at her in amazement. He could not find his tongue, an unusual occurrence for him.

"Naturally, the Great White Father doesn't believe me. If you meet me at the Pink Knob — it is two days ride from here — I will show you."

"I am a very busy man. Can you not describe this weapon to me?" Much against his will, Davis believed the medicine woman might have something that could aid the Confederacy, or at least believed this. Given the Confederacy's plight, he could leave no stone unturned.

"I prefer to show the Great White Father. Your eyes will be far more convincing than my words."

*****

Two days later, Jefferson Davis and his servant Robert Brown rode through the beautiful woods of Georgia near the Tennessee line. A refreshing breeze blew and explosions of orange, yellow, red, and magenta mingled with the dark green of the pines. The last flowers of the year brightened the meadows.

The Confederate president wondered again why he was taking this journey. He again speculated if Shadow Owl was mad, but again decided he could not pass up any chance to help his nation, no matter how desperate. However, he admitted to himself that when he looked into those dark eyes, he sensed that she knew things beyond his ken, maybe beyond the ken of any white man. He was also impressed by her assessment of the Confederacy's current situation. He would view this "weapon" and listen. Maybe she did have something that would aid the Confederacy. Davis, an accomplished equestrian, also enjoyed the ride. It certainly gave more pleasure than listening to the Army of the Tennessee's generals practice innuendo and character assassination.

Davis and Brown turned down a rutted lane and approached Pine Knob. Soon, they noticed a woman standing in the shadow of a large pine. When they neared, the figure proved to be Shadow Owl.

"Good afternoon, Shadow Owl."

"Halito, Great White Father."

Davis dismounted and gave his horse's reins to Brown.

"Follow."

He did so and Shadow Owl led him toward the mountain's base, to a spot where two saplings stood over gravel and dead leaves forming a pile against the mountain. Shadow Eagle withdrew a rattle from her medicine bag and shook it to the rhythms of an incantation. Davis almost jumped and did gasp in surprise when the saplings disappeared and the gravel, leaves, and rock swung back to disclose the passage of a cave. He began to believe the woman really possessed a weapon that could aid the Confederacy.

"Enter."

They walked back through the passage, dry limestone without any formations. They passed through a chamber with a large pool of water in its center. Shadow Owl knelt to fill a white man's canteen. They walked down another passage into a large cave.

"Look."

The president gasped in amazement. Against the far wall rested a long skeleton – he estimated its length as at least 90 feet, from the end of its tail to its massive skull with large protruding incisors. A skeletal wing was folded against the side he could see, and it rested on four massive legs.

"That is remarkable. I've heard of such things of course, but I never thought I would see such a magnificent fossil."

"It is far more than a fossil, Great White Father. Watch."

Shadow Owl withdrew some herbs from her medicine bag. She ate some, washing them down with some water from the canteen, and set others alight in a small clay bowl with strange patterns. She used small pebbles of quartz and feldspar to make a circle about the pair. She threw the rest of the water over the fossil. About her neck, she placed a necklace of spent cartridges, pinecones, bits of pottery, and small wooden carvings of deer and eagles. She withdrew another rattle, dried pinecones at both ends of an oak twig, and began shaking it while she intoned another incantation and danced. Each line of the incantation ended in a hiss, and she also hissed at every seventh step. Davis, a brave man, felt the hair rise on his nape.

After seven minutes, or seven eternities, Davis gasped when black mist coalesced about the bones, gradually forming scales. The eyes opened a slit, revealing red orbs, then closed again.

"I can scarce believe it. A living dinosaur!"

"It is not a dinosaur. It is the dragon Kinepikwa."

"A dragon? Those are myths."

"Is that a myth before you, Great White Father? There are more than things on heaven and earth than are dreamt of in your philosophy."

He was dumbfounded for several minutes, almost as astonished at her reference to *Hamlet* as at the dragon. He finally whispered: "Dragons belong to the mythologies of Europe and China."

"Not true. The Choctaw and several other first nations have accounts of dragons. I imagine the black people of Africa and those who live south of America do too."

"How do we control it? As I recall the story of St. George, dragons were inimical to humans.

"Choctaw magic can control it."

Davis hesitated. This was the 19th Century, and he was a rational man who found this hard to believe. He looked again at the skeletal behemoth and thought of the Army of the Tennessee, of the bitter feuding between its generals, of its poor morale.

"All right. When will you first use Kinepikwa?"

"Very soon. I think the Johnny Rebs will need help at Chattanooga."

*****

And they did.

On October 24, 1863, the Union army opened the Cracker Line, about the same time as General Ulysses Grant arrived, and began to break to break the siege of the railway junction. No longer would the Billy Yanks have to fear starvation. More troops came, some of them under the leadership of Fighting Joe Hooker.

On November 4, 1863, Braxton Bragg ordered James Longstreet to take 12,000 gray soldiers to Knoxville to attack the Union forces in control of the city, a move that further weakened the Confederate side.

On November 24, 1863, Hooker led troops through the fog to the top of Lookout Mountain which overlooked Chattanooga across the Tennessee River. Grant and George Thomas watched the Union troops win the Battle of the Clouds.

On November 25, 1863, 20,000 Union soldiers charged across the fields at the base of Missionary Ridge, paused for a few minutes in the rifle pits at its base, the pits the Confederates had abandoned. General Phillip Sheridan drained a pint of whiskey and threw it on the mountain's slope. He led the roaring troops up the mountain to attack their astounded enemies. The Confederates were veterans, but began to waver, and it seemed the Army of the Tennessee was about to sustain one of the worst Confederate defeats of the war.

Then Kinepikwa flew from the southeast to attack. Soldiers of both armies paused in wonder. Its scales of purple, vermillion, navy blue, and gold shone in the afternoon. It appeared to be a multi-colored comet, it flew so fast, and some of the troops thought it the most beautiful thing they had ever seen.

The dragon opened that huge mouth and breathed flames on the slopes of Lookout Mountain and Yankees died by the hundreds. Its great wings created hurricane-force winds that blew other soldiers, including Sheridan, off the mountain to death and horrible injury. Many Yankees fired their muskets, but the balls bounced off those iridescent scales.

Kinepikwa swooped to the northwest, and the Confederates began to cheer while the Union officers tried to rally their troops. Kinepikwa swooped back at Mach 2, sonic booms buffeting the ears of the troops, and again it slew with flame and wind.

The Yankees, brave men who had fought at Shiloh, Vicksburg, Stone's River, and Chickamauga, could stand no more. The fled back to the plain. On the plain, Grant and Thomas tried to rally the Union troops. Kinepikwa made another pass and hundreds more, including the generals, perished in the flames which incinerated the grass. Some artillerists elevated their cannon and fired at the dragon. Most shots were misses, but two balls struck Kinepikwa, one in the left foreleg and one in the tail. But bullets continued to bounce off its scales, causing more panic, and soldiers began to rout.

Confederate General William Hardee saw his chance and ordered his men to charge down the slopes and attack the fleeing Yankees. They did so with enthusiasm. They wanted a smashing victory after the dismal disappointment of Chickamauga. Hardee's men reached the plains and attacked their foes to the eerie accompaniment of the Rebel Yell.

The combination proved too much for the men in blue. They threw down their muskets and ran back to Chattanooga, some diving into the Tennessee River to swim across. One young private from Minnesota looked in horror as Kinepikwa landed near him, breathing more flame at the Union troops. The private and others fired at the dragon, but with a swing of that great tail many more fell.

Kinepikwa took two limping steps and began chewing with great pleasure one of the burnt bodies. The private could barely move since his leg and two ribs were broken. He watched in helpless horror as the dragon devoured another blackened corpse. He screamed and prayed: "O God deliver me from this evil. Don't let me be eaten, dear, merciful Lord."

The dragon looked at him with those enormous glowing crimson eyes and chided: "You need not worry. I prefer my food cooked."

*****

After Kinepikwa assailed the Union forces beneath Lookout Mountain, the Confederates moved north. The Yankees had seen the dragon and abandoned Chattanooga. They scattered before the invading force, especially after Kinepikwa attacked a small force near Athens, Tenn. A few days later they had little trouble driving the Yankees from Knoxville.

Joseph Pemberton returned to Vicksburg and the Confederates besieged it. The Yankees had left only 5,000 troops to guard the town, so important to commerce on the Mississippi. They could not leave except by river after Pemberton's men had invested the town. When they entered the trenches to defend a Confederate assault, Kinepikwa appeared and burned down men. The Confederates took the works when the Yankees retreated into Vicksburg, and the commanding officer soon surrendered.

The Yankees used that fabled ingenuity in New Orleans. They impressed freed slaves to haul cannon to the tops of buildings. They strung heavy hawsers, both of rope and steel, from roof to roof to make huge nets. They waited with a terrible and fearful patience.

On a moonless light, Kinepikwa entered the Mississippi 20 miles north of New Orleans and swam underwater to the city. It poked that massive head above the water and set all the Yankee ships afire. As the Yankees scrambled to put out the flames, it crawled ashore and slithered through the streets like a great snake, breathing flames at the blue-coated men and rending them with fang and claw.

"Come on, you gray maggots. Fight for your freedom if you be men."

The Yankees on the roofs had trouble depressing their guns, and Confederates rushed out from hidden places where muskets had been hidden. They fired with enthusiasm, eager to revenge the town's occupation. The Billy Yanks were brave, but no match for Kinepikwa and the Rebels, and, once again, New Orleans was a Confederate city.

*****

Jefferson Davis was surprised when the visitor was announced. General Robert E. Lee had been communicating by letter, and those missives were usually informative enough. Still, there was no officer he would rather see. He thoroughly liked and respected Lee, not least because he did not quarrel over trifles like Joe Johnston and Beauregard.

"Pray be seated, General."

"Thank you."

"How are things along the Rapidan?"

"Our horses could use more forage, but the men are getting more to eat. Those people have assumed a defensive posture, I think to protect Washington. The morale of our troops is very fine."

"No doubt they are inspired by our success out west."

"I think many of them are, Mr. President. However, I question the means by which we are securing those victories."

"What do you mean, sir?"

"Mr. President, we are using a dragon. I must confess myself astounded that one still survives. However, that is not important. I need not remind you of what creature is mentioned in St. John's Revelation. I am afraid this creature is from the Pit."

"I disagree, General Lee. With my own eyes, I saw Shadow Owl bring it to life from a skeleton. Before she cast a spell, Kinepikwa was nothing but a pile of bones. It may be a formidable creature, but I do not think it is the Dragon of the Pit."

"That is still heathen magic, Mr. President. That is not blessed or permitted by God."

"Nevertheless, Kinepikwa will most likely grant us the victory we week, the victory I believe Almighty God has ordained for the Confederacy."

"I still must question why we use a dragon. The Bible is very clear, Mr. President. If this is the Serpent of the Pit – and, in all honesty, I am convinced that it is – then we are risking our immortal souls, all of us, in dealing with the Devil. If it is Choctaw magic, once again Scripture is clear. 'Thou shalt not suffer a witch to live.' 'There shalt not be found among you anyone that maketh his son or daughter to pass through the fire, or that useth divination or an observer of times, or an enchanter, or a witch.' We are trafficking with the power of darkness."

Davis swallowed to conceal his rage; he didn't like to be crossed. However, he had known Lee for a long time. He knew the strength of his faith. More importantly, he needed him.

"I, too, have read Holy Scripture, General Lee. May I remind you, sir, of what our nation's state was a short time ago? The Yankees had driven our troops out of Kentucky, Tennessee, and much of Mississippi and Louisiana. We could not get supplies and men from Arkansas and Texas. Had we failed at Chattanooga; the Yankees could have driven to Atlanta. I do not fault your performance in the field – no one can do better – but you and General Meade were at a stalemate in Virginia. Is that not an accurate description of our past fortunes?"

"Yes, it is."

"We're regaining much of that lost territory."

"We'll regain more, maybe even more than western Virginia. We're driving toward Missouri. We're in contact with the Copperheads of Indiana and Illinois, and they promise to arise."

"I cannot deny the truth of what you say Mr. President."

"I know how much you love Virginia. Tell me, General Lee, do you want to see your home state continue to be plundered and ravished by the Northern barbarians. Was not losing your home in Arlington enough for you?"

"Obeying the edicts of God is infinitely more important than my property. I had rather see the South under the dominion of the Yankees than of Satan."

"I think we are obeying the edicts of God. I think he ordained slavery for the benefit of both the white and black races. We use the slaves to build a good society for ourselves. Without question it is a better society than that of the Yankees. We have freedom, charm, grace, and civilized manners. We are also lifting the Negroes out of savagery. We are teaching them Christianity.

"God uses less than perfect men to accomplish His great purposes. Moses killed a man. King David was a murderer and an adulterer. Paul of Tarsis held the coats of those who stoned Christians to death. God used all of them.

"The Lord of Hosts will use Kinepikwa to secure our liberty. Count on it, General."

"Yes, He did use those with blemishes." For the first time, Davis heard anger in Lee's voice.

"However, there is no evidence from Scripture that they committed other crimes after those for which they were rebuked. Moses refused to believe the word of God when he fetched water for the Israelites, and he paid a grievous price for it – he was not permitted to enter Canaan, as I'm sure you know. They were our fellow men, not a creature of hellish sorcery. This end does not justify the means, sir. A freedom gained by trafficking with evil will soon be corrupted. It will not stand. Our nation will not stand if it uses Kinepikwa. I will not be a party to this. You will have my formal resignation on your desk in the morning. Good day, sir."

And General Lee strode from the room.

*****

The man's face radiated infinite weariness, infinite sorrow. None would call him handsome, but that face deserved to be carved in stone. Abraham Lincoln surveyed his cabinet, and none of its members looked any happier than he did.

"Yesterday, I received a communique from Lord Lyons. It seems the British are once more seriously considering recognition of the Rebels. He assured me this will happen soon unless we find a way to check the dragon."

"We're defeated then," said Postmaster General Montgomery Blair. "I'm surprised the damned Rebels haven't set the beast to burn the capital down."

"It has found a better occupation," said Secretary of the Navy Gideon Welles. "It is burning our ships. If we lose many more we cannot maintain even the pretense of a blockade."

"Can it not be hurt?" asked the President. "I understand it was hit by a cannon ball or two at Chattanooga."

Secretary of War Edward Stanton replied, "Yes, but it has taken to striking our forces at night. It can fly so fast that is upon our soldiers and sailors before they can act. It can swim, too, and strike from underwater as it did at New Orleans. I swear Jeff Davis sold his soul to the Devil to gain the use of this creature. I think it is the one mentioned in the Book of Revelation."

Secretary of State John Seward said, "Gentlemen, I hate to say it, but the war may be lost." His voice trembled as he struggled not to weep.

"The election will be in two months, and the Democrats are howling for peace," Lincoln said. "You all know they claim the war is a failure. As long as the Rebels have that dragon, they may be right."

"They may be wrong, too," Stanton snarled. "Our spies reported Lee has resigned. He's the only reason we weren't able to drive the damned Rebels out of Richmond."

"Who replaced him?" Lincoln asked.

"James Longstreet."

"That is not good news for us. Longstreet is a pretty fair general."

*****

Shadow Owl's name became great in all the nations west of the Occochappo, from the Teutons to the Rio Grande, from the Badlands to the Pacific Ocean. As one Great White Father contemplated victory and the other contemplated defeat, she issued a summons and they all came:

Red Cloud, Crazy Horse, Sitting Bull, three promising young warriors of the Oglala Lakota. A young medicine man named Black Elk accompanied them.

Satanta, a chief of the Kiowa.

Tuekakas, a chief of the Nez Pierce, and his son Hin-mah-too-yah-lat-keht, a man known to the whites as Joseph.

General Stand Watie, who commanded the Confederate forces in Oklahoma.

Peta Nocona, a chief of the fierce Comanches, and his son, Quanah Parker, born to a white woman.

Ouray, leader of the Tabeguache Utes.

Black Kettle, chief of the Cheyenne.

Cochise, a chief of the Apache.

They viewed Shadow Owl with respect and some wariness. It would be difficult to deny her anything she wanted, not after the recent Confederate victories and a treaty that gave them Oklahoma and a free hand in the rest of the West. They passed the peace pipe, and Shadow Owl spoke:

"Greetings, mighty warriors. I have summoned you to discuss the future. Much of the western lands now to belong to us, thanks to President Davis. I think we need to discuss our future plans and how to keep them in our hands. I think we need to discuss an alliance of all the tribes. Never again must we fight among ourselves and let the white man advance to our sorrow."

"Have you received an assurance from General Lee? He is the greatest warrior of the gray men," asked Peta Nocona.

"That is true, but I do not think he will interfere."

The wily Santana asked: "How do we know they will abide by the agreement? Most white men speak with forked tongues."

"President Davis is an honorable man," Watie said. "He will keep his word."

"That may be true of him, but what of the men who will follow him. Do you think they can be trusted?"

"As long as we have Kinepikwa, it does not matter," Shadow Owl said.

"You are the greatest of all medicine chiefs," said Black Elk, "but that is a fell and crafty demon. It cannot be trusted. How many more days can your magic control it?"

"I need not control it forever. It is not making any efforts at present to break my spell. It told me it likes the flesh of the white man better than our flesh. They have more fat and are more succulent. There are also other dragons. If need be, I can summon and control them. I am sure you remember Unhcegila, which caused the Lakota so much sorrow, and Gaasyendietha which harried the Eastern Nations."

"Yes, but how long can they be controlled? They are not servile creatures."

"That may not matter, I think." She gestured, and a young brave stepped forward from the shadows behind her. "This is Raven's Tongue. He has been an assistant to one of the white men who seek old bones, the ones they call paleontologists. Tell them what you have learned, Raven's Tongue."

"I have been helping a man called William More Gabb. We have found the bones of monsters from long ago. They are great monsters who shook the earth with their stride. They have maws large enough to engulf a man and teeth like obsidians."

He produced buckskins covered with drawings and passed them around.

"They were mindless so our medicine men will be able to control them with ease. I am sure you great chiefs and warriors have heard of the Thunderbirds, maybe even seen their bones. We can bring them back, too,

"There were also monsters that swam in the sea. We can use them against the white man's great navies."

Cochise, who stilled burned with rage at the cessation of New Mexico and Arizona, said: "The white men are still more numerous than the stars and have their formidable weapons. I have met the gray warriors. They strut like roosters and they will soon come west or south to find new lands for their slaves and cotton. They will not be easy to defeat."

"Those white men may soon have other problems," Shadow Owl said.

*****

Abraham Lincoln walked the gardens of the White House, melancholy head upon his breast, brows knotted in thought. The election loomed ever nearer, and he feared he would lose. He believed the Democrats would have no choice but to make peace with the Confederacy, and the United States would be broken forever. He could not see how the Union could win the war. Not without Grant, not with Kinepikwa.

"Mr. President?" a familiar voice called and roused Lincoln from his mournful reverie.

"Good evening, Mr. Douglass. Under most circumstances, I would be delighted to converse with you. However, I would pass on that pleasure tonight. I am too filled with sorrow and must plan for what I think inevitable, as painful as that might be."

Frederick Douglass smiled. He, too, had not been pleased by recent events. "I understand, and I would not disturb you save that I bring two who can give you hope." Lincoln noticed two figures standing a few feet behind Douglass in the shadows. One stepped forward at Douglass' gesture. "Allow me to introduce John Henry."

Lincoln saw the figure of a massive black man with the largest muscles he had ever seen. There didn't appear to be an ounce of fat on that mighty frame. Even though Henry wore a blue-striped engineer's hat, denim overalls, work boots, and shirt of white, he possessed a dignity equal to his strength. He made Lincoln think of a figure from legend, a black Rustum or Achilles or Siegfried.

"I'se a railroad man, Mistuh President. I told Mistuh Douglass about a plan I have. We can get a train and head it down South. I understand that debbil's in Kentucky. When he flies down to attack, we can set off a blast of gunpowder. If that don't kill it, I can drive a silver spike through its head. Silver's proof against all things evil." He flexed those powerful arms, and Lincoln believed he could do it. "That'll kill it."

"I admire your courage and willingness, Mr. Henry, but I fear it will kill you and anyone with you."

"That don't matter. Plenty of Negroes will help me. You gave us our freedom. We're willin' to die for it."

"How can you lure it down to its doom? I am afraid Kinepikwa is a wily monster. It appears to be more intelligent than any of our remaining generals."

Douglass made another gesture and a second man stepped from the shadows and Lincoln saw Robert E. Lee and could not speak for astonishment.

Lee saluted: "Mr. President, before the war, you offered me the position of commanding general of the Northern armies. Now I would like to accept that post. If you refuse my offer, I am willing to serve in the ranks as a private. I think I can devise a plan with this gallant gentleman's assistance," he nodded at John Henry, "that will lure Kinepikwa to its death."

"I would gladly offer you that post, General Lee. However, I would point out that the Emancipation Proclamation will still be in effect. The slaves will be freed. I will not rescind it, sir, not even if Kinepikwa were to alight before me. I also must ask why you have changed your mind after these years of the effusion of blood."

"Mr. President, I fought for the state of Virginia which I love so much. I can no longer fight for a government which leagues itself with the powers of darkness. I fear for what Almighty God will inflict upon Virginia, upon the rest of the Southern states for this use of diabolism.

"As for the Emancipation Proclamation, I cannot deny to you gentlemen that I originally opposed it. However, if the end of slavery is the price to be paid for trafficking with Hell, so be it. I would save Virginia. I would save the South.

"I will accept the Emancipation Proclamation."

"Then, General, welcome to our side."

"Thank you," and Robert E. Lee shook hands with Abraham Lincoln, Frederick Douglass, and John Henry.

THE SEARCH

by Derek Paterson

By strength of will alone Marina stopped herself from fainting, as the pungent smell of the fish soup assailed her nostrils.

She gazed down at the plate the servant had placed before her. Pieces of fish floated in cream. To other people, it must smell delicious. To Marina it smelled like death and corruption.

"Eat up, eat up," Sir Edwin said, and though he appeared to direct his words to all his guests sitting at the dinner table, Marina could not help but think he was speaking to her and her alone.

She did not think she was being paranoid. In fact, she knew she was not.

Sir Edwin, a close neighbor, had invited her to his house before, curious about his new neighbor, but Marina had always politely refused. However, having learned that the guest of honor this evening was to be Lord Dareth Cavendish, the celebrated naturalist, she had immediately sent an acceptance note.

Sir Edwin said, "Is the soup not to your taste, Miss Pesci?"

She did not correct his mispronunciation of the surname she'd taken upon moving to this area and occupying the old house on the edge of the marshes. She was aware of the probing nature of his question. And aware also of the naturalist's penetrating gaze, his interest in hearing her answer.

But of course, she saw it now. Lord Cavendish was not here because of the fauna unique to these sprawling marshlands. Sir Edwin must have appraised him in advance of his suspicions. Those suspicions had arisen some weeks ago, Marina knew, when he had gone for an early morning stroll, and had glimpsed a shape in a pond that had startled him. Marina had not swum in the pond since, she had found a more remote place, far from human eyes, but clearly Sir Edwin had not been able to forget the incident. Marina had hoped that perhaps tonight she might convince him that he had been mistaken, that the swirling mists had played a trick upon his senses, that his imagination had painted a fanciful sight that did not exist. She realized now the folly of her plan. He was beyond convincing.

The young man seated next to her said, in the act of filling his glass from the jug, "May I offer you some water, Miss Pesci?"

Oh, how devious, she thought, watching as the jug came to hover over her own glass before she could say no. He tilted it so water began to pour from the spout, carefully, very carefully. But then—oh!—an unfortunate tap on the glass's rim, and it toppled toward her. The spilled water ran off the table and cascaded onto Marina's lap, drenching her skirts. *As was intended.* At least he hadn't tipped the soup over her as well. That would have been disgusting.

"Oh, my goodness, how clumsy of me, I am so terribly sorry," the young man said. He offered Marina his napkin, but she ignored him and used her own napkin to dab up the water. As she did so, her gaze wandered around the table. She saw it then. Not just Sir Edwin and Lord Cavendish. All of them. They were all expecting the water to have affected her.

The young man wouldn't stop apologizing. She sensed his genuine embarrassment at being part of a ruse that had clearly backfired and made its originator, their host, look quite foolish. Marina raised her hand, silencing him, but she also smiled to soften the gesture.

She pushed her chair back and stood up. "This is most unfortunate; I am quite soaked. I shall have to go home and change my clothing."

Sir Edwin cleared his throat. His cheeks were red. "Most unfortunate indeed. I shall have my carriage brought around at once."

"There's no need, Sir Edwin, the walk is a short one and the air will do me good. I bid you goodnight. The soup smelled delicious, by the way."

She left the room to an awkward chorus of good nights. A servant opened the front door for her and she went down the steps carefully, trying to keep control over her legs, willing them to remain legs. It had been close, so very close.

The winding gravel driveway took her away from the house and in no time, she was screened by trees, which gave her a sense of relief. She did not like being scrutinized by prying eyes. It was part of her makeup, part of her natural defense instinct. To be exposed invited death, or worse.

The sun had sunk below the distant horizon and now night fell across the land. No one could possibly see her now. She changed direction and headed down to the river that flowed through the estate. The chuckling water called to her. She could feel her legs trembling. Further downstream, the river ran past her house. It was the quickest way home.

Stepping close to a tree, she undid her fastenings and slipped off her still-sodden skirts, and also the waterproof oilskin leggings she'd worn beneath, having been forewarned by some sixth sense that such precautions might be necessary. The leggings had prevented the water from reaching her skin. If it had... she doubted whether she could have maintained her form. She would have transformed in front of a roomful of people. The very thought made her shudder.

She was about to remove the rest of her clothing when a Lucifer sparked in the darkness; the match's crimson glow reflected upon the river.

"A fine night for a walk, Miss Pesci."

She recognized the voice at once; it was Lord Cavendish. He must have left the house soon after her, must have taken another path to arrive at the river moments ahead of her.

"Or *are* you walking?" He gazed at the river and his meaning was clear.

Marina said, "Do you make it your business to follow women into the night, sir, and cause them alarm?" She was surprised she could still speak; fear of being unmasked constricted her throat.

"I apologize if I startled you," he said. He used the burning Lucifer to light the shag tobacco in his pipe. The smell was acrid and unpleasant. "Sir Edwin thought his trick with the water jug would cause you to change before his very eyes. And perhaps it might have." He gestured with the pipe stalk, indicating the oilskins. "But you were more clever than he."

"If you know what I am," she said, knowing that he did, "then perhaps you have encountered others? Of my folk. Elsewhere in this land."

The silence between them stretched interminably. She began to doubt if he'd even heard her question.

He stared at his pipe for a few moments longer before he slowly shook his head. "Truthfully I had thought your species gone, Miss Pesci," he said. "It pleases me greatly that you are not. And yet...." His eyes came up to meet hers, and he sighed. "I am so very sorry."

She'd wanted his expert knowledge, not his sympathy. The fact he could not offer her any information broke something inside her. Her anger should have been directed toward Sir Edwin, not

Cavendish, but her fragile veneer had been torn away by tonight's events and she threw herself at him. Before he even had time to cry out, her widened jaws closed over his head and came together with a terrible crunch, ending him.

She feasted with an abandon she could never have shown at the dinner table. As she did so, she pondered what his next words might have been. No doubt he would have suggested she accompany him to Edinburgh, where he might study her in his laboratory, while also offering her protection. As if she could not protect herself. In time he would reveal her existence to the world; science would never be the same again. Which was guesswork on her part, but Marina knew she was right.

And if she'd refused his offer? Would he have turned and walked away and kept her secret? No, she did not believe Lord Cavendish, a famed naturalist, could have ignored such an opportunity. Far more likely that Sir Edwin's estate workers would have crept to her house during the night, bringing nets with them so they could capture her and drag her off to become a fantastic exhibit. Or a laboratory experiment. She shuddered at the thought.

When she'd had her fill, she stood up and removed the last of her clothing. She could bear this form no longer. She walked into the river and the cool waters surrounded her, nurtured her. The change came quickly, she only just had time to drag Cavendish's remains after her. And his pipe. She stuffed him and her clothes under a large rock near the river bottom, where they would never be discovered. His disappearance would forever remain a mystery.

She let the current take her.

She quested ahead to the limit of her senses, for any trace of her folk. And as always, found none. Their scent had long since vanished from the rivers, the lakes, the sea.

She would never stop looking. But she remembered the sympathy she'd seen in Cavendish's eyes, and thought troubled thoughts.

The End

THE ALEBRIJE

by Christopher R. Muscato

The clanging of trolley bells alerted Henry to his present state of danger and he smartly skipped out of the path of the oncoming cart, the metal tip of his cane rapping against the stone pavement. He would not be the first person whose journey ended at the married hands of distraction and the railways of Oaxaca. And it was easy to fall prey to distraction. The old colonial plaza bustled with energy, vendors competing as they barked the prices of dried chilies, ornamented socialites exchanging their gossip in enthusiastic whispers. Mexico seemed poised to burst into the new century, bubbling with life and wonder.

In his crisp white suit, Henry presented a strong contrast to the vibrant and varied colors of the market. Leaning on his fine cane, he also seemed many years older than he was. War had that effect, and the British Empire offered many opportunities for war. However, it had also offered its own forms of compensation. Henry was traveling in pursuit of such recompense when the dreams began. Dreams of the snowy peak of

Popocateptl. Visions of cenotes in Yucatán limestone. Flashes of emerald feathers.

A playful breeze wove through the market, gifting Henry with a waft of posole boiling in a vendor's worn cauldron. He sniffed the air, the smell calling to him. He wished he had time for a quick bite, but there was another meeting he could not afford to miss. With a sharp turn, he left the main plaza, marched into a small alleyway, and then through a wooden door so unassuming that most people would not notice it at all.

The air inside the pulquería swirled with smoke, the haze a mixture of incense, cigars, and logs burning below an old stove.

"You know they banned pulque," a voice drifted through the dim beams of light that penetrated the smoky fog. Henry, hat in his hand, squinted as his eyes adjusted and a discernable figure emerged.

"Never tried it," Henry admitted, taking a seat at the bar and accepting a wooden cup full of the thick, sacred beverage.

"Few have. Not anymore. The government tried to make Mexico a land of beer, more like Europe. But Mexico will always belong to its people. Chinese phoenix?"

Surprised, Henry glanced down at the polished silver handle of his cane.

"You've seen one?" He asked between sips of pulque.

"We both know that such things do not really exist."

"To know *is* to exist."

"Professor Linares?"

"Yes."

"If Linares sent you my way…" the man at the bar chewed his lip for a moment, seeming to fade in and out of the cloud of smoke that continued to swirl hypnotically around the dim interior of the pulquería. Finally, he nodded to himself and produced from the depths of his baggy poncho a single egg, a fan of feathers, and a deck of cards. While the colorful designs reminded Henry of the popular Mexican lotería game, these were not symbols he had ever seen before, catching glimpses as the deck was shuffled between the weathered hands of the stranger.

"Yours is the element of air," the man mused as his fingers danced between the cards. "And you've already begun. How many have you captured?"

Henry found himself unable to answer, eddies of smoke pooling around him, obscuring the rest of the world. The man continued to shuffle until finally he snapped the deck back together and produced three cards, laying them on the table. Cautiously, Henry picked them up, breathing deeply the smoke and incense as his heart pounded. On the first card, Henry saw a barn owl. On the second, a bat. On the third, a coyote.

Henry started to ask the meaning of this strange game, but his mouth went dry as he looked up. The man was nowhere to be seen. In his place sat only a small, wooden figurine.

*****

Back at his hotel on the plaza, Henry chewed on his cigarette, smoke escaping in deliberate, punctuated puffs. Normally, the evening breeze would have carried the smoke away, but a menacing wind was rattling the shutters and so Henry had locked the windows shut. So, the smoke lingered in diaphanous clouds as he turned the polished wooden figurine in his hand. It was a beautiful piece. Copal wood, he assumed. He would have paid handsomely for it, he certainly had the ability, and was struck by the oddness of the stranger leaving such a fine piece behind. Henry continued to turn it over and over.

The body and face of the creature was that of an owl, a barn owl by the looks of it, but the feathered wings stretched into bat-like fingers of skin. Its tail was canine, as were the pointed ears that protruded from behind the owl's large and knowing eyes. The entire thing was brightly colored, clearly painted by the loving and steady hand of a practiced artisan, the vibrant dots and lines constructing and deconstructing patterns through each other. Henry turned and turned the figurine. The impossible creature felt inexplicably more familiar with each rotation.

Henry did not remember drifting away into a deep slumber, but then again, one rarely does. What he did remember, vividly even after he woke, were the dreams. Rich green plumage, swirling like smoke, surrounding him, enveloping him. The rumbling of massive wings stretching to the horizons and a cry that seemed to pierce the heavens. The great beast reared its head above its coiled body. He'd found it. Henry could see himself standing there in the nest of the feathered serpent. Air and storm incarnate. This was why he had come to Mexico.

In that moment, unexpectedly, there was a silence that crept into the back of his mind, muting the roars of the giant. And from that silence, a whisper. The serpentine body rustled its feathers as it tightened around him, and Henry became acutely aware of the sensation of being watched. In his dream, Henry craned his neck, trying to see the wondrous creature's eyes but the massive beaked face towered too far above him. Despite this, Henry could sense a pair of large eyes. The feathered serpent tightened its coils.

With a start, Henry awoke from the dream gasping, his forehead and neck glistening with cold sweat. The first thing he saw when his eyes adjusted was the colorful wooden figure of an owl with bat's wings and a coyote's tail at the edge of his nightstand, staring directly at him.

Despite the fact that he slept very little for the rest of the night, Henry had rarely felt more awake as he sat stiffly at the edge of his bed in the darkness, examining the figurine. The hunt was on. This was the thing that gave Henry purpose, the only thing to truly excite him since the wars. As a young man, Henry had been a youth of little direction, and found himself blowing around the empire like a gust of solitary wind. There were ample distractions to be found in war, and in the age of Victorian imperialism there were always wars to be had. There was also, as Henry soon discovered, plenty of wealth to be made from war, if one possessed a certain degree of cleverness and lacked restraining moral scruples.

However, it was not until his vessel caught the wrong end of a German naval patrol in the waters of the Orient that Henry truly found purpose. It was here, washed up on an unknown shoreline, that Henry first encountered the phoenix, rising with the Sun and showering him in golden rays of fortune.

That phoenix now resided in a large estate Henry had purchased in the remote American West, Montana in fact, safe from the world behind bars of polished silver.

As the sun rose the next morning, Henry departed Oaxaca and headed east towards the Yucatán lowlands. He was not entirely sure to where he was being called, but what little he could discern of the landscape in his dream the previous night indicated jungles far more coastal than Oaxaca. As the bustling colonial city disappeared behind him, Henry sat unmoving in his private cabin on the train, eyes still fixed on the wooden figurine.

"Feathers from the jungle, señor?"

The unexpected voice caught Henry by surprise, and he looked up to see a young boy working from cabin to cabin, a basket full of bright green feathers under his arm. Normally, Henry was not one for frivolous expenses but something about this intrigued him and without thinking he extended a few pesos to the boy, receiving a single feather in return. It was long and soft, and nearly glowing with its resplendent sheen.

"Quetzal?" Henry asked and the boy nodded.

"Sí señor!" And with that he skipped off to the next cabin. "Feathers from the jungle, señoras?"

Henry admired the feather a moment longer and then deftly poked it into the brim of his white hat, the bright green a splash of welcome color against the white fabric. Henry glanced at the figurine of the owl. It seemed to approve.

The warm southern sun and the percussive clacking of the train tracks soon worked in tandem to produce an enchanting lullaby, and Henry found himself yawning. Giving into the instinct to nap, he stretched his legs across the seat and pulled his white hat with its single green feather low over his eyes. It was not long before he was asleep.

In his dreams, Henry found himself surrounded by the thick foliage of a Yucatán rainforest. The birds chirped and chattered, but from between these sounds there was something else. Henry strained to listen, and the whispers steadily became evident. Although still too soft to decipher, they were louder than they had been before, and seemed to continue to grow. Then, another sound, a rustling in the brush. Henry turned just in time to be overwhelmed by a flurry of colorful feathers and fur and the beating of bat-like wings against the wind before he fell head over heels backwards into the massive sinkhole.

"Valladolid! Last call for Valladolid!"

The conductor's call jostled Henry from his dream, but the vision had awoken a sense of urgency within him, a need to hear the whispers again, to respond. Hurriedly, he gathered his immediate belongings and secured a driver to bring him to the hotel, brazenly shoving pesos into the hands of the train attendants in order to get his trunks unloaded as quickly as possible. The sense of urgency growing ever more prescient by the moment, he at last burst into the hotel, panting by the time he arrived at the concierge.

"A room, señor?"

"Yes, but first," Henry stammered. "I need to charter a guide. Cenote."

It was not long at all before Henry's luggage had been stashed by the hotel staff and a guide secured, although the guide needed relatively little effort for this particular charter as the great cenote was not far from the city at all. Henry was escorted to the sinkhole, which remained relatively quiet and free of bathers today, and he tipped the guide to watch over his things as he descended alone. Quietly, Henry worked his way down the gentle slope leading into the limestone basin, removing his clothing at the edge of the turquoise pool and sinking himself into it. As he bathed in the sacred waters, he listened to the droplets falling from stalactites and the steady rumbling of a small waterfall at the far end of the sinkhole. And through it, for just a moment, Henry could have sworn he heard the faintest of whispers. When he finally emerged from the pool, the colorful figurine of the owl sat neatly on top of his pile of clothes, although he did not remember leaving it there.

At the hotel in Valladolid that night, Henry perched in front of the mirror preening as he combed his hair with methodic obsession. It was something he did to help him focus, although on this evening that proved to be far more difficult than expected. The flames from the gas lamps in Henry's room cast seductive shadows against the wall, dancing rhythmically as the breeze flitted through the open windows.

To ease his mind, Henry organized his papers, research, and findings he had accumulated over the years. Finally, he procured a key from his pocket and opened the largest of his trunks, withdrawing from its mysterious depths a bundle of cloth. The wrapping unraveled on his bed. Henry set to work inspecting the tools of his carefully practiced trade. The nets of silk and steel, the tranquilizer darts with their secret venom, the traps. These instruments of calculated science were what had allowed Henry to capture the Chinese phoenix. And the Hercinia bird of Germany. And the Huma of Iran. And so many others.

It was not pride or vanity that motivated these hunts. Henry knew that much about himself. He did not collect for the sake of collecting, nor to demonstrate his mastery over nature. Henry's encounter with the mystical Chinese phoenix had convinced him of the precious rarity of such magic in the world, a world being plowed over by industrial machinations. And so, Henry had resolved to preserve such wondrous things, to keep them locked away from an ungrateful and destructive world, to protect them.

His remote sanctuary in Montana thus boasted the most remarkable aviary ever known to humankind, not that Henry expected to ever share it with humanity.

Henry was in the Baltics hunting for Stymphalian birds when the dreams first came to him of the feathered serpent, calling him like a siren to Mexico. His first stop was at the Museo Nacional, where the nation's *cientificos* had busied themselves in cataloging and preserving the cultural history of the Mexican people. In his time hunting mystical creatures of the air, Henry often found that many of the best clues survived in the realms of folklore, and so he sought anthropologists and ethnologists wherever he went. It was in this pursuit that Henry encountered a Professor Linares, an expert in the myths surrounding the feathered serpent, and to whom, after many days engaged in rigorous academic debate, Henry had ultimately revealed the true intention of his inquiries. He intended to capture and preserve a feathered serpent in his wondrous aviary. While Linares declined to join the expedition, he had agreed to set Henry a meeting with a man in Oaxaca that was promised to be most enlightening.

Henry snapped the trunk back shut and locked it, satisfied that his supplies were in working order and prepared to perform their designated tasks. But before he went to sleep, Henry resolutely set the owl figurine at the edge of his bedside table, facing him.

The owl appeared to Henry in his dreams in its entirety that night for the first time. As Henry wandered the jungles of his subconscious, the owl emerged from the underbrush, rustling its feathers and wagging its tail. If the lacquered figurine was painted in vibrant colors, it was nothing compared to the actual animal, whose feathers, fur, and skin all radiated in dancing hues that glowed in the darkness of the tropical forest. It whispered, and Henry slumbered contentedly.

Over the next few days, Henry set out to learn from local experts and the keepers of folk wisdom all he could about Valladolid, the cenote, and the connection to the stories of the feathered serpent. The entire time, the figurine remained safely secured in his pocket, his fingers constantly wrapped around it, turning it as if some enchanted talisman. Wherever Henry went, he listened for whispers on the air, trusting them to guide him.

From this exhaustive research, and several open palms that had been covertly warmed with an exchange of pesos, Henry learned rumors of an ancient, lost temple in the rainforest, a mighty pyramid where he may find evidence of the feathered serpent. Without delay, Henry set to securing porters, guides, and supplies to service an expedition to reclaim the secrets of these ruins from the jungle.

The expedition came to fruition without pomp or circumstance, as is possible with enough money to finance discretion.

"Tie these around your waist, señor," the guide instructed. Henry looked at the three red bands of fabric.

"Why?"

"So, we can always find each other in the jungle." That was all the explanation Henry would receive, as the guide was called away by a porter who needed assistance in securing a tarp. Henry examined the rough pieces of cloth, shrugged to himself, and fastened the bands as instructed.

From then on, the expedition worked its way into the jungle, clearing trails and exploratory swaths that seemed to be consumed by the foliage as soon as they were abandoned. On the first days, they found very little but leaves, although Henry did come across a number of very fine feathers, each of which he secured into his hat alongside the one he had bought on the train. Then, gradually, small pieces of scratched stone and broken ceramics started to emerge from the dense underbrush as the expedition continued its search.

Henry micromanaged the entire procession, personally examining each miniscule artifact for clues as to the activities of ancient inhabitants of these lands. Very steadily, pieces of an elaborate puzzle began to emerge that promised to reveal a path to the sacred temple. Every feather found in the jungle was also commissioned into the ornamentation of Henry's hat, an article that was steadily disappearing into a cone of plumage.

Each night, Henry placed the figurine of the owl next to his head while he slept, and the creature appeared in his dreams. He danced with it through the forest, and in the morning had internalized new directions for their quest.

After nearly two weeks in this pursuit, Henry again found himself in the dream, surrounded by whispers he could not understand. This time, however, the luminous owl brought with it a bag of cornmeal that it clawed open with its talons and winged fingers. The owl grabbed the bag with its beak, dragging it around Henry. Only when Henry was completely encircled by the cornmeal did the owl stop and stare at him, unblinking. From that night on, Henry surrounded his tent with a circle of cornmeal before bed each night.

Another week of the expedition passed like this, leaving the porters and diggers to wonder at the strangeness of their employer. Amid hushed whispers in Spanish and Mayan they exchanged their concerns, none of which was ever noticed by Henry, who was becoming more obsessive in his habits by the day. In the mornings, he preened until satisfied, and then spent hours obscured by his feathery hat pecking through every object revealed from the jungle.

Finally, at the end of the week, a shout from a digger alerted Henry to the news that a discovery had been made. Nearly tripping over himself, he rushed to the edge of their worksite and felt his heart jump into his throat. Although the limestone block was still half buried in the soil, there was no mistaking the figure. Henry stared, grinning, and the statue of the feathered serpent stared back.

Henry insisted on setting his tent next to the ancient carving and including it inside his circle of cornmeal and that night he dreamed of this exact site, finding himself sitting next to the stone head, now fully exhumed and polished as if new. As Henry studied the object, the owl appeared, feathers rustling and tail wagging.

"It's not right, the wind trapped in stone," Henry said to the owl, stroking his chin. He looked down at the little bird. "I suppose you know about that, being a wooden figurine, don't you? How wonderful you would look in my aviary." Henry continued to scratch at his chin. Suddenly, the owl leapt upon stone head of the feathered serpent, hopping about impatiently. Henry, eyebrows raised in concern, was unsure what to do. He tried to calm the bird, but failing to do so, hesitantly reached out to stroke it.

The owl shuddered for a moment as Henry's hand brushed against its colorful feathers, which Henry found cool and soothing to the touch. Then, quite unexpectedly, the owl jumped back and pecked at Henry's hand, cutting him with its sharp beak. As Henry started awake, his last vision in the dream was of a single drop of blood falling upon the stone statue.

The diggers and porters were unclear as to the nature and origins of the injury on their employer's hand, and over the next few days many rumors circulated, none of which Henry seemed interested in discouraging. The hand swelled with infection and Henry took a fever, spending long hours in restless delirium but maintaining enough of his senses to insist that the work be continued and that his tent be encircled with fresh cornmeal each night. The workers wondered at his condition, some debating abandoning the expedition to seek him better medical help than they could provide, for none of their medicines seemed to provide any relief. But Henry was insistent that the work of clearing the jungle be maintained without interruption.

Finally, the day came that Henry was so delirious as to be unable to rise from his cot. He sweated through every blanket given him, until one of the porters fashioned a blanket of feathers as his ancestors had been known to do, a knowledge that had survived more generations than most. Henry passed in and out of consciousness, the owl appearing to him every time, and his fever worsened. The workers all agreed: he would not last much longer like this. The wind began to howl through the trees, rustling the leaves like agitated feathers.

That night, Henry woke from another delirious dream feeling surprisingly improved and opened his eyes, seeing more clearly than he had in days and feeling unexpectedly lighter as he rose from his cot. He immediately looked for the figurine of the owl but was unable to find it. Panicked, he shot upright and began to search through the contents of his tent. A rustling breeze revealed to him that a corner of the tarp had come loose. Henry, still wrapped in the feather blanket, shoved his feather-covered hat on his head and burst outside. There, he saw the unmistakable prints of owl tracks dancing through the cornmeal encircling him.

None of the workers seemed to notice as their employer stumbled from the camp, following the tracks deeper into the jungle, eyes burning as he obsessed over the trail. For hours Henry tracked the bird, sometimes crawling on hands and knees. Although still exhausted, he felt nearly weightless ever since he had risen from his fevered state. A breeze filled with whispers whipped around him, pushing him along the path, giving him strength.

Just when Henry thought he could go no further; he caught a glimpse of radiant color disappearing into the underbrush. Henry shoved the foliage aside and came face-to-face with a wall of stone. He traced the moss-covered structured, eventually finding a staircase, on which was waiting the impossible owl, watching him with unblinking eyes.

"What is this place?" Henry asked it. The whispers in the breeze grew stronger.

445

"Al-ay--al what?" Henry struggled to discern the voices.

"alebrije. alebrije. alebrije." Came the whispers. The owl hopped up the steps of the great pyramid, Henry stumbling as he climbed after it.

"Alebrije. Alebrije. Alebrije." The voices grew louder. There was a rumbling in the jungle around the stone edifice. Henry kept climbing, his hands and body seeming to fade in and out of shadow as he did. His fever had returned. He felt the wind increase, lifting him, passing through him. Finally, Henry, cloaked in feathers and feathery cap, with three red chords tied around his waist, arrived at the top of the pyramid.

"ALEBRIJE! ALEBRIJE! ALEBRIJE!" The owl shouted, passing through Henry with blasts of color.

"ALEBRIJE! ALEBRIJE! ALEBRIJE!"

The rumbling in the jungle grew louder and louder, the foliage moving, shifting into emerald plumage. The entire pyramid was encircled with emerald feathers, churning like an angry wind.

"ALEBRIJE! ALEBRIJE! ALEBRIJE!" Henry shouted, the air from his lungs becoming wind, an offering to air and storm incarnate.

"ALEBRIJE! ALEBRIJE! ALEBRIJE!" Henry shouted, unsure if it were arms or feathered wings he raised above his head, the wind swirling inside him. His spirit seemed to soar with the breeze, loosening its tethers with every gust.

"ALEBRIJE! ALEBRIJE! ALEBRIJE!" Henry shouted and then the rumbling stopped and from the night a monstrous serpentine head emerged, not in stone but in feathers, its eyes peering directly into Henry.

Far, far away, in a remote part of rural Montana where curious visitors were absolutely never permitted to trespass beyond the posted signs, a strange wind blew that night. For years afterwards, residents of those parts would talk about the gale that erupted from nowhere, destroying the strange mansion and ripping its very foundations from the ground. Some people swore they saw the most wondrous birds ascend with the tempest, dispersing from the mysterious house as the storm dissipated, but then again, such folktales were common in this region and everyone knew better than to take them seriously. What was a mystery, however, was the solitary object the residents of that town discovered when they inspected the wreckage the next day. Nobody fully grasped the meaning of the small, colorful figurine but all agreed that it was quite a beautiful piece, this wooden owl with the wings of a bat, the tail of a coyote, and three red chords tied around its waist.

Liked
These
Stories?

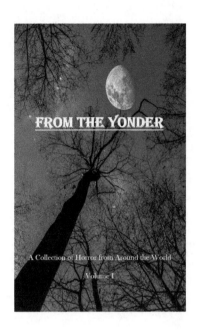

Don't forget to read
From The Yonder: Volume I

And other releases from
War Monkey Publications

Online at:
www.warmonkeypublications.com